Forgiveness

DATE DUE

Forgiveness

Cover Art by *Nicola Martinez*

Harbourlight Books, a division of Pelican Ventures, LLC
www.pelicanbookgroup.com PO Box 1738 *Aztec, NM * 87410

Harbourlight Books sail and mast logo is a trademark of Pelican Ventures, LLC

Library of Congress Control Number: 2016934856

Publishing History
First Harbourlight Edition, 2016
Paperback Edition ISBN 978-1-61116-860-0
Electronic Edition ISBN 978-1-61116-859-4
Published in the United States of America

Dedication

During the course of my writing ministry, there have been so many who graciously lifted me up, believed in me, prayed for me. To list you all individually would be impossible, but you know who you are, and you also know you hold a precious place in my heart. So, to my family, my friends, my incredible readers ~ I'm beyond grateful to each and every one of you. Our God reigns!

What People are Saying

This talented author satisfies both heart and soul. ~ *New York Times* Bestselling Author, Ruth Ryan Langan

On Devotion

Winner, Booksellers Best Award for Best Inspirational Novel

Winner, ACRA Heart of Excellence Award for Best Novel with Romantic Elements

Evans writes a book with a wonderful message of forgiveness filled with hope.
                    ~ 4.5 Stars, Long & Short Romance Reviews

Love one another, for love comes from God. This is love: not that we loved God, but that He loved us and sent His Son as an atoning sacrifice for our sins.

1 John 4:7-10

1

Chase Bradington slid a pair of large-frame sunglasses over his eyes, twisted a smile into place, and walked into the sickest form of choreographed PR nonsense he could imagine.

The main entrance of Reach came open; likely a receptionist or some other nearby staff member had been recruited to clear a path between the substance abuse rehab center and the salvation of a black stretch limo that waited for him at the head of the curved drive, engine purring.

So close, and yet so far.

Reporters, gathered at least four-deep along the stone walkway, went wild with shouts for attention. A batch of fool cameramen trampled moist soil which was now dotted pink, purple, and white by destroyed hyacinth. Brightly colored petunias and phlox fared no better. All that appealing greenery laid to waste in an over-charged blitz to score something as meaningless as the image of a troubled country music star leaving a life recovery center. Chase fought back a self-condemning wince at the circus display.

A few weeks ago, he had spent hours on his knees planting those flowers, gaining some familiarity with horticulture, enjoying warm sunlight on his back and the feel of damp earth pressed against his fingertips. Surprisingly, he'd enjoyed the flower-spiced landscaping sessions while he talked things over with his mentor and sponsor, Mark Samuels.

That same aroma filled the air now, amplified by the dewy release of crushed petals.

Heathen journalists.

Nevertheless, he didn't flinch...and he didn't stop. He sank behind the protection of this orchestrated exit and coached himself the whole way. *Smile. Wave. Move fast. The first cut is the deepest.*

Camera flashes ignited like strobes; clicks, whirs, and shouts pounded against his temples as chaos built to a nasty crescendo. "Chase! Welcome back! How are you feeling?"

"A whole lot better than six months ago, that's for sure. Thanks for comin' out, y'all!" The words formed the only sound bite he felt comfortable offering, but they came wrapped in a carefully warmed tone and his easy, trademark smile. The world at large, however, was kept clear of his eyes, and his struggles, by the mask of dark shades.

"The Opry...are you headed to the Opry?"

"After checking in at home, yeah, you bet. The Opry is my comfort zone; performing at the Country Classics benefit tonight will feel mighty good." This time the smile was real. He meant every word—even if terror gripped him at the thought of a return to the stage without...

He clenched his jaw, disengaging the thought as he neared the door of the limo.

Survive this and you've officially crossed the starting line to re-finding your feet. Move, Bradington. Get to the car and move on.

One reporter, a TV gal, judging by her carefully primped style, that slick business attire and shimmery blonde hair, kept her back to him. Instead, she spoke into a mic and addressed the lens of the camera positioned before her. "Thirty-year-old Chase Bradington, the man fans and industry insiders once called the next country music legend, is seen leaving the confines of Reach this afternoon. Located in Franklin, Tennessee, Reach is a secluded and exclusive retreat for addicts on the mend."

From there, words faded to smoke and haze, burning off until just one remained. Addict. He was an addict. Chase flexed his jaw until it relaxed, forcing himself for the millionth time to face and accept that truth—harsh as it was. Into that acceptance came a loosening of the shoulders, along with the words of his sponsor, Mark Samuels.

Chase, you're addicted to alcohol, and that addiction overwhelmed you for a time, but the addiction didn't win. You've learned how to beat it. Remember the lessons; use the tools you've been given, and don't ever let this battle define you. It's part of your journey, sure, but it's not the full story. Nor is it the end of what your life is meant to say.

Chase bucked up and tossed a last wave to the crowd, smiled while he folded into the rear seat of his plush ride. The door closed immediately; cool air and blessed silence wrapped him in welcome arms. He melted into the seat, tipped his head back and closed his eyes. He whipped off the sunglasses and tossed them onto the leather seat. A long, heavy sigh passed through his chest as the vehicle rocked, pushing off from the entrance of Reach...and the safety net that had caught him when he fell so hard.

While distance grew and northbound traffic along Highway 65 led him closer to his condo, Chase rubbed his lower lip with a fingertip, lost in the passing view of fieldstone viaducts, green space, cars, homes, and office buildings.

Thoughts swirled into the memory of his evaluation session this morning, his exit interview.

"I'm a little concerned about the level of intensity you'll face. The demands placed upon you are going to be grueling and tough. It's a return to everything that brought you down in the first place, now isn't it?"

"You doubt me?" Chase bit back a rise in defensiveness while seated across from the facility director, a seasoned and sensible middle-aged man who had most likely overseen a great deal of human tribulation during his tenure.

"No, I don't doubt you. I wonder about what's best for you. I hope you're not pushing toward freedom before you're fully prepared."

"Meaning?"

"Meaning it's only been half a year since Shayne's death. Six months since you were found unconscious in the bedroom of your home, inebriated to the point that you required immediate medical intervention. You missed a performance, lost ground on your career."

"Those are the facts I've dealt with ever since I entered rehab. I'm not proud of where I was, but that's not where I'm at now. It's time for me to start living again."

Elliot Carmichael pulled a pair of readers from the

bridge of his nose and fiddled with the ear stems. "Chase, you've made great strides, but returning to music, to the road, to the parties, and all the trappings of tour life might wear you down. It's easy to retreat and hide behind the life of a performer—"

"But music, performing, is my home. That home busted apart because of my own stupidity. I get that. I own that. I've had to take responsibility for my fall, but I've also got to build it back up, repair the damage and start over the best way I know how. Right?"

Chase's words were quietly spoken, chosen with care, but nothing less than resolved. They formed a slicing lance through the topic. But just then, his thoughts flowed from the past to the present, and his gaze happened to rove the buildings, the rush of traffic that formed a slight blur outside the car window.

At a stoplight, he spied a small single-story building made of brick that was part of a retail strip center. This particular shop featured a nondescript, one-word sign out front. The word on that sign whipped up an impulse so strong that his throat instantly burned, stirring an urge so acute it knocked him out of breath, left him licking his lips to somewhat alleviate an instant and parched dryness.

The sign read, simply: Liquor.

His hands shook. His fingertips were unsteady as they hovered over the intercom button that would connect him to the driver up front. Heat flowed beneath his skin—paired with a mind-dizzying need. He pushed the button. Hard. "I need to make a stop before we get to the condo."

❧

Minutes later, Chase stared ahead at a square, gray granite headstone placed in neat alignment with dozens of others along the rolling grass of a carefully tended cemetery. The scent of freshly mown grass swept far and wide, but humid air closed around him, causing his chest to tighten, intensifying a lump that clogged his throat.

He'd made it past the liquor store. Barely. Still, he had forced his way past that temptation and won a small victory.

The first cut is the deepest.

Instead, he stood amidst the grave markers at White Chapel Cemetery. Towering trees with gnarled and twisty branches laden with late-summer leaves brought life to the landscape. The scene painted a serene, soothing view, but the comfort didn't sink any deeper than the surface of his skin. He wasn't clutching a bouquet of flowers. He wasn't standing before the headstone of his closest friend—the nearest thing he'd ever known to a brother—hand-in-hand with a loved one or family member. Rather, Chase confronted death's blow the same way he had for close to a year now.

Alone. Guilty.

Life's not about the birth date. Life's not the end date. Life's about that dash in between.

Chase had come upon those words, that phrase, more than once during recovery. Right now, they struck home. Most likely they were part of the lyrics of a poem, or maybe a song. That's how he processed most of life anymore—in stanzas, in melodies and rhythms. Composing verses helped him to cope—and breathe.

Regardless, the origins of the phrase didn't matter,

only its truth remained and he embraced it the best way he knew how. Chase scuffed at a pair of rocks near the toe of his cowboy boots. Bending, he cleared overgrown grass from the base of the stone. He tossed the excess aside.

God, Grant Peaceful Rest to Shayne Williams
Beloved Son, Beloved Friend

Shayne. Just six feet beneath the spot where he stood. Chase choked back the clog at his throat, blinked furiously against the sting in his eyes. The inscription on the headstone stirred him to reach out, to slide restless fingertips against the deeply grooved words. At his request, the last two words had been chiseled to permanence.

They had both been 'lonely-onlys,' neither having siblings to mess with or dream with. They were brothers not by blood, but by choice, especially when they'd discovered a mutual passion for music.

Shayne had always been the more sensitive one. The poet. The word crafter who possessed a natural gift for song writing. Critics always said Shayne Williams could pack a lifetime of emotion into a three-minute song, and they were absolutely spot-on.

"But we weren't ready for the ride, Shay. I certainly wasn't mature enough to handle what came at us, and you looked up to me. You followed my lead because I was the front man. In the end, I'm the one who fell, and you...the more talented one to be sure...died because I wasn't paying attention. I was swept into an attitude of excess that ruined everything." Chase gulped and choked on the husky words. Hot tears tracked. "God, I'm sorry. I'm so sorry."

Chase shook his head—a futile attempt to force

clarity. He wavered, and tried to home in on anything but the end date on his friend's headstone. A sweeping glance of the graveyard should have given him a small measure of peace; instead, Chase felt only heat—the flames of a hell that licked inexorably at the heels of his feet, no matter how hard he continually battled.

Bracing, he stared into the distance, able to see the shimmering waves of steam that crested through the air. A laden wind kicked up layers of dust that blew irritating particles into his eyes. He pressed a thumb and forefinger against the bridge of his nose. The instant he closed his eyes, memories rushed in as thick and oppressive as the heat that kissed this late July day.

All of a sudden, he was seventeen-years-old again, living with his folks in a rundown but serviceable ranch just outside of Murfreesboro. Like a lot of would-be musicians, Chase dreamed of The District, of downtown Nashville and honkytonks lit by neon signs and the scent of success. These were the hot-spots, the golden tickets to stardom. Country music—was anything better? Early in his high school years, Chase discovered, and built upon, a passion for singing and performing. He and his rough-hewn posse of four created a garage band. With their rangy good looks, tattered blue jeans and simple black t-shirts, they formed a band, which their audience—young ladies most especially—seemed to enjoy. At school dances, at neighborhood gigs, on amateur, small-scale stages, they covered the latest songs. Back then, he'd been all playful attitude and confident swagger. Music was something he didn't have to struggle to understand. It was natural. It spoke to his soul. It drove him.

But then came an unexpected meeting with a

producer who had heard and fallen in love with their debut song "Color of Life". A record deal followed. What came next was a rocket ship to venues across North America and the kind of airplay that turned "Color of Life" into a country/rock anthem and brought about a level of exposure the likes of which Chase and his friends had only dreamed.

Especially Shayne.

Trouble was, it became easier and easier for Chase to move from spot to spot like a target and believe his own marketing spin and press propaganda than to keep his increasingly troubled head on straight. His world had spun out of control.

The first tour was Chase's first taste of success…and he wanted more. The first and second albums were his first taste of financial security…and he wanted more. Music provided his first taste of affirmation…and that one tipped the scales against him, and he ended up taking Shay down as well.

Chase had spent long months struggling in recovery to come to terms with the fact that he had failed his friend so miserably.

Shayne married his high school sweetheart, Corrine Lucas. Corrine and their little boy, Gunther became constants on the road. Soon after those joy-filled events, Shayne was dead.

A vivid streak of red flashed through the air just in front of Chase, jarring him from his thoughts as it landed in a graceful swoop directly on top of the curved slab of gray stone. A cardinal. The bird hopped and flitted, then launched into the branches of a nearby tree and began to chirp. Birdsong. From a male cardinal. If that didn't beat all. Nowadays Chase knew enough to recognize a blessing from heaven when he received it.

The strident chirp and warble of his red-feathered companion left Chase pondering the advisability of his return to the stage tonight at the Opry. Was the clinic director right to be concerned? Chase wasn't sure. All he knew was that music wrapped him like battle armor. Music was his gift and call, his salvation…and his disgrace. All the same, music provided a healing that medications never could.

Shayne was gone, and nothing would bring him back, but Chase had made life-changing decisions during the past six months. Never again would he fall prey to self-destruction. Somehow, someway, he'd find a way to redemption. He'd find a way to repair the damage he'd done to Shay's wife and son; he'd honor the man he had loved like a brother.

2

A compulsion to pray overcame Pyper Brock. Seated on a leather couch in the Women of Country Music dressing room back stage at the Grand Ole Opry, she attempted stillness and calm, but couldn't quite get there. Instead, a spiritual deluge took place. Urgency. A weird and uncomfortable foreboding tightened to a coil through her chest.

She submitted, closed her eyes and drank in the sweetness of heavenly breath moving through her body.

I come to you in the light; I come to you in the darkness; I come to you always. You're Mine, and you're precious to Me.

The Spirit's words worked against Pyper's skin. The moment of assurance lent strength to a night she knew was going to be huge for her and her entire family.

What mystified her, though, was a subtle vibration of warning, a sense of being called to…to what? To battle? To some form of preparedness? Foreboding didn't fit into the puzzle pieces of her life at the moment, but she opened her eyes and straightened against plump pillows and focused on her mom who stood near a picture covered wall not far away. The jitters quieted, yet didn't quite go still. "Mama, can you come here a sec? Can we pray together before makeup invades and we're not alone anymore?"

"Sure, Pyp." They sat together, but Pyper's head continued to swim in an ocean salted by disquiet.

Her mom's brow puckered. "You thinking about the performance to come?"

"No. It's…" She couldn't figure out specifics quite yet, so she shrugged. "No. I just want to find some peace."

That dodge didn't lie, but it didn't tell the whole truth, either. Pyper sensed something momentous on the horizon, but it felt like blinders obscured her vision. For now, anyway.

So, she sent her trust to God and joined hands with her mom, but didn't begin to speak right away. Patient as ever, Amy Brock waited on Pyper in a silence that gradually worked against Pyper's rattled nerves. "It must be the magnitude of the honor dad is about to receive, but I feel edgy…like something big is set to explode."

Her mother stroked gentle fingertips against Pyper's cheek. "Something big *is* happening, sweetheart. You're helping to spring the surprise of a lifetime on your dad. It's going to be great. You're going to be great."

Pyper squeezed her mother's hands. "I know…and you're right…but it's more than that. It's…"

Rest in Me. Call on Me. Seek Me and you shall always find Me. Trust Me with what's to come.

An instant later, Pyper's body relaxed. Anxiety dissipated and a supernatural surrender took place. From there, prayer came as easy as her next heartbeat. "Father," Pyper began quietly, in a voice that bore testament to her Tennessee upbringing, "watch over us tonight. Bless Dad, and help us honor You as we use music to bring praise to Your name. Calm my restless heart; still my nerves and touch this night with the power of Your love."

"Amen and amen."

The response was tender, but no less emphatic. That made Pyper smile. She squeezed her mother's hands once more. Everything would be fine. Everything. Sustained, Pyper leaned forward to deliver a tight hug. A sharp knock sounded at the dressing room door which came open a moment later, admitting the makeup and costume team.

An entire *team*. The idea made Pyper chuckle. When she stood to move from the couch to an empty makeup chair, she captured her mother's gaze and delivered a sassy smirk. "Can you even believe the amount of effort that goes into making me presentable for the stage?"

Her mother laughed. "I guess I better leave them to it. I'll be right back. I'm going to check in on your dad and your brother or they'll wonder where I am and get suspicious. We can't have that."

"Give them both a hug from me."

For the next quarter hour, Pyper sat straight and tall in the makeup chair, centered behind a wall-length, stage-lit mirror.

Her mother reentered the room followed by a production assistant.

"Fifteen minutes, Miss Brock," he said.

"Thanks, Sam. Appreciate it." Pyper flashed him a smile. Following the call to arms, she looked at her mother via mirrored reflection while makeup techs finished brushing a thickly waved tumble of dark blonde hair. "Mama, how am I going to get through this duet with Dad? I feel like bawling, and I'm not even on stage yet."

Her mother fingered a curl of Pyper's freshly styled hair. Not that it needed much work. Pyper's trademark was a mane of hair that twirled and spun to the mid-point of her back with a life all its own.

"Sweetheart, think of tonight as just another show. You've sung with your dad a thousand times before, right? Tonight is no different. Just enjoy the music. Your brother'll be right there with you, too, playing in the band. It's going to be great."

Yeah, no different except for the fact that Tyler Brock, her step-dad—*dad*, she amended with a fierce sense of love—was about to be honored with an invitation to lifetime membership in the Grand Ole Opry performance family.

Pyper tilted her head to cuddle her cheek against her mother's palm. "This...tonight...what's to come for Dad, it's so important to me. I want him to be proud. He's done so much for me."

Her mother leaned against the makeup counter and turned Pyper's chair by the arm rests so they were eye-to-eye. "You already make him proud, Pyp. Always have. And that goes triple for me."

Pyper's chin quivered, but before sentimental emotions could gain traction, the dressing room door came open once more.

Sam, the PA, made a return. "Miss Brock, we're ready to set up. Need you in the wings. Your dad and brother are on the move, too."

Pyper expelled a pair of fast, steadying breaths. Anticipation's shiver swept through.

She wore a pair of well-used, well-loved cowboy boots of deep brown. She snagged a pastel blue sequined jacket and slipped her arms into the sleeves while her mom finessed the fall of her hair and arranged the lay of curls against her shoulders. Her white lace dress swished against her ankles; jeweled fringe and sparkles captured the light and set it free with flashes of brilliance. Perfect stage attire.

"I'm out of here, Mama. See you from the stage, and I love you!"

She took stock of the one who had seen her through the worst and brought her to the best. An indomitable, petite blonde, Amy Brock was Pyper's hero. A rise of tears threatened once again, set to spill over and do damage to the skilled workmanship of the Opry's makeup artists.

Blast the way her emotions always lifted right to the surface.

With full understanding, her mom shot her a teasing glower. "Don't you dare cry, Pyper Marie Brock, or I'll be a mess, too." That said, she yanked a few tissues free from the nearby box and handed off a couple so Pyper could dab her eyes while she did the same.

Restored, Pyper moved fast. "Thanks, Mama. You're the best. The very best."

"Knock 'em dead, Pyp. I'll be cheering—for both of you."

She was right. This was all about Dad. Tonight belonged to Tyler Brock—the man who had changed their lives, their hearts, forever.

Pyper dashed into the hall, looking over her shoulder just long enough to give a last wave before the door closed.

And she collided hard into a tall, strong body that stopped her as solid as a wall made of bricks.

"Whoa, there…"

A smooth deep voice registered. Her breath

whooshed on impact, but Pyper found herself grabbed at the forearms and carefully steadied. She looked up, way up, and took in a pair of pitch-black eyes and the olive-skinned features of a man who caught her attention, held it fast. Black hair tumbled in well-styled waves that curled against the collar of a supple, tan leather jacket worn over a plain white t-shirt. Her eyes skimmed down, then up again—he wore faded blue jeans like a dream—and she focused once more on a strong, compelling face, full of male charm and a dangerous, edgy charisma. A layer of stubble shadowed his chin and square jawline…

"So sorry."

Her murmured apology and auto-smile died when something else registered. *Chase Bradington*. Oh, for the love of mercy she had nearly been upended by Chase Bradington?

All that wonderful female appreciation, the sparks and tingles, died cold against her skin. Not to be judgmental or anything, but facts were facts, and as a member of the Nashville music scene, she knew the guy's history. He was sexy as could be, but ten-thousand shades of trouble.

"No problem." His grin spread slow, warm as sweet melted butter, just as tempting, too. Her throat went dry and heat worked through her body in spite of every intention otherwise. She fought the sensory pull and gathered her focus until it rested on one thing alone: the performance to come. "See ya, crash."

His close caused Pyper's lips to curve. She stared down his insolence and propped her fist on a cocked hip. "Whatever you say, bad boy."

She spun smooth on a booted heel and his rolling laughter followed her to the wings of the Opry stage.

3

"I'll get you for this, Pyper Marie Brock, if it's the last thing I do. Same goes for you, Zach. I can't *believe* what you guys pulled off tonight!"

Her dad's decree stirred Pyper's laughter into a merry twinkle, left her heart to soar as she tucked her arm through his and slipped her free arm around her brother Zach's waist. "Empty threats, empty threats."

Post-performance, she danced on air as they exited the stage. A crew followed headlined by triple-platinum inductee of two years ago, Jeff Stockton who tugged Tyler close for a final chest bump and a celebratory hug. Jeff had a jet to catch for a gig in Tulsa, so while farewells were exchanged between the two men, Pyper took note of nearby activity as Chase Bradington made ready to step into the spotlight.

Tyler rejoined her. "I swear, when I saw you tearing up at the end of "True Justice," when I heard your voice wobble a bit, I knew something was happening, but it wasn't until we finished, when Jeff strolled on stage, casual as could be, that my knees about buckled, and I almost fell to the floor. I couldn't believe it. What a night." Pyper's mom bounded forward and launched into her dad's waiting arms. He laughed and spun her in a circle. "I do believe I've been ambushed by my family."

"True enough. We're kinda brilliant like that."

"No argument here."

Her parents' conversation faded to static once Pyper saw Chase take the stage with a confident, powerful stride, waving and smiling as the emcee performed an introduction.

"Ladies and gentlemen, the Opry is pleased to welcome back to its historic circle two-time Grammy nominee and three-time CMA award recipient Chase Bradington!"

The crowd went wild. Folks pressed against the front lip of the stage and stretched forward, accepting Chase's high-fives and handshakes. The women in particular seemed bent on out-screaming one another.

Whatever.

He stood before the iconic WSM microphone, a guitar slung against his back for now. "Hey, y'all. It feels real good to be back on stage singing for you, especially here at the Opry." Applause rang out along with cheers of support. Pyper found it tough to breathe—and even tougher to look away—while she watched him gear up the crowd with a level of energy that was electric. Then there was that gorgeous, sizzling smile...irresistible to some, Pyper thought, but she steeled herself against its power.

Almost.

"I've missed you guys more than I can say. Thanks for the welcome home." Crowd noise distorted everything, amplifying, building, until he calmed matters by simply going still, studying the hallowed circle of oak at his feet and shifting so he could position and strum his guitar. The world faded to a silence that vibrated through the venue.

"As most of you know, I've walked through the badlands lately. In fact, you probably can't read a tabloid these days without mention of my name."

Music built in the form of a smooth, aching ballad. He addressed the house now; his posture struck Pyper as intent—most definitely potent. "All the same, I own my past with all of its blessings and all of its curses. But I also own my future."

Drawn, Pyper edged closer to the nearby curtain line of the wings.

"I've battled tragic circumstances and bad decisions. I'm hoping I can find my way back to what's good, because moments like this are what I love the most. Nights like this are what I dreamed of while I battled the demons in my soul.

"The song I'm about to share with you is a new one that came to life as a result of my recovery from addiction. It's called 'Burning Bridges'."

The band increased its volume. Pyper's heart started to thump—hard.

"A lot of times when we think about burning bridges we think about ruined relationships, or circumstances that've conspired against us. In this case, 'Burning Bridges' is about destroying a bridge that leads us to something bad, and finding a way to transform evil into something good in ways only God can create."

"You OK, sugar beet?"

Lost to poetic words and high ideals, Pyper jumped when her dad stepped close and wrapped an arm around her waist. Fast as lightning, she lit a smile and laced her fingertips with his. "You bet."

Her step-dad could never be fooled, though. He tracked the direction of her gaze. "You seem tense."

"Nah, I'm OK."

The evasion caused Pyper's nerve endings to skitter, but then, comfort rode in. The easy, gentle presence of her truest dad always worked on her spirit that way.

Her attention drifted back to Chase Bradington; the song he had crafted was evocative, an ode to heartfelt wishes, to wanting more than life and life-choices had delivered. She listened, captivated as he painted a world of redemption and hope with nothing more than his voice and his words. The song featured a definite country vibe, but remained unapologetically Christian.

The song was pure gold.

"Mr. Brock? I'm Joan Bradley, a hostess here at the Opry." Jarred once again from the view on stage, Pyper tuned in to more immediate concerns as a lovely woman with short, curly hair and a dynamite smile joined their group. "If you'll follow me, I'll lead the way to the green room."

Reluctantly, Pyper left Chase Bradington's music behind. Then, like the answer to a building wave of disquiet, Darren McCree fell in step next to her and delivered a great big smile.

"You did it, Pyp!" Darren kissed her cheek. "Great job."

"Thank you." She leaned against him and gave him a quick kiss in return. After a year of sharing space in Tyler's band, Pyper and Darren moved closer and closer to the crossroads between friendship and romance. "If I looked as shaky as I felt on the inside, I don't think I'll want to watch the broadcast when it airs next week."

"Yes, you will. Trust me, you were fantastic."

"Gosh—do ya bias much?"

"Yeah. Much."

He was so warm, so engaging. Even if Darren

didn't set her world on fire, Pyper loved his companionship and affection.

Joan guided their team. "To be honest, I don't like to refer to the space I'm taking you to as the 'green room'. For me, that feels way too impersonal and Hollywood. The staff of the Opry would like you to consider this your family room. Make use of it as you wish."

They entered an expansive area off the right wing. Walls were decorated by legendary performance photos and a wall-sized mural that featured caricatures of the biggest names in the industry. Comfortable seating invited folks to linger within the ebb and flow of service personnel and VIP's.

"I'll leave you here," Joan said, "but again, I want to welcome you to the inductees of the Grand Ole Opry, Mr. Brock. This is your night to take over the premises, and I hope you enjoy every second."

Visibly absorbing their surroundings, Pyper's dad acknowledged their hostess. "I already am, ma'am. Thank you again for everything."

Pyper continued to move in step with Darren like a perfectly synched puzzle piece. This was comfort. This was relationship as it should be—warm, steady and thoroughly compatible. She was blessed, and she knew it.

"You rocked the stage tonight."

Pyper looked into Darren's clear, green eyes. She dipped gentle fingertips against the soft fall of an errant wave of his light brown hair.

"I've always loved the guitar riffs in 'True Justice'," he said. "You and Zach really know how to bring them to life."

"What a beautiful flatterer you are."

He kissed her temple, and Pyper closed her eyes, absorbing his touch. She sought passion—heat. She sought connection and a tingle of awakening but instead came upon a solid, ready tenderness.

That was good, and that was enough.

She forced her enthusiasm upward and let Darren lead the way toward a buffet table that bowed beneath a fragrant variety of warm finger foods, an assortment of fresh fruits and veggies, and even a selection of succulent desserts. Pyper crossed the room at his side, but felt a somber chill sweep the length of her arms as her gaze rested upon a thin line of dark wood installed against the far wall. The simple piece leveled at a spot just above Pyper's waist, a poignant reminder of just how far flood waters had risen within the gorgeous auditorium during the late spring of 2010, destroying everything in its path.

Gliding her fingertips against a section of the trim, Pyper remembered the desperate way she and her family had stuffed sandbags and stacked them as tight as they could, as they'd prayed hard and chased the clock while a nasty deluge caused the Cumberland River to spill over its banks. A destructive crush of water washed through downtown Nashville, toppling history, toppling beauty, but never once toppling the city's hope and determination to rebuild and overcome.

She surrendered that memory in favor of the rebirth she now enjoyed, smiling at the way God had provided for the town she lovingly and resolutely called home. She focused on Darren.

"Now that my nerves have settled, I'm starving. Are you hungry?"

"Why else do you think I'd be dragging you to the

food table?"

He cast a grin, and Pyper laughed at the same instant she heard a familiar voice. "Hey there, superstar!"

As soon as she heard the greeting, Pyper spun from Darren's hold and squealed like a teenager, landing straight in the middle of a tight hug from her best friend, Anne Lucerne. "Annie!"

A statuesque brunette, Anne had a lovely, heart-shaped face, huge green eyes, and enough energy to fill the entire room. In honor of tonight's occasion, Pyper's surrogate sister wore cowgirl attire—right down to a flouncy denim skirt, a white button down shirt and a pair of black leather boots that were showroom fresh.

Issuing a teasing huff, Pyper decided to give Anne the business about that particular fact. "OK, seriously, you need to stay here with me forever so you can break those in. They need some scuff and wear."

They giggled and hugged all over again, spinning into a timeless dance. "Consider it done. My word, but you're completely gorgeous. I hate you."

"Oh, I am not. This face is the result of skilled makeup technicians and nothing more. But what about you? You look like a fashion model with those mile long legs. I've always resented that about you."

Anne struck a dramatic pose. "So true, but you've always been an adorable little shorty, so I've opted to hang out with you anyway."

A fresh round of laughter ensued; they talked over each other all over again, forcing their time apart to vanish beneath the history they had shared since childhood.

"Where are your mom and dad?" Pyper asked. "Did they come, too? I hope they made it."

Her wish was answered when a quick scan of faces revealed Ken and Kiara Lucerne. The pair stood not far away, nearly swallowed within a buzz of afterglow chaos. Ken's searching gaze lighted on Pyper, and he gave her a nod along with a smile that mirrored Anne's. He moved their way with his wife in tow.

"Wow." The cadence of Ken's deep voice, punctuated by a Midwestern twang straight from Michigan, was a slice of heaven to Pyper's ears. "Honestly, all I can say is wow."

Kiara wore a dazzled expression as well. "So, this is how life is lived in the big leagues."

Pyper fell into a fresh round of hugs and welcomes that filled her heart to overflowing. "It's the big leagues now that you're here! I am so glad to see you!"

"We're honored you included us. What a night for Tyler." Ken continued to take in the faces and energy of the room. Dressed casually in a polo shirt and jeans, he sported salt-and-pepper hair and remained strong of build, even at close to sixty.

Kiara settled her purse strap on her shoulder and fingered back strands of shoulder-length, honey-colored hair just barely touched with dashes of shimmering silver. Soft green eyes—a replica of Anne's—danced with happiness. "Speaking of music, I can't believe the way Tyler's life—and now yours—has become such a powerful mission field. Pyper, you're honoring his legacy in ways that are just incredible. I'm amazed at what God brought to life for you all."

If she didn't crack a joke, she'd lose it and cry, so Pyper gave her extended family a saucy glance. "Kiara, please, you're not in Michigan anymore. You're in

Tennessee. It's not you all, it's y'all!"

While laughter burst between them like sparkling confetti, Pyper's mom bounded toward their gathering, letting out a happy exclamation when she caught sight of their visiting dignitaries. "Ken! Kiara! I wondered where you were. I knew you had checked in with the VIP's, but I didn't have a chance to connect with you in the theater; I'm so sorry for that."

Kiara tugged Amy close for a long, tight hug. "You were a little busy, Miss Thing. We loved the performance! Where's Tyler? I can't wait to see him!"

Miss Thing—that was the nickname Kiara had given Pyper's mom decades ago, during a different, tragic season—in a life so different than the one Pyper now knew. Michigan memories, Michigan love, took her under. In a blink, Pyper was five-years-old all over again, battling monsters, battling hate and an innocence-robbing fear—and winning the victory. God's grace had seen to it that she and her mom circled away from a life marred by abuses both physical and mental.

During the height of battle, Pyper and her mom had found a safe harbor with Ken, Kiara, and Anne. Shortly thereafter, Tyler had entered their lives, and the nightmare ended for good and for all. These were the people who formed a precious framework for Pyper's heart. The celebratory evening wouldn't be anywhere near complete without them.

She surrendered her link to the past when her dad joined their group, explaining once again how he had been conned into thinking tonight's performance was just another routine show at the Opry.

"I don't know how they pulled it off. There I was, completely unaware, tucked behind the doorway of the Stars and Stripes dressing room, strumming with Zach and chatting with friends like I always do, yet I had no idea what was brewing."

"Well you deserve the accolades. Oh, man—do you remember the mission trip to Appalachia?" Ever stylish in wide-leg slacks of gray and a hip-length blouse of soft pink lace, Kiara gave Pyper's dad a grin and a nudge. "The entire trip to and from Pennsylvania was full of you and Amy with your teenage dreams and connections. Even then I knew your love of music would play itself out, Tyler. And I knew, somehow, some way, you and Amy would find your way to each other."

Tyler didn't answer. Not with words, anyway. Rather, he kissed Amy's lips. Pyper sensed the way her parents lost themselves in one other for a few precious seconds and her heart sighed. *That's what I want. That level of passion. That level of joy. God, please show me that sureness of connection, the spirit-melt that leaves two people in the shape of one.*

Hmm. Now those were song lyrics. Definitely. She'd have to jot them down before dropping off to sleep tonight…

Seeming to realize an immediate visit to the food table was placed on hold, Darren joined their circle and more introductions and chat ensued. Meanwhile, Pyper's mom focused on her friend and mentor, Kiara. "When we visited Michigan a couple months ago, you two had just retired from Woodland Church. How are you and Ken adjusting to the change?"

Updates were exchanged, paired with jokes about Ken never completely retiring from pastoral duties and Kiara not quite relinquishing her involvement in the church's youth group activities. Pyper stood next to her dad, content to rest against his side and survey the action taking place all around—their nearest and dearest gathered close to savor the moment of a lifetime.

Darren, she noticed, carried on a companionable conversation with Anne, which reminded Pyper she had become totally sidetracked and hadn't yet snared a bite to eat. She tilted her head, noticing the way easy smiles and a somewhat solitary focus seemed to encircle Darren and her best friend.

When Pyper paused to study them, she wondered why the exclusive focus she sensed inspired threads of happiness rather than seeds of jealousy. The thought had barely struck home when Chase Bradington entered the room and distracted Pyper completely. Fresh from the stage, he sent her senses into a rush.

Honestly. What was with her right now?

Surrounded by an eager entourage, he offered large, warm smiles and strode straight toward the food line. More folks gathered, shook his hand, offering what seemed to be encouraging comments; the overall presence of support earned nods, a few hugs as well as some hearty laughter. Nothing, Pyper supposed, beat the marketing angle of a fallen angel attempting to rise.

Hmmm. *A fallen angel attempting to rise.* Even more lyrics to memorialize later. She had definitely scored a ten on the inspiration meter tonight.

With her gaze latched onto the iconic singer, Pyper took note of the way folks continued to battle for Chase's attention. Through it all, he remained visibly composed. No small feat, she figured, since he was just hours out of rehab. In spite of the frenzy, she couldn't help but admire the view. Chase's smile was warm and wide; he engaged people in a direct manner and with an energy she absorbed even at a distance.

Mysteriously propelled, Pyper excused herself from her group and prepared to join the food line so she could touch base with her younger brother. Presently, Zach was making his way toward Chase like a wide-eyed groupie.

Darren, along with the rest of the world, faded to black while Pyper moved toward Chase, intent on conducting some reconnaissance and somehow subduing her unexpected reaction to the man.

4

What. A. Stunner.

Three small words, paired with a mouth-watering image, displaced everything else in Chase's world as the spritely blonde who had tumbled into him pre-performance drew near, circling through the crowd. Her level of poise and confidence could leave a body wondering if she didn't in fact own the Grand Ole Opry and its famed after-performance gathering space. Crash—as he liked to think of her now—was none other than Pyper Brock, Tyler Brock's daughter and an up-and-comer in the Christian music scene. She had a great smile. He focused on full, generous lips that tempted with a sweetness he could all but taste. Nice curves, too. She retained an easy, natural grace that set her skirt line skimming against slim legs and drew his attention to them quite nicely, thank you.

When she broke free of her conversational tribe and sashayed toward the spot where he stood, Chase experienced a flood of expectation, a push of wistful desire and heat. He froze against those thoughts and gave that pull of longing a real fast shove to the rear. *Bad idea, Chase. Very bad idea. Stop where you stand. Can you imagine how her rock-solid, upstanding father would react to the display of any interest on your part?*

She stepped into place at the end of the line right next to a man Chase recognized from the show tonight; that's when a whole new development tossed ice water against the warm slide of attraction toward the woman. Evidently she had earned the attention of Darren McCree, a guitarist who had backed her and her daddy during the show tonight. A man in the band. The two were most likely off to a proper and perfect life together. God bless 'em both.

Fortified, Chase ignored the encroachment of an impossible, romantic fantasy and concentrated instead on the more important task of networking. He pressed palms, worked through the growing layers of industry suits, media members and fans. All the while, he remained easy-spirited, grateful for every show of support. Yet, his gaze tracked to the sweet innocence of Pyper Brock. A pierce-point struck home at the center of his heart. He could have sworn he felt a bleeding start deep within—a hemorrhaging for something he could never have.

Too much time wasted ever to be young again. Too much time wasted ever to taste pure again. To be worth more than…

Forgiveness.

Just like that, a flash sent his mind far from the charms of a fascinating woman. He tumbled headfirst into a song that came to life, breaking free from a spot in his soul he hesitated to approach, let alone open wide. He stood immobile, fearful and exhilarated at the same time.

Forgiveness.

A song with meaning like that would be great, but it would also require exposure—the kind of soul-deep exposure that would only come after exhaustive revelation. Could he do it? Right now, he just didn't know. After all, once chains like that were unlocked, who knew what might spring free—good or bad?

Risky? Yes, absolutely. Worth the gain? In the end, who knew but God?

Forgiveness.

Chase's focus returned to Pyper. Something about the woman kept pulling at him. Maybe it was those soft, ruby lips he had enjoyed perusing. Maybe it was something in the radiance of her eyes and demeanor— as if she bubbled with love and simply let it flow over the ones closest to her. She captivated him because she was alive and unguarded. Self-assured. She walked with a degree of confidence that could only come after being brought up right, with a careful blend of love and discipline that had obviously molded her into a formidable woman.

In short, she possessed all the benefits he wished like crazy he could have found in his own life.

"Excuse me...ah...Chase Bradington, right?"

Thank goodness for interruptions. Chase delivered himself to the moment at hand, placing his smile even before he turned to face...

A kid? A teen? A handsome, earnest youth with an almost familiar look to him. The eyes of blue in particular, spoke of something familiar, but...

The boy extended his hand with smooth aplomb, like a polished adult. "I'm Zachary Brock." Only then did he shuffle his feet a trace. "Zach, actually. I just wanted to say hello and tell you how much I've always loved your music. Great to see you back on stage again. You did an excellent job tonight and everything."

Chase's smile warmed from 'performer' to authentic when he met Zach's straight-on gaze. No wonder the kid looked familiar. He was probably a replica of his father when he was in his mid-teens.

Chase saw the resemblance clearly now.

"It's a pleasure to meet you, Zach. Thanks for your kind words. I appreciate them. Your daddy is incredible. He's a mighty tough act to follow."

"Tell me about it." Zach's gaze flicked to the spot where Tyler stood, then to the ground as if somewhat embarrassed by the admission.

Chase's comment had been innocent, an ice-breaker, but it visibly shook the kid. Chase recognized battle lines—stress fractures waiting to expand. He did his best to countermand those developments. "You have a great family. Count yourself lucky. I've known them for years by reputation, of course, but it's nice to get to meet them officially."

"You sounded amazing. Will 'Burning Bridges' be on the next album?"

Obviously Zach wanted to drop the topic of family. Fair enough. Chase didn't push. Besides, the kid's optimism was a panacea, the best form of medicine he'd received since exiting Reach. "I sure hope so. I'm looking to get something started for certain."

Zach went silent for a moment. "You will. You're an incredible musician." He hesitated again and Chase absorbed another resemblance.

With eager optimism and innocent enthusiasm, Zachary Brock put him in mind of someone else. Shayne Williams, back in the day.

"I hope you're feeling OK. You went through a terrible set of circumstances, and I can't wait to watch you prove what you've got all over again."

The words were like a mystical response to the connection Chase had just made. God at work. Zach seemed bent on conveying his support, yet cautious of stepping into territory best left alone. Shayne would have reacted just the same. This youngster's warmth left Chase wanting to open up and respond in kind.

"I won't lie. That kind of affirmation is something I'm awfully glad to hear right about now. Working the stage tonight was equal parts terror and adrenaline rush."

"Man, I can't even imagine how cool it must have felt to—"

"Mr. Bradington. Good evening."

Conversation stopped immediately and Chase's world froze as Pyper strolled into place next to her brother. Inky lashes fluttered against an ocean of luminous blue; her lips tilted upward as their gazes connected, and held.

Chase caught his breath, steeled his spine. "Pyper Brock. I'm delighted to meet you, formally that is."

She chuckled. "I see. So, that little body blow from earlier wasn't quite formal enough for you?"

"Not nearly. You OK, by the way?"

"I don't intend a lawsuit, so rest easy. Thanks for the great performance tonight. You rocked the house. Congratulations."

What awesome sass and personality. Chase's regard for Zach faded to the background fast, though he noticed the way Pyper's brother kept close tabs on their interaction. "I'd like to say the same to you and your daddy. You must be awfully proud, crash."

"To levels I can't even contain, but, excuse me, 'crash'?"

She moved a step closer then another—whether for food or connection Chase couldn't quite tell. Handing her a plate then nabbing one for himself, he delivered a negligent shrug. "If the name fits…"

Chase went to work retrieving a cluster of grapes, some strawberries, a couple skewers of chicken satay and a handful of veggies accompanied by a dollop of creamy dip. He munched on a few of the grapes, avoiding her eyes. Next he snagged a small stack of crackers and some cheese cubes.

"I shouldn't have referred to you as 'bad boy.' That was mean and uncalled for. I apologize for that."

Chase flicked a glance in her direction. Those eyes of hers were breathtaking. "Don't worry about it. I knew you didn't mean any harm. Let's start from scratch." He extended his hand to pave a road to fresh starts. Also, he wanted to touch her—to feel her hand in his.

She accepted the gesture, but a sudden and shy hesitance filled the space between them. Chase pondered that reaction. Had he just earned the upper hand? With Pyper Brock? He sensed that didn't happen often. Lips twitching, he nudged her gently out of the way so he could nab a couple crispy ovals of garlic toast. At least that way he got to invade her space a little. She jumped back slightly. He grinned. Playing with her was kind of fun.

All at once, she stopped filling her plate and an expression of intrigue colored her features. Chase tracked the line of her gaze straight to a spot on his right wrist where a rolled up shirt sleeve revealed a small purple cross that had been inked into permanence by a tattoo artist.

"You're a believer."

The observation, so simple and straightforward, struck against the most important facet of his rebirth, recovery, and commitment to life. "Very much so."

"A tattoo?"

"Yep. A memorial, and a reminder."

"I sense there's a story behind your story."

He discovered he liked being the recipient of her intrigue. "There is at that. In short, the cross memorializes my best friend, and it's also a permanent reminder of who I belong to from here on out."

"Shayne Williams and God."

"Yep."

She set aside her plate and took hold of his hand, cupping it in both of hers so she could examine the tattoo. She brushed her thumb light against the surface of his skin; his pulse took off as heat built and stirred his senses.

"I wanted to honor him and the changes I went through as I dealt with...recovery."

One look into her eyes and he knew she didn't need a roadmap through the terrain of his past and his very public fall from grace.

"You're all about your faith now."

Chase nodded.

"I could that tell by the lyrics you wrote. You've found Christ."

He nodded once more, relishing the sensation of her touch.

"It's purple. Why's that?"

"Think about it, Pyper. What does the color purple symbolize?"

Puzzling briefly, she blinked—then made a connection. "Royalty."

"The lady isn't just beautiful, she's smart, too." Chase registered the quick touch of pink that tinged her cheeks at the compliment, then he looked down, glad their connection lingered. Her skin formed such a soft and creamy contrast next to his. "Christ is the King of kings. I thought the color fit."

"It does. It's perfect. I love it."

She released his hand and her smile worked through him like sunlight.

"About the whole 'bad boy' thing...I really was just being a smart-mouth, and I also hope the nickname doesn't fit you anymore. After all, tonight was about winning back trust, right? A chance to shut up the critics and regain loyalty? After listening to your new song, I promise I'm one of the folks cheering for you, Chase. Come back, y'hear? All the way back. Your talent's too good to waste."

Now carting a full plate—when had that happened exactly?—she tilted her head, delivered a tender wink before turning and walking away. Enchanted, Chase stared, wondering. Did she practice that pretty little spin move in her spare time? The decidedly feminine exit worked on him like a spell, especially when she added that mind-blurring smile, and the sparkle of those warm, beckoning eyes.

For the rest of the night, Chase lost himself in the afterglow, but his attention stayed glued to Pyper.

5

Chase's world patterned into a weird form of black-and-white. He was backstage at the Ryman Auditorium, but he wasn't set to perform any time soon. Instead, he was stretched on a gurney, right arm held down by a person's hand…a person he couldn't see. He didn't hurt, but didn't feel altogether comfortable, either. Why wasn't he afraid?

Maybe because of the amazing light show. Sunbeams poured through stained glass, painting a multitude of colors across the stage, the carpet of the theater, the stairs and pews that now acted as seating spaces rather than spots for worship.

"You ready?"

A man's voice, vaguely familiar, came from the right; a whir and a buzz filled the air. Chase nodded, but found himself transfixed by the dozens of colorful stage lights rigged to the ceiling. "Yeah, but where's the audience?"

"They'll be here soon enough. You wanted this first, right?"

Wanted what? And what was that buzzing?

Beside him, on a surgical table, he saw a hammer, a long, thick nail. Why wasn't he scared?

Suddenly, the nail point came to rest against his wrist. He saw a hand pick up and lift the hammer. Turning his head, Chase tried to attach a face, a person, to this odd vignette, but the buzzing increased and a blaze of fire hit the nerves of his right wrist. A pierce point? The start of a stabbing blow? No. As fast as they materialized, the hammer and nail disappeared, replaced by a tattoo machine, held by the guy he now recognized as the one who had inked his cross.

A scene shift took place.

"You're a believer."

Chase came upon the sound of Pyper Brock's soft, south-kissed voice. A blink later, there she stood, gorgeous as could be, wearing her show outfit from the Opry. They were face-to-face outside the Women of Country Music dressing room, where their worlds had collided. Without a word, without reservation, he took a dive into those tempting blue eyes, admired the perfectly styled tumble of dark blonde hair that his fingertips just twitched to comb through…

"Jesus saved me," he replied.

It was the purest, simplest admission he could manage, the truth of his life encapsulated into a brief trio of words.

"He did, Chase, and I'm so glad for that."

All at once, the eeriness of the previous vignette morphed into a rushing tingle, into a warmth so soothing he nearly weakened at the knees. All at once, a need took him over; a longing pulsed through his chest and filled him. In that instant, he knew she was all he'd ever wanted.

His world came to a standstill that echoed with all-over peace, a tranquility he craved more than any shot of alcohol he'd ever consumed. All he felt right now was homecoming. A sense of fulfillment.

Pyper stretched to tip-toe; her hair smelled of jasmine and spice. Chase closed his eyes, surrendering to the touch of her lips against his left cheek, then his right.

"I'll see you, Chase. Have a great show."

The tattoo machine amped up again and the inking resumed…

Chase awoke against a harsh snap of consciousness, bathed in a sweat that chilled his skin. He heaved to a sitting position. The conversation with Pyper last night had obviously tripped a few of his less-than-steady mental wires. Still battling the shakes, he angled his wrist, rolling it, pondering the cross tattoo—the mark of his Savior's sacrifice, the symbol of Christ's supreme act of forgiveness and redemption. He traced the image, but his memory took a taste of Pyper's sweet smile; into his mind drifted the image of clearest blue eyes. The soft touch of her fingertips still echoed—a touch that had obviously slipped past skin-level to something much deeper.

And terrifying.

Odd dreams weren't an uncommon companion, but this one proved more powerful than most. Had to be the result of leaving rehab and taking to the stage again.

And the impact of Pyper Brock.

He padded from the bedroom to the kitchen. There, on the green quartz countertop, right next to his keys and wallet, rested his cellphone. And he had forgotten to latch the stupid thing to a charger.

"Smooth, Chase. A bit distracted, were you?"

All over again, the perfume that was Pyper Brock swept through his psyche. He plugged in the device which started to juice, then lit like a mini firework. There were a good number of congratulatory texts. Nice. He would read through them while he sat on the balcony outside and devoured a stack of pancakes and sausage patties.

A grumbling stomach prompted him toward the stainless fridge, but before leaving the phone behind, he scrolled through a long string of missed calls. Two came from Mark Samuels. That made him smile. Maybe they could meet for lunch. Sooner rather than later. It would be great to reconnect and absorb some of the man's ever-present reinforcement—and wisdom.

Chase whisked batter, cooked and plated, pausing just long enough to look out the floor-to-ceiling windows that lined the living area of his condo. His home featured a sparkling view of downtown Nashville spread across the land like a jewel. It had shaped up to be a perfect morning to enjoy a leisurely breakfast alfresco, so he grabbed his half-charged cellphone and carried his plate to a small bistro table of black metal. The outdoor space was expansive, dotted by spiky green plants his housekeeper had tended to faithfully during his absence. Most of all, he enjoyed the privacy afforded by walls that enclosed each side of the balcony. He had spent much of the last three years both dodging and courting the paparazzi. Home, however, was his sanctuary. Here he coveted one thing—mental rest. Solitude.

He settled into one of the chairs and then glanced at his phone. In addition to calling to Mark, there was business to be done after he ate. His gaze rested on one of the tallest, most prominent markers in the city skyline. A lot of locals referred to it as the Batman Building, due to the way its twin antennas sprouted from each side, pushing to the sky against a slightly arced topline. Right now, as Chase studied the structure, he saw only one thing—hope—hope in the form of an entertainment agent who worked within that glass and metal skyscraper. Kellen Rossiter.

Instinct left Chase wanting to call Kellen first, but he knew what would serve him best, and he was equally determined to follow that call. He needed the reinforcement and guidance of his recovery sponsor first. So, once he finished breakfast, after dropping his dishes in the sink and replenishing his mug of coffee, he dialed up Mark Samuels and resumed his seat outside.

"Chase!"

"Mark. Have I interrupted you mid-packing?"

Mark's laughter crossed the cell connection. "You wouldn't recognize my office anymore. It's barren."

"You gonna be paying a visit to the new Reach facility in downtown Nashville anytime soon?"

"On my way there in a couple of days, actually. I leave South Carolina on Wednesday. We need to finish set up and get ready for launch now that I signed a lease on an apartment in Tennessee. You doing OK?"

Muffled background noise came to life, drawers opening and closing, items being moved around, but it only took a split second for Mark's tone to switch from easy going to intent and concerned. Mark was on his way to Nashville from the Reach flagship facility in South Carolina where Chase had first met him. Mark had followed Chase to Franklin, Tennessee to take on a permanent position in Nashville at a new facility. During the interim, he had finished Chase's counseling, and assumed a few cases that would carry over to his new position. The man never seemed to quit on his patients. That level of commitment—that drive to be present to those who needed him–was assuring, and had always filled Chase with confidence.

So, he stretched his legs and crossed them at the

ankles, looking ahead, at the curves and glitter of the Cumberland River as it ambled through town. "I'm doing good so far. No worries."

"So I hear."

"Oh? How's that?"

Judging by the sound, Mark seemed to drop a few heavier items into a box. He chuckled. "Hey, I'm tech savvy. I know how to check out social media feeds. Your name was all over the place this morning. Country music fans and critics alike are singing your praises loud and clear. Seems you hit the comeback trail with a rock-solid swing. Keep it up."

"Yeah, thanks. I received some interesting nibbles as the result. Your arrival in Nashville couldn't be more perfect. I have a meeting coming up later this week with an agent, Kellen Rossiter. Seems he wants to take me on as a client. I'd love to see you first and take your temperature on things. I'll even help you unpack."

"What an incentive. Really. You're too gracious for words." They shared a grunting laugh and a snort. "With all that's going on, everything running at high octane, are you doing OK? Staying away from temptation?"

Chase smirked to himself. Temptation in the form of alcohol, yes. Temptation in the form of Pyper Brock, no...not so much.

"Closest I came to a bottle was the instant I left the rehab center. Nearly stopped at some dive liquor store off the highway. Passed that up in favor of time better spent."

"Yeah?

"Shay. I visited Shayne's gravesite."

Silence filled a beat or two of time. "Good for you.

I think that's great."

"After that, the Opry event took up the rest of my focus. I'm doing all right. Really." *So far*, he added in silence, drawing in a breath of cool morning air.

"I'm checking in at Reach North pretty much right after I land. Let's plan to meet after that."

"Absolutely. Talk to you soon, Mark. Thanks."

"I'm praying for you, Chase. Keep your head in the game, hear?"

"Yes, sir."

The term didn't stem from simple affection, it stemmed from a level of respect Chase had felt for precious few people in his life.

Call concluded, Chase continued to rest in the warm sunlight and muffled urban noise of central Nashville. He tipped his head back so the rays could kiss his skin, and he prayed. He relaxed his mind and body completely and surrendered to a quiet interlude, along a fresh wash of memory. An anticipatory smile split his features as he recalled his final moments at the Opry gala and the approach of Kellen Rossiter.

Kellen owned and operated the entertainment agency that bore the man's name, and he had long enjoyed a reputation for fierce and intelligent representation. Kellen managed Tyler Brock's career, and Chase had admired the agent for years based on industry word-of-mouth alone. Chase knew Kellen to be dedicated, loyal and dogged in his approach to client management. He possessed a knack for recruiting great artists, but he kept them in place by displaying tenacious fighting skills tempered by a solid core of decency that Chase had uncovered in far too few players within the mainstream media.

Last night's introduction had been the first time

Chase had spoken to Kellen directly, and the agent had made it very clear he was interested in fostering Chase's return to the industry.

"Keep up the kind of performance I witnessed tonight, and I'd like to talk to you about what's ahead."

"You'd be interested in representing me?"

"I am if you're serious and committed to a road that's straight and narrow."

"That much goes without saying, I promise you that."

Kellen cracked a broad smile at the disclaimer. "I hope so. Like everyone else, I paid attention when you hit bottom, but I also paid attention when you pushed through recovery. I paid attention to what I saw and heard tonight. If you intend a return to the gifts you've been given, if you stay strong, I see a lot of good things in your future. I sense you've changed. If that's the case, I'd like to talk about taking the helm of your career and building on tonight's momentum."

Kellen extended his hand and Chase accepted the gesture at once. "I'd appreciate the opportunity."

"I'm looking forward to it." Tugging a business card from the inside breast pocket of his suit coat, Kellen extended it to Chase. "Call me, and let's meet next week."

Chase palmed the offering like a gift; Kellen delivered a final nod and blended into the crowd.

When his eyes came open in the here and now, the first thing Chase saw was the Batman Building. He fiddled briefly with Rossiter's business card then picked up the phone and dialed. He was ready.

It was time to make music again.

6

"Hey, Pyper, and Tyler, it's good to see you."

Pyper's affection bloomed like a spring meadow when Kellen Rossiter rose from his desk chair and crossed the length of his office to greet her and her dad. Dashes of silver highlighted Kellen's dark brown hair. Olive skin was touched by light lines that curved against the corners of his mouth and formed a faint spray against his eyes. Her dad's agent and their long-time family friend was sharp and intense, but soft-hearted when it came to the ones he cared for the most. Knowing full well she was counted among that circle, she stretched to tiptoe and kissed Kellen's cheek. Tyler accepted a firm handshake before Kellen directed them to a pair of chairs in front of his desk.

"Thanks for meeting me on such short notice. I wouldn't push if it wasn't important."

"Timing's no worry, Kellen, but I have to say, our curiosity is definitely piqued." Tyler answered Kellen's concerns while Pyper settled, and waited. "What's going on?"

"The short story is I want to talk to you both about an idea I have." Kellen returned to the chair behind his desk.

"An idea. With that, I'm all set to hear the *long* story." Pyper stifled a laugh while her dad shared a teasing smirk with his agent.

"Then I'll start at the beginning. First off, I've

signed Chase Bradington as a client."

No denying the flush—the awareness—that skimmed through her system when Kellen dropped that piece of news. Pyper stiffened against the memory of dark, fathomless eyes, a strong build, and a heady vibration of charisma. She abandoned those thoughts when she noticed the way her dad's brows pulled.

"So, you're on the Bradington comeback train?"

"As his agent, I might even be considered its conductor. I'm behind the guy, yeah. I believe there's a lot to him."

Her dad sat back in his chair and stared, his concern palpable. "Yeah, there's a lot to him, and don't get me started reviewing it all."

A tense form of energy flooded Pyper's body while her dad went on offense, refuting Chase quietly and calmly, yet with a finality that told Pyper everything she needed to know about a future with the handsome icon. Alcohol. A powerful, alpha bad-boy image. Battles small and large in his personal life. What was she thinking letting a purely chemical reaction run wild like this?

Resolute now, Pyper nodded in agreement with her dad. "Kellen, due respect to you, truly, but isn't he a tremendous risk?"

Kellen accepted that query with a nod. "Maybe. And, yes, I understand where you're coming from. The arguments aren't unfamiliar to me."

Her father gestured wide. "Of course they're not. You know the business inside and out. That begs the question. Why would you—"

"I get that he's a risk, but to my mind, he's a *calculated* risk." Kellen's interruption was emphatic, accompanied by a glint of light that dawned in his eyes, a light sparked by challenge…and something a bit more that Pyper couldn't quite define. "I intend to help give him a second chance."

Pyper sighed inwardly, but figured, case closed. "I hope it works out well for both of you, but you're making me wonder why you've asked to meet with me and Daddy. It's certainly not our business who you represent."

"Actually, Pyper, my representation of Chase just might involve you directly. As such, I wanted Tyler's take on my plans as well."

That nervous stiffness returned all over again—with added strength this time. Pyper straightened against an onslaught of complicated, mixed-up feelings. Kellen, meanwhile, focused on her dad for a second or two before continuing.

"Pyper, sometimes life gives us an opportunity to start over again. I know what it's like to lose something I cherish then use everything I am to claw my way back and return to what's good. From where I sit, that's what Chase is doing right now. He's determined to succeed. His effort has earned my attention and my opinion that he deserves an opportunity to prove himself again."

Pyper set her jaw. What argument could be made? None.

Lifting a pen and tapping it restlessly against his desk, Kellen pressed on. "Finding him an opportunity circles to the reason I've asked for this meeting. As I put together a rundown of songs for Chase's new album, I came up with an idea to include you on one of the recordings."

Pyper stared, slack-jawed. "Include me?"

To combat a roll of fear and disquiet, Pyper forced

herself to relax against the back of her chair. She assumed a composed, professional air, but all she could see was Chase—all she could feel in the air around her, like inevitable fire and flame, was the man who had struck through her like a streak of lightning. He was mysterious, compelling and most of all—for a number of reasons—extremely dangerous.

So, she faced off with her dad's agent, chin lifted, gaze unflinching. "Kellen, I'm working on my second album as we speak, and I'm also ramping up my own workload in the months to come. I don't see how this will work."

"Hear me out before you issue any final decision, OK?"

She delivered a playful smile. "I'm all braced."

Since Kellen was used to her sass, Pyper wasn't a bit surprised when he simply grinned right back.

"Thanks for that," he said. "Here's the situation. I watched Chase's performance of 'Burning Bridges' and it occurred to me that the song calls out to be a duet. It's got a push-pull style that calls for harmony along with the touch of a woman's voice, and emotion. I connected the dots, and they created a line straight to you, Pyper."

Pyper's eyes went wide. She shook her head. Contributing a few lines of harmony to a song or two with some combined vocals that could be blended post-production was one thing. Working with Chase Bradington on a tug-your-heart-out song like 'Burning Bridges,' in the intimate confines of a recording studio, sent Pyper into full panic mode. The heat index in Kellen's office seemed to soar.

Kellen worked a preemptive strike by lifting his hands to stem an outburst. "Judging by your expression, I can see you understand where I'm headed with this."

Her dad leaned forward, propping his elbows on his knees. His eyes glinted, and Pyper could tell his protective instincts had kicked in at max capacity. "You're treading on very dangerous territory, Kellen. You know Pyper's history. You propose pairing her in a song setting with the king of bad behavior?"

"The *reformed* king of bad behavior, Tyler. Give the man his due for emerging from recovery and displaying a solid effort to this point."

At last, Pyper found her voice—and a small piece of sound logic. "Kellen, you know I adore you. You're the best there is, but you can't possibly be serious." Forcing a demure attitude, she rested her elbows on the armrests of her chair; she fluttered her lashes, pouring on a dose of friendly charm. She needed to catch this fly with sugar rather than vinegar.

Kellen didn't flinch. Nor did he back down. "Pyper, I'm very serious, and I want you to give this proposition full consideration."

Kellen Rossiter had been part of Pyper's life long enough to know just how to gauge—and just when to push. Her deliberately winsome smile faded when shadows danced against the walls of her soul, when dastardly ghosts crept like evil itself through her spirit. Her alarm system blipped loud as every escape hatch drew slowly, inexorably closed.

"No. No way."

Three short words were delivered with fierce conviction. Pyper wouldn't revisit her rocky childhood. Not here. Not now. Chase was sexy, attractive and a total charmer, but his battle with addiction would push her into a land of pain she refused to inhabit ever again.

Sensing a temporary impasse, Kellen lifted smoothly from his desk chair. He walked to a beverage service stationed against the far wall of his office and cracked open a trio of water bottles. He delivered them to his guests and kept one for himself before continuing the battle.

"Working with you would be good for him, Pyp. Plus, I think you'll be incredible performing together. I bet you'd have a great sound, probably some great chemistry, and—"

Pyper answered that praise with a guffaw that came out overdone and a bit too strenuous. Her prior attempt at sweetness turned steely in a flash, and she drummed her fingertips against the bottle rather than taking a sip. "Kellen, with all due respect to your instincts as an agent, my answer is no. A hundred times, no."

"Then I'm asking a hundred and one." Kellen was firm, determined, once again proving a truth she had known from the start of her career. Kellen Rossiter was nobody's pushover. "Look—I know where you're coming from, but your past makes you the perfect person to interpret this song with him and bring it to life and add to its authenticity. All I'm asking you to do is sing with the man. It's not a big deal. It's music. It's professional. It's what you do. What's the problem?"

Pyper tracked Kellen while he resumed his seat.

"I can't be part of that story, Kellen. I can't. I won't be able to handle it." Relentless in her own right, Pyper pushed on. "I respect the guy as a musician, but I'm not going to be used to build a roadway for him. You know I have a history with this kind of thing. I will *not* do well working side-by-side with an alcoholic."

The combustible reaction poured through her heart and soul with no kind of filter. That's when she noticed something flicker through Kellen's features—surprise—followed by a laden chord of discomfort. That's when Pyper turned and realized the cause of his reaction.

Chase.

Paused at the threshold, dressed in a button-down shirt of blue and pair of thigh-hugging black jeans, Chase leaned against the doorjamb, his focus trained on Pyper. "I'm a *reformed* alcoholic, and I can assure you, I'm determined on that count."

Exhibiting a smooth, quiet dignity, he stepped into the rising heat of the moment by folding into the third chair positioned next to Kellen's desk. "I'm sorry to interrupt, Kellen. I know I'm a few minutes early, but your assistant told me I could come on in."

"No worries. I'm glad to see you again."

"Same here. Apologies for disrupting the discussion."

Pyper wanted to disappear into the floor, or at least be given a chance to rewind the past ten seconds and play them out all over again—with a completely different outcome. Despite the mounting flush that crept upward from her shoulders, she steeled her spine and found her voice but couldn't meet his eyes. "Chase, I'm *so* sorry."

"It's all good. You didn't say anything I haven't heard before. Besides, I'm the type of person who prefers straightforward honesty to polite falsehood."

"We have that in common." Pyper murmured the words, finally hazarding a glance in his direction. She had to give him huge props for graciousness—especially since he had no idea of the minefield he had unwittingly stepped into, nor how deep a nerve this opportunity struck within her.

"I don't mean to short change you, Chase." Her tone rang with sincere contrition. "And in general, my manners are much better than this."

"Thanks for that, but I have no problem with your manners, Pyper." Chase punctuated the words with an assuring smile and steady regard that sent her pulse rate into overdrive.

"It's like I said to you at the Opry," Pyper began in earnest, "I know you've got a hit on your hands with 'Burning Bridges.' I admire what you've done, and how you're trying to turn everything around."

"You mean how I've *turned* everything around." His eyes narrowed just slightly; she sensed the way his resolution dawned sharp and real.

When he refused to yield an inch with regard to his progress through recovery, Pyper's temperament eased. She knew she had to place a fair and honest end-note on the moment. "And the outburst you just walked in on? It was about me not you, OK?"

"More than. And I appreciate that."

Chase's focus trained on Pyper and stayed firmly latched until Kellen resumed the meeting.

"I'm with Pyper. There's no question 'Burning Bridges' will be a hit."

"And artist to artist, I agree as well," her dad interjected. "But the song and its story belong to you. Are you sure you're OK with all of this?"

Just like that, Pyper's longed for escape hatch yawned open, offering her a means by which to avoid this dizzying sense of magnetism, the pounding of her heart. *Thank you, Daddy,* she breathed in silence. *Thank you so much.*

"I see my dad's point." Pyper shifted to address Chase directly. "Why complicate a great piece of music you created from the residue of your own sweat and tears?"

"Actually, Kellen made this suggestion, and I agreed to it when he signed me on as a client. Naturally, he didn't mention potential co-performers by name. He knows the lay of the land better than anybody, right? He probably wanted to find out who'd be willing to work with me first. I'm surprised it's you as well, Pyper, but I think it makes a lot of sense."

Her respect for the man grew exponentially. Blast it all. She could brush aside arrogance, ego and entitlement, but Chase bore none of those trappings. He was equal shares toughened and humbled, forming a whole that fascinated her in spite of every instinct and inclination otherwise. Pyper pursed her lips. "I don't mind the idea of working with you, Chase. I have more than a few black spots in my own past that put us on even ground, but are you sure you want to share the spotlight on a song that would easily launch you to the front lines of the music industry as a solo artist?"

"Pyper, let me make something real clear." By now, a layer of weariness dimmed his eyes. "I'm not about the *industry*. I'm about making great music. To my mind, that'll follow a Christian contemporary theme enhanced by a country vibe. As such, if you have something meaningful to add to a song I've created, it'd be a win-win from my point of view. Why fight it?" All at once his gaze intensified, sliding against her slow and as alluring as a finger stroke. "Besides, I have other songs in the works that'll showcase my talents just fine as solo pieces."

Silence ensued. Pyper drifted into the shared

moment. "So, what you're saying is you've been writing a lot these days."

"Call it a silver lining against some very dark and stormy clouds. The title track will be called 'Forgiveness.'"

"And producers at Imperion are already behind the album." Kellen spoke, refocusing the meeting. "Label execs liked the idea of infusing a woman's tone, some female sweetness into the mood of 'Burning Bridges.' They believe that kind of emphasis will serve to make the piece even stronger. As for the title track, producers have heard rough cuts of 'Forgiveness' and they're ready to sign off on making the song its first release. They figure it'll become the anthem of his comeback. To generate some positive media buzz, I'd like to pair the two of you in a live setting, maybe at one of the bigger-name spots in The District like Tootsie's or The Stage. I'm thinking we could polish up a three-song set and test the waters in front of a crowd before hitting the recording studio next month. Any thoughts?"

Chase shifted, appearing uncomfortable. "Anywhere in The District would be great—but I don't think I'll be welcomed back at Tootsie's any time soon. Not after being a public-broadcast no-show."

"Maybe not welcomed yet, but you will be soon enough. I'll check with my contacts and get something in place while the irons are still hot from the fire you lit at the Opry."

Nearly an hour of strategic planning followed that decree. The large, circular clock on Kellen's office wall inched toward noon. As the meeting wound down, Chase cast a glance toward Pyper.

"Are you hungry by any chance?"

What was it about his voice? The sound of it—silky and low—poured through her body like warm sunlight. Uncertainty lost a battle against the attraction that tugged at her chest. "I'm getting there."

Chase quick-scanned faces, first her dad's then Kellen's. "I was thinking it might be a good idea for Pyper and me to hang out for a bit, go a little more casual. We could grab a bite to eat and just...I dunno...get to know each other better."

Probably a good idea, but as fast as a pleasing sizzle burst against her skin, a rush of ice quickly followed. Caution swept into place. "I'd have to rearrange a couple things, but, yeah. Sure. That'd be fine."

Pyper realized her acceptance was stilted. Chase was the last type of man she'd ordinarily spend time with—personally or professionally—yet here she was, initiating a relationship. For better or worse.

Chase stood and extended a hand to guide her to her feet. Their fingertips brushed, curved and held. Back came every single one of those sensory tingles. The *need*. There was a deep, elemental need here that took her completely by surprise. That, more than anything, kept her moving toward him—as though there were no other choice. That recognition stopped her short, but Pyper regrouped fast.

As a team, the foursome made promises to meet again soon and revisit to the ideas they'd discussed. After that, Pyper departed Kellen's office with Chase leading the way. And her emotions were nothing more than a tumbled mess.

7

While Chase drove, Pyper thumbed the buttons of her cellphone, crafting a text to Darren to cancel their lunch date—or, at bare minimum, postpone her arrival. She needed to work out this curveball with Chase, pronto, and she knew Darren would understand.

So sry. Have a professional fire to put out. Meeting w/Kellen didn't go as planned. Will explain l8r. Give Anne a call and pick her up. She's dying to see Nville again. I'll meet u both @ Pucketts ASAP.

Just seconds after Chase parked his pickup in the restaurant lot, Pyper's phone beeped with a reply in the affirmative. That gave her a rush of relief and happiness. Thank goodness for Darren.

Schedule clear for now, she followed Chase through the doorway of Gabby's, a simple but delicious staple of the Nashville burger-and-fries scene. Their arrival at the small, diner stirred an immediate buzz of conversation, and a few folks reached for cellphones, trying without success to be discreet while they snapped photos.

Chase took it all in stride, which helped Pyper move smoothly past the reception as well. He seated her at a round wood table tucked into a far corner of the eatery, and they promptly lifted laminated menus to explore lunch options.

"I have to say, you took me by surprise today, Pyper Brock."

Her eyes lifted and she found him studying her intently. "How so?"

"Well, you've been handpicked by Kellen Rossiter to perform with me, but when I entered the meeting, I heard talk about your history. Then, there was that strong reaction to alcoholism. Given all that, I guess I just don't understand the mix. Why you? You don't seem eager to work with me, and you sure don't seem like the type of person who'd have many burning bridges in their life."

Pyper's spine went taut. "That's where you just might be surprised."

Chase watched her for a few seconds. "Care to share?"

"No. Not yet. I don't know you, Chase. In fact, all I seem to do is tumble and fumble around you."

"I'm not complaining."

"Me neither." The moment cooled, and their smiles mixed, delivering a push of pleasure she tried—and failed—to deny. "All I can say is this: the territory you're asking me to cover is very painful, very private, and still leaves a bitter taste on my tongue. Not your fault. You had no idea you landed in the crosshairs, and that makes me feel bad. You're kind to ask, and you're kind to care, but I'd prefer to keep things—"

"Comfortable?" He arched a brow, a playful light making his eyes sparkle because the word comfortable was about the last adjective she figured either one of them would use to describe their interactions thus far. Like it or not, something vivid and electric coursed between them—heady, captivating, but not at all comfortable.

"I want you to understand me," Pyper said at length, "but it's hard to verbalize, and harder still to revisit."

"All right then. For now, let's explore something easier."

"For example?"

"For example, when did you first know you were gonna be a singer?"

The unexpected question, the warmth in his eyes, stirred a joyful burst of laughter. Pyper propped an elbow on the table, looking into his eyes, saturating her soul with a source of nourishment she hadn't even known she needed until now.

"Happened when I was five."

"Oh, my. That's completely awesome."

Chase's rumbling chuckle, the crinkle of his eyes and his smile tugged her closer, and closer...

"Music, singing, consumed me the first time Tyler let me play the piano. Chopsticks, of course."

"Is there any other starter song for piano?"

"Not in our world. Anyway, we plunked the keys and laughed and sang and played. After that, I sat in on a recording session, and he let me sing with him. To this day, I have a CD of that session, and that's a disc I treasure. From that point on, game over. I was done. I knew I was going to sing. Music equals magic. No other way to explain it."

"I hear that. Some things are just destined, right? Ordained. That's how I always felt about music, too."

A young waitress stopped by and following a pair of autographs, accepted their orders for the house special—burgers and fries. They also opted for a couple large cherry colas.

Chase handed Pyper a wrapped set of silverware and a straw. "Me and Shay...we had dreams. He'd write the words. I'd craft the music. We'd perform.

Together. Brothers. He was a poet. There was no emotion, no picture, he couldn't paint with words. He was an incredible writer."

"What a gift."

"The plan was foolproof. Shay'd craft the words, and I'd supply the melody. From there, we'd take the music world by storm."

"What happened to the dream?"

"It came true."

Flat and sardonic, Chase's words hit Pyper hard.

"Losing him wrecked me, as everyone in the world seems to know, but with a lot of help, I fought my way to a better place."

Drinks and food arrived. He peeled away the thick tomato slice and the onions while Pyper opted to decrease her offering by three large circlets of dill pickles. Following a cheeky wink, he swiped her pickles and Pyper laughed. But then, he drew up short. He backed off and looked away.

Pyper absorbed his somewhat awkward withdrawal. "What's wrong?"

"Nothing. I was distracted and in a hurry this morning. I was anxious to get to the meeting and everything. Had to run back in and grab this, then I forgot about it until now." He tried to be dismissive while he hiked a silver container from his jeans pocket and dropped a few pills into his palm. As though wanting to stem any concern, he addressed her quickly. "Antabuse and some vitamins. I forgot to take them before I left."

She wanted him to know the medication didn't scare her—only his need for it. She stilled his hand for a second then worked his fingers gently open so she could examine the doses. She gave his forearm a squeeze that she hoped conveyed support. "Ironic, isn't it, that the pill is formed in the shape of a stop sign?"

Chase grinned, relaxing a trace. "Very true."

A few seconds later, the medicine was washed down with iced water. The stark reality of the addiction he fought created a dual-force reaction—respect for his commitment to recovery, and fear for her heart. What was she doing? She was increasingly attracted to a man who battled the demon of addiction. Wasn't she smart enough to recognize trouble on the horizon and protect herself from pain?

But for the first time since meeting Chase, confronting his past—and her own—didn't fill her with dread. Rather, in the face of his quiet determination, when she came upon the added layer of embarrassment she sensed at his medicinal interruption, Pyper felt nothing but admiration. She could work with that emotion.

"You don't have to be worried, right? I mean, it's not like you'll be drinking or anything…you're doing OK."

"Yeah, but for the time being, when I take this, it's much easier to fight temptation."

"How so? Do you mind me asking?"

"I don't mind. Are you sure you want to hear it?"

"Absolutely."

Chase didn't speak right away. Instead, he studied her for a time, as if somehow gauging her temperament. Did he worry about condemnation? Judgment? Pyper waited in the soft-building silence, determined to meet him halfway and try to understand the places he had been, the circumstances he faced. If they were somehow expected to forge a path ahead, professionally that is, she could do no less.

"I spent four months at Reach's founding facility in South Carolina. Everyone thought it would be best for me to leave Nashville for a while and get out of the spotlight so I could find my feet with some peace and privacy. When I first started rehab, I was a self-absorbed, cocky jerk. I thought for sure I could control my impulse toward alcohol. I was convinced they could preach and teach all they wanted about twelve-step philosophies and self-love and the whole touchy-feely thing. Shocker, right? Me having an attitude?"

Only because she knew he had learned, and grown, Pyper allowed his wry entrée to stir a smile accompanied by a brief chuckle.

"When I was first administered anti-addiction drugs, I told 'em flat out there was no way I couldn't control myself. I knew...I just *knew*...I could still enjoy a social drink, a light buzz, every once in a while. I refused delivery on my dependence. Completely denied it. I offered no apology, no willingness to change my world when it was everyone else who was off kilter."

Pyper braced, steeling herself against the dark places Chase had inhabited, the parallel path her life had taken down a painful road littered by empty liquor bottles, physical pain, and despair.

Stretching his legs, Chase leaned back in his chair. "In a tightly controlled environment, rehab specialists gave me the chance to prove my theory. What they really did was give me a chance to fall flat without anyone having to learn from the lesson but me."

"How so?"

"I took the medicine as prescribed, but I told 'em I wanted a beer. They let me have one. Went down good, too, all cold, wheat-filled and tasty. I wanted another. They let me have it. Let's just say that one didn't taste nearly as good, and it certainly didn't stay in my system for long."

"Retraining your body, and its cravings."

"Exactly. I'm stubborn, though."

"We have that in common."

Chase delivered an accepting grin. "I battled every step of the way, wanting to prove them wrong. I wanted liquor that much. I shudder to think what my preferred drink—whiskey—would have done to my insides."

"All the while, they were breaking a stallion."

"That's a nice way of putting it. Moral of the story is, when I know the Antabuse is in my system, I remember the times the folks at Reach taught me to fall, and rise again. I can battle the temptation. I can overcome it because in the end, if I don't, I'll be sick—literally and figuratively."

While they ate, Pyper considered everything he had revealed. "What was the hardest thing for you to handle during rehab?"

"That's easy. Guilt."

Pyper reared back. "Guilt?"

His chest rose and fell, drawing her attention to the clean, crisp lines of his dress shirt, his broad, strong shoulders. "I had to come to terms with surviving." There he stalled, and studied his folded hands, avoiding a direct connection. "Shay was so much better than me. He had so much to live for, so much in his life that was worthwhile. So much to offer. Why did God take him instead of me? It's a struggle I still deal with on my bad days. It should have been me, not him."

"Chase…no…please, no." She pleaded, because

his words tore at a soft spot in her spirit, a spot that opened to him in spite of pain, in spite of fear.

"Physically I was a mess. I wasn't used to illness. Then there were a lot of emotions I had to get under control. I had to learn to forgive myself for all the way's I'd failed. That's something else I struggle with. Guess that's where 'Burning Bridges' and 'Forgiveness' came from." Chase chowed on his burger and polished off his lunch.

While conversation paused, in spite of the heavy topic at hand, it occurred to Pyper that the meal and the company went down surprisingly easy.

At last, he met her gaze and delivered an eloquent smile; his look lingered. She was drawn to the man like magnets to steel. Needing something cold and bracing in her system, Pyper sipped through the straw of a condensation-kissed plastic tumbler, savoring the peppery-sweet burst of cherry cola.

"OK. My turn. I want to know your story, Pyper. All of it."

Her head dipped and curls of hair fell across her shoulder, sliding against her arm. She noticed the way Chase watched as she tucked them away quickly—nervously. A shy glance followed. His attention never once wavered. Pyper had to admit she loved that fact.

"I hit a nerve with you, and I never saw it coming. I'm sorry for that. Truly. Obviously you have a history about which I'm completely unaware. That shocked me. What black marks, what fears, could your past possibly have, Pyper? You've been raised by parents who embody everything that's good and decent. You have a great family."

"I do. They're my greatest blessing, but that doesn't mean my life has been perfect, Chase. Not by miles."

"So then, tell me about it. Please? Tell me about you."

So very tempting, but Pyper deflected on sheer instinct. "C'mon. For the most part, I'm an open book."

"No, you're not."

She froze, and he took hold of her hand, carefully and gently, as though begging her forward with nothing more than the sliding touch of his thumb against her wrist. She dissolved. Pyper tried to gather herself, but couldn't hold back from him any longer. Nor did she want to. This man was remarkable—battered and healed, just like her—though he had no idea of that commonality. Not yet, anyway. After his openness, how could she refuse to be equally straightforward and honest?

Following that moment of truth, she found the words she sought. "Not many people outside of a select few know this, but…my dad…Tyler Brock…he's not my biological father."

She waited for shock, for a surprised exclamation of some sort. Chase remained steady. She was grateful for that. He watched her with gentle eyes—dark, deep eyes into which she could easily and willingly lose herself.

"I had no idea." The quiet reply smoothed a balm against her jagged nerve endings. "You and Tyler seem as tied and tight as can be."

"Because we are." Fierce words emphasized a fierce, loving loyalty. "He's a gift from God, to me and to my mama. I was abused as a child, Chase. My mama was abused, too. By the man who I'll refer to as my biological father, but never as anything more than that."

Chase blinked, but didn't speak. Likely, he didn't expect such anger from a person generally full of confidence and sassy positivity.

"I was four—almost five—when we left him, but until that time, I was bullied and abused. With words. With strikes of the hand. With hostility. Worse yet, all that garbage fell on me from my father. From the man I should have been able to trust and rely on implicitly. For the longest time, I wouldn't have anything to do with men. My father's behavior scarred me that bad. Until Tyler."

"Your father...your natural born father...he hit you? I can't even begin to imagine..." The rasped tone, the expression on his face let her know Chase was appalled.

Pyper nodded. "His drunken rages left me with nowhere to hide. He'd lose a job, or he'd have a bad day or ten at the gaming tables in the casinos of downtown Detroit, everything set him off. Sometimes all I had to do is walk into the room and he'd fly into a fit. He hated me, and I figured all men were just like him. I figured all men used fists and yelled." Her lips quaked. "I wasn't even five. I didn't know any better. His brand of fatherhood was all I knew. Until Tyler."

"I didn't mean to travel into territory that hurts you, Pyper." Chase appeared agonized. "I'm sorry I pushed."

"No worries. You can't push me where I don't want to go."

"I believe that." There was a smile in his tone.

Fingering a last pair of fries, then lifting them toward her mouth, she shrugged, softened. "It is what it is, right? There's no changing the past, and my future belongs to me, not him; so in the end, I like to think

65

I've won the war."

"You sure have, and that's a wise outlook. I know the feeling. Learned the hard way that the people and circumstances in our lives—whether good or bad— make us who we are in the here and now. Don't hate on him too bad without considering the fact that—"

"Oh, no. Stop right there, Chase. I truly don't want to hear it." Pyper cut him off with a ruthless hand slice. "I never see him. I never hear from him. He took an exit from our lives and none of us has ever looked back. Speaks volumes, don't you think? I don't want, or need, the ghost of someone I despise, someone I don't even care about, to slip into a happy moment like this and wreck things. I'm enjoying getting to know you. Let's leave it at that, OK?"

"Pleasant. Uncomplicated."

"Yeah." In a way, Pyper knew she was running from herself, but her biological father hadn't been part of her life for nearly two decades. Why stir tidal waves when they were unnecessary? Conclusion drawn, she figured it was time to shift matters from the past. "I'd love to hear your new songs sometime."

He shrugged lightly, and she enjoyed his sudden display of shyness. "Yeah. Sometime."

No, not sometime, she thought. Soon. So she moved forward, whether it was the smart thing to do or not. "We'll need to rehearse."

Chase faced her straight on but didn't say much right away. He sipped his soft drink. "Nothing's set yet. Rehearsals and such might be jumping things a little, don't you think?"

"You don't know Kellen Rossiter the way I do. Trust me. What he talked about today? He'll make it happen. I want to be prepared. Besides, the momentum will be good as you set up production, right?"

He nodded.

"My, but you're the chatty one all of a sudden." Masking uncertainty with sass and a playful grin, she considered the sudden realization that this gig meant something to her. Chase meant something to her— neither of which made a lick of sense. "Even if the shows don't come to be, would it be so tough to spend a few hours making music together?"

Chase reached across the worn, speckled surface of the tabletop, aiming for the spot where her hand rested. He slipped his fingertips beneath hers, held on snug. "It'd be a lot of fun, Pyper. I'd really enjoy it."

She fought off a shiver of need that started deep in her chest and rolled outward. "You could come over sometime. We could work on the live set and you could share your new songs. You could have dinner with me and Zach and the folks. Zach is crazy about you, you know."

Mention of Zach prompted Chase's smile—the seductive, lazy smile that slipped into her head without any effort at all.

"He's a good guy, and I'd love to spend time with y'all." He paused very deliberately and looked her straight in the eyes. "Will Darren mind you hanging out with me as we put this thing together?"

Languid heat vanished. Her brows shot upward. "What a loaded question. Is that anything you really need to concern yourself with?"

"I'm just askin'." Not a bit put off, Chase's intensity zapped her senses. He didn't relinquish his physical or visual hold.

"No need to ask, and there's no need to worry." Could she be any more defensive? Pyper wanted to duck for cover.

"Got it. The topic is closed."

Not quite, Pyper decided. "In the meantime, what about you and Emily?"

"Emily?"

She could tell he drew a complete blank. Shocking. "Emily Nelson, the woman who headlined for you on your last tour. Surely you haven't forgotten her...ample charms."

Recognition struck and Chase shook his head, lips twitching. "You don't hold much back, do you, crash?"

"Nope. Your entire tour was punctuated by pictures of the two of you at bars and clubs and concerts and premieres, with her slinky, sexy self poured all over you like honey."

He laughed outright. "And you're starting to sound just a little bit jealous there, Pyper."

"Hardly." She sniffed and tilted her head, waiting.

"Mmm-hmm." Chase just grinned all the wider. "She once referred to life as her one-time-only-playground, and for a while, I was her toy. The pictures don't lie. Back then, I was more than happy to bask in her glow. I liked the attention. I liked the heat level. But that was then, and this is now. Emily doesn't have a spot in the framework of my life any longer, and she never will again."

"Got it. The topic is closed." Pyper parroted his words, seasoned them with a smile, but what she couldn't quite get a handle on was the relief she felt that Chase was unattached and the assurance that swelled in his absolute rebuke of the life that was.

When Pyper came upon his continuing regard, the heated shimmer in his eyes, her pulse quickened. She had overplayed her interest in him, and she knew it.

Now, all of a sudden, she reverted to self-conscious nervousness.

And what *about* Darren? What was she going through with Chase? Was it simple chemistry? Was it the idea of working together? Sharing a mic? Creating music?

The prospect of creating music with him was all it took to pull her right under. On cue, those tummy tingles and nerve sparks danced through her senses all over again.

"I have another idea we could work on together." Chase spoke, interrupting that alluring chain of thought.

"What's that?"

"My sponsor followed me from South Carolina to Franklin about a month ago to complete my rehab. He's been recruited to stay in Tennessee permanently and head up a new facility in downtown Nashville so he's closing up shop in South Carolina and moving here. To assist in the launch of the facility, I intend to help him raise funds and build awareness."

Pyper perked right up. "Really? That's awesome. Can I help at all? What can I do?"

"The opening of Reach North is coming up next month. Maybe you and I could do some PR beforehand. There'll be a pre-opening benefit. Maybe we could sing. Gather a few artists to join in. It'd attract attention, that's for sure. I'm all for that, if you're game."

"Count me in. I'd love it." She refused to even glance at her phone to check incoming messages or missed calls, but all the same, thoughts of Darren and Anne prompted her to bring lunch to a close. "I'd love to stay, but…"

"Oh—yeah." Chase drew out his wallet and led the way to check out. He settled their tab, refusing Pyper's offer to contribute. "It's been a pleasure, Pyper. Let me know when you want to get together again, hear?"

She added his number to the contact list of her phone, and he did the same with hers.

A promise lifted from her heart to her lips. "I'll grab some dates from Mom and Dad and let you know right away. I'm looking forward to it. Truly. I enjoyed today."

"So did I."

8

Courting support for the launch of a new album meant a whole lot more than just song writing, production meetings and studio time. Chase knew he had to network and earn back some much-needed positive PR. He needed to spend face time with label execs for Imperion Records. He needed to reconnect with DJ's, station owners, and promoters.

That meant parties. Lots of glitz and maneuvering at events where frenzied fans and over-solicitous attendees bent over backwards to make certain a celebrity felt welcome, pampered, and important. The ultimate ego snare. That was the trickiest part of his return to the entertainment industry. Plus, he had to be "on." He had to live up to a persona he wasn't comfortable with nor fully reconciled to any longer. He wasn't the same Chase Bradington of six months or a year ago, but that didn't change circumstances, or the responsibilities he faced. He needed to show up. He needed to promote himself, market, and win a way back to full houses and record sales. If he didn't, the label support that was now tentative at best would vanish altogether—and so would the music he burned to share.

Just days after his meeting with Kellen and the Brocks, a brief limo ride took him south from downtown Nashville to the exclusive suburb of Brentwood. The sun had just set behind the darkening juts of mountain peaks that etched a jagged line against the paling blue sky. His driver executed a smooth turn into a curved driveway that framed the front of a huge brick colonial. Chase came aware of the swarm of paparazzi, then the line of cars that paused in front of open double doors at the main entrance of the stately home. Each vehicle released recording artists, media personalities and A-list producers who posed for cameras and chatted briefly before disappearing inside.

When his turn came, Chase unfolded from the car and made comments to reporters about how excited he was to celebrate Alex Monroe's twentieth anniversary with Imperion records, how he looked forward to spending an enjoyable evening with friends and colleagues who shared roots in country music.

"Chase, how tough has it been so far to hold to the straight and narrow and uphold the promises you've made to remain clean and sober?"

An eager reporter, recorder in hand, posed the question. In the strongest and most unexpected way, Pyper Brock's face materialized in Chase's mind. "It's easier than you'd think once you put your heart in it. Thanks, y'all, and have a good night. I need to get inside before I forfeit my invite."

The words filled and spilled before he could think them over, but they provided the perfect exit and spoke truth in the type of succinct, sound-bite terms necessary to the moment. He slipped inside the grand foyer of Alex Monroe's home and took a deep breath, grateful to have—

"Nicely done." Pyper's voice drifted his way from behind, causing a jolt and then a hot, eager sizzle. Chase felt a breath of air, then the brush of a petite body as she sidled past in a pale pink dress full of lace and shimmer that fell to her shapely calves and suited her curves to perfection.

"You heard that?"

"We were right behind you."

"We" was Pyper, who stood next to her brother Zach, followed by Amy and Tyler. Tyler seemed to battle a grin.

"Mind if I tag up with you?" Pyper craned her neck to search his eyes. "Dad's already got a date, and Darren had a gig at The Bluebird. I love my brother and everything, but..."

Zach rolled his eyes and gave Pyper a shove but extended a hand to Chase who accepted the gesture.

"Good to see you again, Z."

"You, too." Zach's smile went wide at the nickname, which crossed Chase's mind on automatic.

Chase's attention didn't stray long from Pyper and those luminous blue eyes. "So, you gonna be my chaperone?" He shot her a teasing smirk meant to goad her on.

"Ha. That's not my job, pal."

Sweetness flavored that salty piece of sass. Chase laughed, snagging her hand, and drew it through the crook of his arm. "You're a piece of work, crash."

"You really need to come up with a better nickname."

"Nope. If the moniker fits, you gotta wear it."

She gave a playful huff, her stride a relaxed and easy sashay that Chase admired and kept pace to as they crossed the threshold of the great room. There, the party was in full swing jammed with folks in suits, dresses, jewels. The assemblage formed a humming vibration of conversation with a gentle undercurrent of jazz that accented the atmosphere from a nearby sound system. Glassware chinked and chimed, adding a melody to the surroundings.

"So, Darren's tied up, eh?"

"Yeah. I recruited Annie to hang out with him so he won't be alone. He's got an acoustic set in the round with Jack Paul."

"Jack Paul? Nice score."

Suddenly, Pyper's lips flattened and her eyes went narrow as she surveyed the crowd. "Well, joy is me."

Full of snark, the muttered comment drew Chase's focus from the party and the idea of Pyper and her man in the band. "What's up?"

"Petra Goode is here."

Chase snorted. "Ah, yes. Gossip columnist to the stars. My sullied rep has helped her sell magazines for years. Why does that bother you? She's got nothing on Pyper Brock."

"Maybe, but she never gives up trying. She's been after me for the last couple of weeks for an interview. Not sure why. Lately, I've been laying low, wrapped up in Dad's induction and coming up with new material for my second album. The PR machine won't start humming for a couple months yet when I hit the studio and start recording so I'm not sure what's got her so eager."

She shook her head and Chase noticed the creamy line of her slender neck. A gold chain rested at her throat; a small, sparkly diamond pendant dangled from the end. She wore her hair in a loose French braid tonight; he found himself longing for the loose, wavy curls that always tempted his fingers to go for a long, slow dance.

"Oh, great. She just caught sight of us, and her eyebrows about disappeared beneath her hairline."

Chase's laughter erupted, and he turned Pyper smoothly in the opposite direction from Petra; he leaned close enough to whisper. "You know, we could always just dodge the woman. Messing with the press is an art form I've perfected over the years."

Pyper's eyes twinkled in the light of an elaborate, crystal chandelier that graced a soaring ceiling. "So, you're tellin' me that hanging out with a bad boy just might have its advantages."

"Definitely." In the face of that playful tease, a newfound comfort fell between them, and Chase thoroughly enjoyed the fact.

"You're sweet, but I think I'll deal with her head on. Find out what's creeping through that nosey little mind of hers."

"Great attitude, Pyp, and great sense of humor."

A visual rove of the crowd revealed a number of folks he needed to see. He spotted one producer in particular who had recently offered a ringing endorsement to Imperion of the "Forgiveness" rough cut. The guy deserved a huge kudo for the show of support.

Chase gave Pyper's waist a gentle squeeze. "Tell you what. You go conquer Petra. I'm going to spend some time with Tony Edwards. Meet you at the food table in a bit, OK?"

"Deal."

Graced by her smile, Chase released his hold, making tracks to the small group where Tony stood. In a nod to good fortune, it looked as though present conversations were winding down. Chase stepped into the mix with smooth ease and sank into the process of returning to the ebb and flow of networking and schmoozing.

✦✦

"Pyper, you look incredible, as always. What a gorgeous dress. I love it! Who's the designer?" Petra Goode stepped up and air-kissed Pyper's cheeks, a gesture Pyper returned only because decorum demanded it.

"Thanks so much. It actually comes from a local talent, Becca Bique. I'll be sure to let her know you like it. Are you enjoying the party?"

"Absolutely. I wouldn't miss celebrating this milestone for Alex."

"Neither would I. Alex is a wonderful mentor to so many folks in the country and gospel music scene. I'm honored to have worked with him, and I can only hope his career spans another twenty years."

OK, I delivered a flawless sound bite for your pub, Pyper thought, *can I now be left in peace?* Instinctively for some reason, she sought Chase. He remained happily engrossed in a conversation with Imperion producers. Her lips curved soft. Good for him.

"You're such a sweetheart. Head to toe."

Petra's high-pitched, over-done southern drawl pierced its way into warm thoughts of Chase.

"It never ceases to amaze me that with all your well-deserved acclaim in the arena of Christian music, fans and even objective media types like me have been so taken in we don't do much ground work on where you've been, or where you've come from."

In dismissal, Pyper brushed a hand through the air and beamed a mega-watt smile. "Oh, honestly. What's there to know? I'm simple and basic."

Petra shrugged, answering Pyper's stand-off with

a shrewd look. "Why not let my readers decide on that? I've been hoping for a phone call."

"I'm so sorry if I seemed rude. Between pre-production meetings, the Opry induction, and everything in between it's been insane. Besides, I'm afraid my history would bore folks to tears." She infused as much kindness and charm into the statement as possible.

"You're hardly boring, Pyper. In fact, the older you get, the more you intrigue me. Everyone has a story to tell—a life worth revealing and using to reach others, right? Isn't that part of what drives you and your mission?"

Pyper couldn't gracefully bow from that observation. "Of course it is, yes."

"You've lived a storied past, raised at the heart of a loving, talented family. It isn't top secret knowledge that you were adopted by Tyler Brock, but your past remains a tantalizing, foggy mystery. I guess I'm becoming an aged cynic, but I have to wonder what's been covered by your beauty, your charming poise…and the good name of Brock."

A sneering emphasis covered Petra's final words, and Pyper took immediate offense, nearly dropping her glass of ginger ale. "Hidden? I'm an open book, Petra, and I'm not at all sure what you mean."

"Then let's discuss. Let's meet next week and talk. I'll make the interview part of my plans to spotlight you and Chase's efforts to fundraise for Reach North. The exposure would help both of you, as well as spotlight a worthy cause, don't you think?"

Wait—huh? Was this interlude somehow connected to Chase? Was the reporter angling for some kind of a kiss-and-tell about her and Chase simply because they had walked into a party together? Petra knew they'd be performing at the opening—had she already caught wind of the prospect of their duet on "Burning Bridges"? Man, oh, man were the media sharks circling—sniffing out anything having to do with the return of Chase Bradington.

And she was falling into the center of a target by listening to her heart instead of her head.

Pyper's confident posture faltered.

The uncharacteristic response seemed to fuel Petra's wide-mouthed smile, which was emphasized by a garish hue of red lipstick. "Pyper, darlin,' I just want to talk. You said it yourself"—the reporter's posture went from kitty-cat soft to biting in an instant—"what have you got to hide? You're a role model."

"I'm no role model, Petra. I'm simply a music lover and music maker on God's behalf. He's the role model. Not me."

"Like I've always said, you're a sweetheart from head to toe. Talk to me about it, Pyper. All of it. The past, the present, the future."

A hissing coil cut loose in the depths of Pyper's chest, but she schooled herself to reply in calm neutral. She was smart enough to recognize a goading reporter on the hunt. Petra and her style of publication wanted a slick, dirty oil spill, not the affirmation of cool, clear water.

The only way to combat the dark, Daddy had always taught her, was to shine a light. So Pyper put an end to the pressure by delivering a gracious smile and a nod of agreement. "Call Kellen. Set up a time and place."

Petra wanted to go fishing in the river of Pyper's

past, uncover tidbits about her life before Nashville. She'd skated around the press before; she'd simply have to do so again. Pyper wasn't a novice. Although she loathed the idea of being interviewed by the woman, she intended to place a smooth and concluding stamp on the matter of her past.

Seeming to figure she had aced her serve, Petra didn't linger. Instead, she fluttered her lashes and smiled knowingly. "Enjoy your evenin' now. I look forward to our chat."

෩෪

Emily Nelson was five-feet seven-inches of female come hither parked on spiked stilettos so high they nearly brought her eye-to-eye with Chase. Once-upon-a-Bradington, that form-fitting silk dress, all that lush tan fabric draped snug but shimmering against a long, lean form, would have tempted his body heat to skyrocket and his hands to launch into a fast, greedy field day. Layers of long silver chains draped their way from her throat to her waist—there was nothing in the world subtle about this woman, or her intent.

She slinked toward him, gaze latched, eyes flashing in an intimate form of invitation. Crossing through a pair of wide open French doors at the rear of the Monroe estate, she angled straight for the spot where he stood and had been happily enjoying a few moments of solitude in a peaceful corner of the outdoor veranda.

She carried two crystal tumblers, both half-full of golden liquid poured over ice. Slow and sleek, she wet her lips, gave her brown, chin-length hair a toss and sidled close. After a deep, long guzzle from one of the glasses, she kissed him full on the mouth without invitation, without compunction and without a single word ever being spoken.

She tasted of the world that had nearly ruined him—whiskey on the rocks. Emily's beckoning moan and the way she slithered against him repulsed Chase. He took hold of her forearms and pushed her back. Insolently, she swigged from her glass once more, offering the second one to Chase.

"You don't feel like havin' some fun again?"

She laughed over the words, pushing aside the months he had spent in agonizing reform, the painful battle lines he still struggled to maintain when it came to liquor. Even the briefest remnants that had lingered on her lips, even the smell, left him aching to toss back the contents of the glass. Instantly, he craved the infusion of warmth, that heady rush of confidence, the strength a few shots of strong liquor would provide. He needed the reinforcement so bad…

Nothing but deceit. Three words later, Chase shook free of that hedonistic call. "I'm not after the kind of fun you seem to be talkin' about, Emily. Not anymore." He removed the second tumbler from her grip, refusing to pay it the merest glance. Instead, he emptied the contents onto a patch of manicured lawn to his right and then set the glass on the cement railing. He needed to get back inside, find some food, and meet up with Pyper again.

Emily stalled his exit by exerting a strong tug against his arm. "C'mon…don't go all cold and hard. I've missed you so much. We always had such great times together." She hooked her arms around his neck.

He unlatched her invasive grip and shoved her hips back and away. He wanted nothing to do with

Emily Nelson. He'd never fall back into a bed full of nothing but fleeting pleasure that always ended with soul-crushing emptiness and regret.

Nevertheless, and God help him, he now ached for the burn of alcohol, for the way it would soothe away the rough edges and erase his discomfort at being forced into an environment he had worked so hard to leave behind. But he knew the score. If he didn't find a way to fit in, his chance at rebuilding a career in music would be lost forever.

"Chase? I'm sorry to interrupt, but—"

What a saving grace. Pyper's voice cut through hot uncertainty like a cool, sweet breeze. "Yeah?"

Fortunately there was plenty of distance between him and Emily. Nothing inappropriate could be seen, except for one empty tumbler, and one full tumbler, resting side-by-side on the nearby railing. Pyper noticed the glasses. Chase saw how she took in the view with deliberate calm, a head tilt and quiet, sad eyes.

Just as fast, she perked up, fashioned a smile he recognized instinctively as false. "My dad was just chatting with Phil Anderson and they were looking for you. Wanted to see you real quick if you've got a second."

"Absolutely. I'm on my way."

"Thanks." With that, her eyes turned to stone, even as a polite smile curved lips soft and full.

The instant Pyper was out of ear shot, Emily snorted over a laugh. "Oh, man. Are you seriously considering Miss Sweetness and Light there as a potential conquest? Do you honestly believe you're going to scale that monument to good, wholesome living and strong Christian values?" Emily snorted

81

once more. "More power to you, Chase. I guess it makes sense in a roundabout sorta way. Using Pyper Brock'd be a nice way to clean up your image—you know—hanging out with the good girl might rub off on you."

She melted against his body all over again, her eyes smoky and wanton. "But once that particular adventure loses its luster, I hope you'll remember what's waiting for you on the other side. You know…in my world it's always been about the thrill of the…Chase…" Emily launched into him like chocolate dessert all over again, mouth latched to his, lips moving in expert motions, dewy, welcoming, pliant, coaxing.

When involuntary heat rose, Chase's disgust at her manipulations, at his human weakness and malleability, bubbled to the surface. He pulled away. "Stop it." He pushed her backward, and this time he wasn't as gentle.

Her unwelcomed assault, her mockery of Pyper's lifestyle scraped him with the sharp edge of a blade.

"What's wrong with you?" She smoothed her hair into place, straightened the lavish lines of her gown. Her sneer transformed plastic perfection into every shade of ugly Chase had ever imagined. "You know? You were a lot more fun before you went and got your head all straightened out in rehab."

"Thanks for your support, Emily. For the record? Using Pyper is the last thing I'd dream of and the last thing I know I'd ever accomplish when it comes to a woman as strong as she is." He was on a roll now, and no power in his arsenal could keep him from cutting loose. "Furthermore, here's a clue from my days spent getting my head straightened out in rehab: belittling her life isn't going to make yours any better. Chew on that for a bit, won't ya? I have to go. The CEO of Imperion isn't someone I intend to keep waiting."

Not caring what her reaction might be, Chase turned and beat a hasty exit, crossing into the house where he searched for Tyler Brock and Phil Anderson.

Fortunately, he came upon Pyper first, but she saw him coming and headed in the opposite direction. Chase released a mild curse, and tracked her. Suddenly, Imperion Records could just wait.

"Pyper, wait. Please…wait."

He kept his voice low, but followed at a brisk clip. Long, fast strides brought him even with her in seconds, and he nabbed her forearm and pulled her through the first doorway he could find. They ended up in a tiny, squared off powder room. He jammed the door closed. Pyper yanked free of his hold and twisted the knob violently, shoving him away.

"No!" He banged the door closed all over again and blocked her exit. "You're going to stand right here and listen to me. It wasn't what it looked like."

"Of course not. It never is."

"If you had stuck around, you'd realize I never touched the drink she brought me."

Could she feel and hear his sincerity?

"Whatever. She was wrapped around you like a mink coat. It was sickening."

So that was the issue. In an instant he lost his breath; his heart jack-hammered. "Her choice, not mine." Emboldened by her revelation, he pushed. "And I think you need to make a decision, Pyper. Can you ever really trust me? Will you find a way to believe in me? If not, this…venture…we're starting is dead where it stands."

Venture. So innocuous a word that had popped into his head like a donut shaped life preserver he could toss into the ocean of her rage. *Venture* didn't even scratch the surface of what swam between the two of them and expanded like the movement of waves every time they met. Tonight's proceedings—good and bad—proved that fact clearly.

So he continued to press. What'd he have to lose? "You need to figure out if this reaction of yours is about alcohol or Emily. Is it about my bad-boy past, or might it be about jealousy?"

As good an ending point as any. Chase opened the door. "Think it over, crash. Then, come to terms."

He took his leave at a good clip, never once looking back.

During his stride through the house, he came to the conclusion there must have been something circulating through the atmosphere of Alex Monroe's mini-mansion tonight. On his way to the great room, where he could just barely see Tyler and Phil conversing near a wall-length fieldstone fireplace, Chase happened to glance through an open doorway and came upon a scene that slowed his forward progress.

In a dimly lit room that seemed to be an office, or a den, he saw Zach tucked against the rounded side of a large, brown leather couch, and he was body-to-body with Kimberly Monroe, Alex's only girl and youngest child. She pressed against him, fingers roving through his hair, her white lace dress riding high against her thighs. Zach's hand was splayed against her hip, his lips danced against her neck, her lips…they murmured quietly. Chase heard her encouraging giggle, noted the way her free hand slipped downward against Zach's chest.

Fighting a groan, Chase realized there was nothing he could do to interrupt the moment, not in the middle of a party, not when he'd be calling out the behavior of a pair of teenagers he barely even knew. Nonetheless, danger sounded through his head. Maybe he could bring a close to this necking session by prompting Tyler to seek out his son after this impromptu meeting with Imperion's chief officer.

Head pounding, Chase couldn't wait for the night to end. What was going on? This world felt as foreign to him as outer space.

&∽&

Brimming with rage, Pyper escaped to the food table and got in line to fill a plate. Thoroughly distracted, she worked hard to focus and shine bright. She tried to keep her head in the game, acknowledging acquaintances, colleagues, the smattering of friends who passed by. Pasting on a smile, forcing herself to breathe steady and slow, she navigated the party. At the same time, she wished like crazy this night was already relegated to the history books.

Into that maelstrom glided Emily Nelson. She nudged past Pyper, cutting in front to assemble a plate of hors d'oeuvres.

"Pyper."

The bare-bones acknowledgement was meant to slight, but Pyper ignored the jibe.

That only prompted Emily to continue. "Quite the vision you made striding in on the arm of a fallen angel. He's all kinds of sexy. Take it from someone who knows firsthand. He is delicious."

Pyper fought a gag at the indelicate provocation. Could this evening get any worse? Tossing a few fruit pieces onto her plate, some cheese and crackers, she made to flee.

Emily executed a smooth spin that blocked Pyper's progress. Deliberately. "Question. Do you honestly believe a man like Chase Bradington will embrace and maintain your kind of puritan lifestyle?"

Condescension dripped from the last two words. Pyper bit back a flood of temper and chomped her jaw tight, opting not to dignify that barb with a response. When she tried to leave, she found herself stonewalled once again.

"Do you honestly believe he'll rebuke the bottle, the parties, the women, forever? Frankly, I'm shocked to see you anywhere near him. I suppose you're sweet and no doubt an intoxicating diversion, but I'm awful afraid he'll get bored and move on. Men like him do, you know? My advice? Make sure you're not living in a dream world, child."

That did it. Pyper's control snapped. "First off, you're only a year older than I am, so you might want to be careful about how you refer to me. Second, what impresses me far more than your worthless attempts to act as a piece of kindling within a forest where you most certainly don't belong, is that none of the character flaws you listed seem to bother *you*. Why might that be? Are you that misguided? That desperate?" Pyper lifted her shoulder into a dismissive shrug. "You were all over him. If he's as bad as you say, then what does that tell me about you, *child*?"

The observation seemed to conclude their tête-à-tête, but Pyper's stomach rolled. She had stuck up for Chase—lost her temper over his sullied honor—despite every instinct to chop him at the knees for what she had witnessed just moments ago. Who said God wasn't in the miracle business?

"Smart-mouth me all you'd like." Emily re-found her voice, and her anger. "That man will move right past you, Pyper. Mark my words."

Pyper slowly turned back around, a smile of pure sweetness pasted into place. "No, you mark mine. This Chase is a different man than the one you used to know. Besides, I'm not his to move past. I'm with him tonight because we're going to be working together. *Professionally.*"

OK, God, please let those words be true. Please don't make a liar of my heart. I don't want to get hurt.

"Well, you go on and have fun, but remember what I said. Chase Bradington is trouble with a whiskey chaser. Literally."

"No, he's not."

Pyper froze at the sound of Chase's voice coming from behind, smooth and calm. When he moved to her side, the scowl on his face, paired with those dark, snapping eyes was enough to make her blood run cold.

"Not anymore, or haven't you read the most current headlines from the gossip rags? Drunken Chase Bradington was so last year. I thought I made that clear when you tried to tangle with me on the veranda."

The princess of pop had the good grace to flinch before spinning away and beating a nose-in-the-air retreat.

Chase started to turn as well. "The meeting with Phil was positive and a great boon to an otherwise miserable evening. You might want to check in on Zach, though. He's been MIA for a bit and I think I saw him lounging a little too comfortably in the den with Kim Monroe."

Pyper barely had time to register agitation at that development and deliver a nod of acknowledgement before Chase walked off, leaving her alone and more confused than ever.

A short time later, as the party wound down, he caught up with her in the great room as she and her family bid farewell to their host. Zach had rejoined the festivities before Pyper could launch a search party—thank goodness—but the evening had run long, and Pyper couldn't wait to get home to the farmhouse in Franklin that soothed her soul like no other place in the world.

Her family followed Chase to the entryway where they stood in line and waited for the car to be summoned.

"Chase, it was good to see you again." Obviously unaware of the evening's drama, Pyper's dad clapped his hand against Chase's shoulder. "I hear you might be stopping by soon to do some brainstorming and creating together. That sounds good."

"I'm looking forward to it, sir."

"Me, too."

Her mother gave him a warm smile. "Chicken stew is my specialty, and a favorite of the house. Let us know when you're available."

"I'll do that, ma'am. Thank you."

Tyler tucked an arm around her mother's waist. Pyper stood to the side, continuing to stare at Chase, to gauge. Would she ever be able to stop watching him as though expecting hell itself to suddenly break loose? Probably not—that was the problem. And after the events of the evening, she stubbornly owned that fact.

All the same, she couldn't quite pull away, no matter how hard she tried.

Just when she was ready to surrender the battle and disappear into the night, Chase edged her to a private spot in a long, empty hallway that stretched beyond the foyer. Very softly, but very deliberately, he settled his fingertips against the raging pulse point at her throat. He swept his lips against her cheeks. All was softer than soft, but powerful—and enticing. Reason and logic melted to nothing. What was happening…?

"I want you to take one thing away from tonight, Pyper." Gently he lifted her chin, directing her gaze to his. His voice was a deep, quiet whisper. "Forget all the theatrics. Forget all the crap that took place. Once the dust settles and you have time to rest, to go still and pray, I want you to ask yourself one question."

"Which is?" Her chest rose and fell on her attempts at a deep breath. She aimed for aloof and cool—failed miserably; on the inside she quaked.

"When Darren looks into your eyes, what happens? Does he make your heart react like I feel right now? When he touches you, what happens? When he shares his dreams, his truest deepest self, warts and all, when he shares his soul with you, what do you feel?" He leaned in, and she melted against the wall at her back. Her knees weakened at the joints. When the front door opened, when her father was called forward to claim their car, Chase slid his fingertips against her arms in a final caress. He backed away and a brush of floral-kissed air streamed in from the outside, moving around her, through her.

"This isn't about physicality or passion, Pyper. For better or worse, we're pushing our way toward each other. We're searching. We need each other. That's the call. That's the vibration that keeps stirring us, and that's the truth. Think about it."

Following a gentle but emphasizing tug against her waist, he broke contact and left her be. All Pyper wanted to do was dissolve into a puddle against the cool, dark tile at her feet.

And figure out how someone so wrong could be so perfectly right.

9

What a mess.

Pyper's first thought the next morning was pretty much an echo of her last thought before dropping off into a turbulent, disquieted sleep.

In dreams, now even in waking, the goading image of Petra Goode came alive. Something about her set Pyper's teeth on edge. The woman was obviously fishing hard for gossip, but what Pyper couldn't figure was why. Next Pyper battled the memory of Emily Nelson and Chase. Ever the unrepentant diva, Emily's behavior was about par for the course, but she had provoked Pyper into a public display of anger that didn't sit well. Then there were those emotional fireworks at the end—the confrontation with Chase, which overrode all else, including Pyper's logic. Sticky cobwebs still spun through the tapestry of her overly-tired mind. The only solution she could come up with to combat the disquiet was music.

She retrieved her guitar from a stand in the corner of her room and trotted back to bed where she sat cross-legged. Stretching, she yanked a wire-bound journal from the headboard and pulled a pen from its resting spot against the coils. She clicked the pen to readiness, glancing outside. Beyond the acres of land she loved to call home, golden light bathed the dips and curves of the Smoky Mountains. Shepherd and Briar—Daddy's stallion and her filly—could be seen in the distance, feeding on dew-kissed long grass that glistened beneath the sun in a hue of green so rich and fertile she went still at once and offered God a huge nod of gratitude.

Fleetingly inspired, she scribbled a few words against the lines of the paper. On re-read, they were no good. Frustrated, she crossed them out. She leaned against the familiar, glossy curve of the guitar and stared, thinking about...

The Spirit melt that makes one out of two...

She inked the words that had come to mind while she had watched her parents interact at the Opry, and Pyper smiled. That particular image would come in handy. After that, inspiration pulled to a stop, most likely because she couldn't work past the idea, the emotion, of a dark angel on the rise, working hard at redemption, a man who had tantalized her thoughts from the moment they met.

She rubbed a fingertip against her lower lip then groaned, giving up lyrics in favor of the slow-building strum she created on the strings of her guitar. Closing her eyes, she let the melody wash over her. It was slow and evocative, governed by a poignant harmony. Awesome. Still, she agonized, in the clutches of a fitful message pushing to be born. Words. She needed words.

Stilling restless fingertips, she studied the journal spread open against plush, white satin down. She took in a pair of lined pages which were rapidly filling with the chords, key shifts and notes of the melody she had begun to craft.

The complexity was there...the layers and wistfulness...but there was more...more battling to burst free. For now, though, the deeper emotions she thirsted for remained elusive.

Her cellphone rested next to her knee and an incoming alert sent it into a skitter along the comforter. Once the ringtone kicked in, her concentration vanished. Sighing, she temporarily surrendered creation and unstrapped her guitar, setting it aside so she could review the incoming text from Kellen Rossiter.

Green light. Looks like you and Chase are performing at The Stage. Coming up quick, too. Call me. Let's discuss. KR

She nearly whooped. Leave it to Kellen. Expectation danced against her skin; a smile bloomed.

"Pyper, where's the blow dryer?"

Distracted by Anne Lucerne's summons, Pyper gathered her hair into a loose ponytail. She secured thick curls with a holder and left her bed behind. The idea of claiming the wooden dais of The Stage next to Chase, singing with him, followed close on her heels, unavoidable and in a strange way, welcome. "Don't blow dry your hair, Annie. It'll frizz."

A Jack-and-Jill bathroom split the space between Pyper's room and the spare room occupied by Anne who would soon conclude her vacation in Tennessee. When Pyper crossed the threshold, Anne issued a scowl. "I am *not* walking around Nashville with wet hair. Fork over the dryer, babe."

Well, if this wasn't like old times, Pyper thought, regarding her friend with a flourish of affection. Anne wore a terrycloth robe and the blue fuzzy slippers she had swiped from Pyper's closet on day one of her visit. With shower-damp hair and rosy, fresh-scrubbed skin, Anne was adorable, and the closest thing Pyper knew to a sister.

Pyper opened a nearby cabinet door and pulled a

hand-held dryer from the shelf. "I just heard from my agent."

"Girl, you are *so* big time." Anne gave her a saucy wink and snagged the styling equipment.

"No, I'm not. I'm just me. Want to see me perform a live set at The Stage before you leave town?"

Eyes wide, Anne stopped pulling a brush through water-dampened locks. "No, you're not big time. Nope. Not at all." They fell into a brief fit of laughter before Anne returned to styling her hair. "Actually, that'd be fantastic. It isn't often I've been able to cheer for you live and in person. When does it happen?"

"Not sure yet. I need to call Kellen and get the details." Pyper handed her friend a bottle of finishing spray. "I'll be performing with Chase Bradington. No big deal, really, just some good PR for him and a good momentum builder for me. I think you'll have a good time and—"

"And you're rushing to explain that development in an overly businesslike way because *why* exactly?"

OK, in fairness, she hadn't been quite as casual and devil-may-care as she hoped. Pyper's heart thumped out a crazy beat. *Because I can't wait to take the stage with him!* Attempting nonchalance once more, she leaned against the door jamb. "I think I'll plead the fifth on that one."

"I bet you will."

High time for a new point of discussion; Pyper didn't need Anne catching the scent of her growing disquiet about—and attraction to—Chase. "Tell me all about last night, and Darren. Did you enjoy The Bluebird?"

"Oh. Yeah. It was great. Fun. Great."

A branding of hot pink crested against Anne's

cheeks. She stared into the mirror, overly fixated on the fall of her hair. Just like that, the tables turned; Pyper's dilemma about Chase Bradington took a backseat to this most unexpected reaction from her friend.

"Annie?"

"I mean, Darren is...fun...great."

Another giveaway? Anne fumbled, and didn't establish eye contact. Instead, she toyed with the tassels that dangled from the waist tie of her robe. An epiphany occurred, dancing through Pyper's mind—freeing a small piece of her spirit she had been holding in check. "Annie—you like him, don't you?"

Anne caught her breath, stared at Pyper askance. Her eyes went wide—pooled by uncertainty, even as she recovered and delivered a wry, teasing grin. "Yeah. I like him. I'm all over your boyfriend, Pyp. That's how I roll."

With that quip, Pyper realized she had uncovered a heart-secret—her friend's attraction to Darren.

And as far as Pyper was concerned, that realization formed the oddest reaction. There was no jealousy whatsoever. Rather, something deep within her melted into relief.

"He's not exactly my boyfriend, Annie. He's easy to be with. He's convenient, and considering the idea of romance just made sense. I mean, intense work schedules and constant contact tend to elevate things between a man and a woman, but I'll be straight up with you, I never really thought he was 'the one.'"

Anne reared back slightly and frowned. "Are you sure?"

"Don't get me wrong. He's a wonderful guy."

"Yeah, he is."

"Annie, he sparked for you, didn't he?"

Anne's eyes went wide, but all she did was shrug. Next, she delivered a thoroughly unconvincing head shake. But then, typical to her character, a strong will rose and she met Pyper's probing inquisition head-on. "Kind of like Chase has sparked for you."

With that, another truth pushed its way into the open. Pyper propped her head against the doorjamb. She released a groan. "I don't know what's wrong with me, Annie. On paper, in theory, Darren is everything I should ever want in a man. He's a lifelong Christian. He's steady and gentle and loving. He's always treated me like a treasure; he believes in my mission, and he sure is easy on the eyes."

"Agreed on that count—on all counts, actually."

Pyper didn't miss the wistful tenor of her best friend's observation. She smiled at Anne and allowed a punctuating nod, but she was mixed up, eager to confront herself as directly as possible. "Here's the thing, though. Even with all that, as good as it is, something's missing. What's wrong with me? Why would a simple equation, a good and logical pathway, leave me feeling cold?"

"Only you can answer that, Pyp. If the pull isn't there with Darren, then maybe you're meant for something different…"

The sentence dangled into the rapidly materializing image of Chase Bradington. It felt so good to be with him, to share time, to reveal herself, to share their battle scars. Sure, to a degree they formed a wonderful equation, but talk about trouble on two long, lean legs.

Reformation. Passion. That whipcord intensity. Those were just a few aspects of the man she found completely irresistible. Maybe she continued to bristle due to issues beyond his control. Maybe she prickled because of her history with men and alcohol abuse. Her own reformation had been neatly skirted in public, even repressed in some ways, but Pyper had beaten the odds via the love of her family. Digging deep, she realized that she battled Chase's entrance to her life out of self-preservation and a supreme need to avoid being shattered. Again.

But life and love were never about playing it safe, right?

Maybe his image drifted to life for a whole different reason—connection. A connection that stirred nerve tingles, awareness, a molasses-style spread of warm want, a gravitation toward tasting something rich and flavorful.

Pyper paced to her bed. Could she possibly be this galvanized, this quickly...by *Chase*? By a man the likes of which she'd normally avoid without a second thought?

"We're wrong for each other, Annie. Seriously. Like, no. We're the wrong recipe by miles and miles."

Anne's perfectly shaped brow arched upward a notch. "Would that be panic I hear in your voice, or poorly repressed attraction? Both, perhaps?"

Pyper folded her arms across her chest, tried to scare her friend with a glower. Anne was unfazed, naturally.

"He's intriguing, sure," Pyper admitted. "He's strong and he's driven to make a comeback. That's an inspiring combination, but he's not someone I can take on."

"Why not? What are you afraid of?"

"Pain."

The answer to Anne's challenge dawned at once,

with clarity and conviction.

Relaxing at the shoulders, Anne snagged Pyper by the forearm and tugged her to the edge of the bed where they folded into place cross-legged, face-to-face and eye-to-eye. "Leave everything else out of this conversation. Talk to me about what's happening right here"—Anne tapped an index finger against Pyper's chest—"and don't hold back. Not with me. I know precisely where you come from, and you've emerged. You're strong. The Pyper Brock of here-and-now would never deny herself happiness out of fear. Did Darren ever inspire you like this? Did he ever make you think things through the way you are right now?"

Such a direct set of questions. Taken aback by their similarity to Chase's challenge, Pyper tried to find honest answers. In the interim, she had no choice but to fight back. "Let me turn those questions around and give them to you, Anne."

"We're talking about Chase here. Don't evade, and don't even try to tell me that one look into that man's eyes doesn't make you smolder and turn into a pile of mush."

Indeed, Pyper thought, remembering the end note of their party encounter. "Annie, you're a bad influence."

"I think there's something captivating about a man like that. A man who can have any woman he wants, a man who's so attractive, and even a bit dangerous, but decides with single-minded fervor that he wants *you*. That's what's going on, Pyper. He's choosing you, and you can't deny the fact that you're awakened by his focus and attention. It's written all over your face and your body language."

"And all over my busted up, battered slice of

history." Oh, great. Now her angel of inspiration decided to show up with some song lyrics. Wonderful. Pyper groaned, snapping up her journal, scribbling the words. "Have you ever come across a guy that you knew was every color of wrong imaginable, but you just couldn't help but be...I dunno...pulled toward him?" Of course she did, Pyper thought. Darren.

"Let me plead the fifth on that question for now. All I'm saying is, I have eyes, Pyp. I know you well. I see what's going on beneath the surface."

"So, then, stop me! Tell me what a fool I am to even look at a package full of explosives."

"I can't."

"Why not?"

"Because he makes your spirit dance." Gentle conviction rode through Anne's tone.

Pyper went still and gaped, taken under by the memories she shared with Anne. "Spirit dance. Remember when we'd talk about whatever guys we were crushing on at school? That's exactly how we'd describe what we felt."

"When we got older, we became a bit more risqué and said 'He makes my toes curl.'"

"That from a pastor's daughter."

They shared grins, but Anne went serious in a hurry. She took hold of Pyper's trembling hands and tugged her forward a bit. "I know what you've battled. I know where you come from." She shrugged broadly. "Who knows? Maybe his danger and his ties to turbulence are part of what draws you in and creates that pull you're talking about. Thing is, you're rattled by the guy. Tough not to be, all in all. He's definitely got a fascinating edge. You need to figure out what to do with the reaction that's going on inside of you."

Precisely what Chase had said. Pyper stared ahead blindly, shook her head. "I swear. Am I looking for trouble? Am I looking for ways to get my heart broken? Maybe I have some kind of defect, some strand of self-destructive DNA in my system that makes me crave stupidity and obliterates common sense. I'm sure that bit of inner chemistry comes straight from my dad. What a mixed up mess of a heart."

"Mixed up mess of a heart? That sounds to me like a country song just aching to be written."

Pyper rolled her eyes. "Figures, right? I mean, when it comes to men, I've been messed up since I was a kid. You lived it with me. I've never known the right guy from the wrong guy, so I steer clear of all guys. It's been kind of fun to play the role of unattainable, and being unattached never bothered me much at all. That's not the case anymore."

"Because of…?"

Chase. Immediately the answer reverberated through her head without any filter or dilution. Anne waited in a silence that stretched; most likely she already knew what Pyper attempted to hide from plain view.

"Pyp, you're incredible. Don't sell yourself short. You're searching for the ultra-safe and perfectly prescribed, like Darren, but you also have this powerful spirit, a passion, that draws…well…"

The bad boy on a comeback trail.

But was he a bad boy any longer? Was she not giving him his fair due: an honest attempt at redemption?

Annie smiled, gave Pyper's shoulder a playful shove. "You're looking for fulfillment. We all are.

There's nothing wrong with that."

"But I'll never find fulfillment in a man. Fulfillment has got to come from God. I only wish He'd let me know if I'm on the right path. I don't want to get my heart chopped."

A telling silence followed, but Anne persisted. "Pyp, no matter what, I just want you to be true to your heart. No matter where it's meant to go. I saw something happen between the two of you. I sense it in the way you talk about him. I want you to be happy. Period. No matter what."

Pyper hugged her friend tight. "Annie…for real…no matter what…I want the same thing for you, too. I'm happy for you. I think you and Darren could be great together, and I promise you this—I'm not jealous or even…" She shrugged broadly, exhilarated. "To be honest, I'm happy. Relieved. What does that mean? What does that say?"

"That he's not the one. But I'd never… ever…ever…"

Pyper reached out fast. "I know that. From the bottom of my heart, I want you to find out if he's the one. Keep spending time with him while you're in town. Enjoy his companionship and see where it goes."

A silence beat by, pulsing with a sense of joy Anne couldn't hide. "Then I have one last question, best friend to best friend."

Pyper felt a tingle skirt the nerves along her spine. "Yeah?"

"Would you have reacted this way if I had told you I was attracted to Chase Bradington?"

A shocked jaw-drop followed. Pyper stared. A red-hot lance struck home propelled by the emotion, the jealousy, the passion she should have been channeling toward Darren. Instead, that swirl of emotions resided with one man alone. Chase Bradington.

In the meantime, Annie's expression melted into lines of understanding and the kind of affection that could only come from a true and trusted confidante. "With that, I think I have my answer. And don't you worry. I'm not. Besides which, I can already tell he's totally off limits."

10

Chase swung his pickup truck into a wide left turn and entered the parking lot of Almedia Court Apartments. Spotting an empty space close to Building Four, he slowed the vehicle to a stop then settled comfortably to wait, keeping an eye out for Mark Samuels's time-worn silver Honda. It was move-in day and Chase had offered to help his mentor and sponsor get settled in Nashville.

He opened the driver-side window to catch a breeze and gave a slight jump when his cellphone issued an incoming call alert. Kellen Rossiter's name lit the screen and Chase engaged receipt with a finger tap. "Kellen. How are you?"

"I'm good, but I think you're about to be even better."

"Yeah? How so?"

"Not this weekend, but next, I want you and Pyper to be ready to hit The Stage."

Chase kept from trembling. How, he didn't quite know. This was answered prayer, on multiple levels. He sank against dark gray leather and pressed unsteady fingertips against his eyes. "Me. And Pyper. Center stage at The Stage."

"That's the offer I'm extending. Management is billing it as a single-set, three-song, special event next Saturday night. In other words, they stepped up with prime-time visibility."

Prime time, meaning a weekend gig, during the height of summer, at a historic performance venue in The District. As far as Chase was concerned, that glitter equaled nothing when weighed against the fact that he'd be making music with Pyper. They'd prepare, they'd sing, they'd sass and share and create and...

He breathed hard, trying to regroup as fast as he could. This wasn't just any woman, or any performance. This was different—and Pyper was different in a way that called to life all the chambers of his existence he had once surrendered to darkness and futility.

"Kellen, I can't begin to express how much—"

"Hey, this is my job. You don't have to say a thing. Just crush it, hear me?"

His heart took off like a jackhammer. "I do, and we're going to *own* this opportunity. I promise you that."

"I have no doubt."

Chase concluded the call just as Mark's car glided into view. Buoyed—wrapped in optimism—Chase pocketed his phone. Mark nodded in passing; Chase answered with a smile and a wave. While Mark unlatched the trunk and started to haul out plastic bags stuffed with groceries and household items, Chase unfolded from the truck and joined his friend.

Mark gave a teasing smirk. "Hey there, big-shot."

"Whatever." Chase delivered an affectionate thump to Mark's back and arched a brow when he saw the number of sacks still tucked inside. "Cripe, Samuels, did you leave anything for the rest of us?"

"Not much. A man's gotta do what a man's gotta do. Come on in and see the place. It's great."

Chase hefted a load of bags. "Lead the way."

Mark's dark jeans seemed store fresh as did his dark green shirt. "You're polished. Did you stop at the new Reach branch before your shopping spree?"

"Yeah. Had to drop off files and such then set up meetings with the staff before I could call it a day on the job."

Chase admired Mark's professional aptitude, but found greater comfort in the reality of where this man had been, and the demons he had conquered. Mark's edge remained visible; remnants of a rough life had carved grooves against the corners of his mouth and his eyes. A longish fall of sandy brown hair was threaded by silver. A layer of dark stubble covered his jaw. At a glance, Mark's overall impression might be off-putting to a carefully styled or buttoned-down individual, but Mark was just the kind of person Chase could relate to and respect.

A short walk down an open corridor led them to unit 2-D. Mark shifted his baggage so he could insert the key and twist the doorknob. "I'll give you the two-second tour in a little bit. If we don't store the frozen food quick, it's gonna be running to meet us."

Chase's chuckle rumbled. "Moving is big-time fun. Said no one. Ever."

They packed away refrigerated and frozen items straight off. After that, before attempting to make a dent in canned goods and sundry, Mark initiated the two-second tour he had joked about—which took about that long. There wasn't much to the space, really, just a living room split by a kitchen divider that featured a pair of tall chrome stools. Beyond that, separated by pocket doors, was a fair sized bedroom. Tidy and efficient, with nothing left to waste, just like the man who'd be occupying the space.

When they resumed their attack against a sea of plastic grocery sacks, Chase extracted an item that took him by surprise, the latest edition of the tabloid gossip magazine *Nashville from the Inside*. Plastered across the front was a big color photograph of him with Pyper. Her arm was linked through his; their gazes were connected exclusively, and they shared smiles that had been freeze-framed by the magazine's photographer. Chase took in the headline.

Check Out the Angel and the Bad Boy...

His throat went dry when he continued on to the brief summary that followed:

Has Christian music sweetheart Pyper Brock taken up with Nashville superstar and supposedly reformed bad boy, Chase Bradington? The pair unveiled some cozy behavior at a recent party hosted by record exec Alex Monroe at his Brentwood home. Attendees looked on as the couple tried to play it cool, but they kept close tabs on one another during the duration of Monroe's 20-year anniversary celebration with the Imperion label.

The blurb went on to detail Pyper's upcoming plans to release a second album and included a timeline of Chase's future career plans and recovery efforts

"Hey...Mark...seriously? Gossip rags?"

Mark turned when Chase called, and then went unnaturally still as he spied Chase holding the magazine. Chase watched, perplexed as Mark filled his chest with a deep breath.

A second later, Mark shrugged. "Oh, you know how irresistible those tabloid offerings that stand guard at the end of the checkout lanes are. No doubt guaranteed to both horrify and entertain the folks waiting in line. I told you I was keeping up on you.

Quite the cover story to catch my eye. Care to talk about this development?"

Chase looked at the cover once more and wanted to snarl as he took note of the byline. Petra Goode. Naturally. "The only development is a friend of mine has a barracuda on her tail with an axe to grind."

"Meaning?"

"Meaning Pyper Brock is upstanding and decent. Therefore, media-types like this Petra woman are determined to find a way to bring her down and sell papers. She wants to find chinks in the armor, if you know what I mean."

"I do at that." Mark took custody of the magazine and tossed it aside, face down. "So, tell me what's going on beneath the slick headlines and black ink."

"Nothing much, really." Chase turned away, returning to storing soup cans, spices, and other dry goods in Mark's pantry—a deflection that he hoped wasn't as transparent as it felt.

"Yeah, it sure seems that way."

Busted—about as expected. All the same, Chase's world teetered. He had just shelved a couple cans of tuna and his hand rested against the edge of the shelf. He stared ahead then he smiled. Pictures didn't lie, and that photo on the cover of *Nashville from the Inside* revealed the romantic spark that followed Chase straight into his dreams at night. He rejoiced, even as a contradictory flood of dread doused his bloodstream with ice. Evidently things were going to get complicated in a big hurry now that the media had sunk their teeth into personal matters...

"What's she like?"

Mark's question—posed almost like a counselor, as in their days of therapy—helped push Chase out of hiding. He shook his head, yet the all over smile that curved his lips came straight from the heart.

"You want me to describe Pyper Brock?" Chase released a quiet huff of sound. "I'd never be able to do her justice. She's soft and sweet, but she's got this fantastic core of strength and sass, too. Mark, God's in the process of helping me resurrect my life, there's no doubt there. But to be happy like this? For a man like me to come upon a woman like her? It's nothing short of a miracle. She's everything I want. Spirited, faith-filled, loving and true. When I'm around her, I feel like I'm home. Like I'm where I belong...black-marked soul or not."

"Quit that. The soul's wiped clean when we call on Christ and start living for Him. You know that, but it'd be best to start *believing* it, Chase."

"Yeah. You're right." Properly chastised, Chase met Mark's probing gaze. "I'm grateful for the reminder. Still, you know better than most that I struggle with self-worth. The whole time I was in rehab, I dreamed of finding my way to a relationship with a woman like Pyper Brock. I dreamed of her before I even met her." He unloaded a few more groceries. "I'm almost there, Mark. Honest. I'm at the point now where I can almost taste it. I can almost believe in good things to come. I haven't felt like this since..." He paused to consider. Since before Shayne's passing? No, long before that. Long before the excess of life in the fast lane had overrun his soul. It had been almost a decade since contentment like this had filled his spirit. "Let's just say it feels like it's been forever."

Expecting a show of affirmation and support, Chase struck a wall of surprise when he looked Mark's way and came upon a clenched jaw, a troubled shadow through the eyes that wasn't at all reassuring.

A second later, Mark blinked. He smiled, albeit tiredly, and Chase figured his imagination was simply running wild.

"You're doin' real good, Chase. You've worked hard, and you're staying focused. Humble. I couldn't be prouder, and I couldn't feel better about where you are and what you're gonna accomplish. Stay true to that goal, no matter what comes your way in the days and weeks to come."

Where, exactly, was that coming from? Mark's tone and tense posture rang with warning and pulled Chase to a halt all over again. Did his friend refer to temptation, or staying true to God? Chase opted to brush off the disquieting vibration. Mark was under a lot of pressure these days—moving, launching a rehab center, starting a new season of life. The combination was more than enough to tax a person to maximum.

Maybe Mark needed a breather. Kellen's phone call from earlier inspired an idea. "Hey, I've got a welcome wagon idea for you. Why not take some time out to hear me play a live set? My agent lined up a gig. Pyper and I will be performing at The Stage in a little over a week. Next Saturday's the date. Come along and listen in. It'll give you a chance to see her in person. I'd love for you to meet the Brock family, and Kellen, plus you'll hear some of my new music."

"Ordinarily I'd jump at the chance, but I think I better get my feet under me and settle in. I've got a lot on my plate right now, and I really need to focus on Reach North and make it a huge success. My legacy, you know."

Chase nodded.

"Next time, OK? Let me know when and where.

I'll be there, and I know I'll enjoy it."

"You bet. No pressure. Besides, now that you're local we'll be seeing a lot of each other. In fact, Pyper and I intend to perform a song or two at the grand opening of Reach North next month. You'll meet her and her family at that point for sure, if not before."

"Yeah. Sure. Sounds good." Mark rubbed his eyes, heaved a sigh full of exhaustion. The poor guy seemed completely tapped out right now.

Eager to move beyond, Chase shifted the conversation, initiating a discussion of dinner options. There was a small balcony attached to Mark's second-floor unit, complete with a small gas grill so the idea of hotdogs and hamburgers climbed to the top of the menu. The life-switch from South Carolina to Tennessee seemed to drag on Mark harder than Chase previously realized, but that push of disquiet—stronger this time—took Chase under all over again and he had no choice but to set that recognition aside.

For now.

11

On his way to the Brock farm for a rehearsal session with Pyper and dinner with the Brock family, Chase rocked out with Zach to the song "Shake" by Mercy Me. They laughed and sang loud while Chase navigated his truck and swept along a sparsely traveled two-lane highway that cut through rolling fields rimmed by the peaks, dips and lush valleys of the Smoky Mountains.

Once the music faded, Pyper's brother edged forward against his seatbelt, casting Chase a wide grin. "Man do I love that song."

"Me, too. Story of my life." Chase kept an even, easy touch on the wheel, enjoying the feel of the wind against his face, the sun beating down on his arm through the open window. Life as it should be, he kept thinking. Life as it should be. Shaking free of sinful, earthly chains...

"Thanks again for letting me tag along at the studio today. It was awesome to watch you start work on the album. I still can't believe the way you let me step up and play along with the musicians."

"Y'already thanked me, like, a half-dozen times. I pretty much get the picture." Chase's tease and affectionate grin earned an eye roll and a light shove to the shoulder from his passenger.

"Seriously. That session was awesome, and your new stuff is solid."

"Thanks, Z. I hope the team at my label feels the same way. You did a great job; I'm real happy with what we laid down today."

After the episode he had witnessed between Zach and Alex Monroe's daughter at the anniversary shindig, Chase battled back and forth between minding his own business and finding a way to step in and be a friend. Someone Zach could turn to outside the family fold...someone he could open up to and listen to when life turned tricky.

The best way to do that, Chase figured, was by embracing the thread of music and performance that bound them with strands of commonality and shared passion. So much like how his bond with Shayne had begun. Nowadays, as production time materialized for the new album, a few ideas came to mind as to how he could mentor Zach, and help ease the way forward onto a good and fruitful path.

Atonement—in a mighty formation.

Chase realized Zach was studying him hard, which kicked aside that contented thought and tripped a few warning wires.

"Can I admit something to you?"

Zach's question prompted Chase to flick a glance from the road, and he discovered something turbulent in the boy's eyes.

"Sure. Anything."

"Between us and stuff."

"Of course."

"I've been tempted."

"Tempted?"

Zach huffed, banged a restless fist against a folded knee; he drummed his fingertips. "You may not get it, but, sometimes it's hard. It's hard to be the poster child for good behavior and a family that never stumbles, and stands for all these high ideals. We end up being watched all over the place, as if people are just waiting for us to fail." Zach paused for breath, sidled Chase another gauging look. "I find myself wanting to fight the ropes sometimes. Is that bad? I mean…" Zach shifted, expelled a sigh. "I mean…I think you're cool, Chase."

"Big mistake there." And he made sure his tone conveyed utter sincerity.

Zach shot him a bland look. "No, hear me out a sec. I know what you mean, and I know where you're going with that warning. You got into trouble, but you made it through. You stand on your own and you're real. You own your life. I admire that."

"Yeah, I own it, all right. For better or for worse, and I've seen plenty of both. Don't think more of me than what I am, Zach. Hear?" Chase's heart quickened and a growing buzz sounded in his ears. *Careful. Be very, very careful.* "Tell me what you're going through. You say you've been tempted. What are you getting at?"

Zach's chest rose and fell on a deep breath. "Well. Like…"

Chase waited, allowing the silence to force Zach out a bit.

At last the youngster shrugged and ground out a sound. "OK, so, here it is. I'm Tyler Brock's kid."

"Yeah."

"And I'm Pyper Brock's little brother. A guy in her band."

"Yeah. And there's nothing wrong with those facts."

"Nope."

113

Zach shot him a fast, intent look that simmered with conflicted emotion, even in the brief moment Chase took his eyes off the road.

"Thing is? I'm *Zach*. I'm trying to figure out who *Zach Brock* is, and...well...I'm just not sure right now. I mean, I don't want to be some kind of second-rate, carbon copy of my dad, no matter how great he is, and I don't want to live in Pyper's shadow, either. I've been tempted to just try things on my own. Maybe intrigue people by doing something totally different than my family would ever expect, or...I mean, you've done so much, Chase." There Zach stalled.

Chase picked up the ball in a hurry. "Like I already said, don't follow my lead. At all. I paid for every wrong move I've ever made, and I paid dearly. Rebellion might seem an alluring antidote to feeling displaced, but it won't work over the long haul. Trust me on that."

"I'm not talking about turning my back on things like faith and family—but I want to build my own life. There are people I've met who are so cool, and they play hard and work hard and that outlook appeals to me. I like the idea of taking charge and exploring on my own terms. I'm tempted to follow my own ideas, see where they take me."

Chase recognized the drill and understood all too well the lure of diverting from expectation. Heaven help him if he fouled up this interlude. "OK, Zach. My turn. Can I let you in on a secret?"

"Sure. Absolutely."

"I saw you with Kim at the Monroe's anniversary party. She's a beauty. You guys seemed pretty caught up in each other."

"Ah...yeah." Red color spread across Zach's

angular features. "She's gorgeous, and she's into me. I like that. A lot. She's not afraid to horse around, do stuff, and let life take care of itself." He raked back a shaggy tumble of dark blonde hair and speared Chase with a look. "But...you know...I'm listening."

"Here's the secret." How to phrase this exactly? In visual terms, Kim had poured herself over Zach like sweet honey with her innocent yet alluring lace dress, that flowing auburn hair and all that come-hither, touchy-touchy close proximity. Then, there were those impassioned kisses and caresses, the tight body language that made it obvious Zach was swept into her current, and eager to be carried away. "Life doesn't take care of itself, Z. And, feeling good for ten seconds isn't worth ten years' worth of pain. Take it from someone who walked the path and didn't like where it ended."

After thinking that through for a moment or two, Zach relaxed, and he laughed. "You talk like a song."

Just like that, the seriousness of their conversation broke like the wake of lake water. A laugh rolled up from Chase's chest. "I suppose I do. Call it a job hazard, smart aleck." Instinct kicked in, prompting him to not let the topic drop. "Speaking of songs, you've got some serious chops as a guitarist."

"You think so?"

"Without question. How committed could you be to learning new material? Can you handle six or seven new songs?"

"For you? No doubt. Why?"

"Because if you can handle it, I'd like you to join my studio band. You wouldn't be able to tour or perform at most of the live shows because you're too young for the venues I'd start at, but you could be part of 'Forgiveness'. I think today was a huge success. You've got great interpretive instincts and your riffs are wicked."

"Are you serious? I can't even believe this!"

"I'm very serious. You have a gift, Z, and that gift doesn't come from your daddy, or your sister. It comes from God, and it's all yours." Chase liked the spark of excitement that lit Zach's eyes, but felt compelled to issue a warning. "It's going to be intense. I need your promise to keep focused and learn a whole lot of new material. There'd be lots of practice sessions, too." He paused a beat. "Still interested?"

Zach nodded emphatically. "Ah...yeah. Completely."

"It's got to clear channels with your folks."

"That'll be fine." He shrugged off the caveat. "Chase, this is incredible."

"Glad you like the idea. Let's see what we can do together. My concluding advice? If you want to try some experimenting, experiment with music. With creation. Use what you love, not something that may seem tempting but is actually pretty dark and destructive. Y'know?"

Zach shrugged and nodded, but Chase grabbed comfort from the way the kid absorbed the message and seemed to take it to heart.

For the time being, anyway.

രാൟ

The doorbell chimed and Pyper dashed to the front entryway. "I've got it."

She opened the heavy wood door to Chase and Zach who had obviously forgotten his key. Again. Her brother sidled past with a friendly grin and a playful shove. Pyper gave him a shove right back, but paid him no further notice because standing before her, framed in the threshold of her home, Chase formed a striking image. He held a bouquet of bright yellow sunflowers, their long stems wrapped in green tissue paper.

"Ah." In a heady instant, Pyper lost her figurative footing; a flood of heat cut loose through her body.

"Yeah. Ah, hey." He looked over her shoulder.

It comforted her somehow that Chase didn't seem to be in much better shape. That helped Pyper find her poise. She opened the door wide, gesturing him inside. "I'm so sorry. I generally have better hostess skills than this. Welcome. Come on in."

Tentative steps led him into the foyer. "Something smells great."

Pyper pushed for ease, but continued to tremble on the inside. "My aunt, Ruthie Newman, passed the recipe on to mom long ago. Chicken-veggie stew is a staple around here."

"Sounds great." With endearing boyishness, he thrust the bouquet her way. "These are for your mom. Thought she might enjoy them. It was kind of y'all to invite me."

Pyper didn't accept. Instead, she stepped back to lead him to the kitchen where she could hear her parents chatting as they prepared dinner. Delivery honors definitely needed to be extended to her mom directly.

"Oh, and, ah, this is for you," he continued.

Pyper's progress stalled and she turned. Wrapped separately and tucked behind the large sunflower arrangement was a long-stemmed, pale pink rose surrounded by greenery and a delicate spray of white baby's breath. Chase handed her the bloom, his features kissed by a sense of careful reserve.

Pyper stared at him, wordless, charmed. When he passed her the flower, their fingertips connected. Before she could even help it, a welcoming thaw began within the darkest, deepest trench of her heart. Tingles of delight left her smiling. She buried her nose in fragrant sweetness. "Thank you, Chase. How beautiful."

His return smile charged her senses. She continued to the kitchen. "Mom? Dad? Chase is here."

"Chase, it's good to see you. Welcome." Tyler stepped forward, offering a ready handshake. Her mother exclaimed over the flowers and stationed them promptly in a vase. Pyper, meanwhile, clung to her rose, wrapping her head around the fact that Chase was in her home, part of the family for a time, part of sharing some music, some food and…affection. That's what threw her. The care. The emotion behind it all.

In passing, her mom gave Pyper's arm a discreet nudge and glanced at the rose. "Would you like a vase, Pyp?"

"Oh…ah, sure. Please, Mom—thanks."

OK, that was the most awkward response in history. When she brushed past Chase to accept a crystal bud holder, their gazes caught and held. Closer and closer she inched to a fire she couldn't yet begin to understand—or avoid.

❧

"Mmm…this dinner makes me miss Aunt Ruthie a little less. She walks through the dining room door every time we have her chicken stew. It's wonderful, Mama."

"Thanks, Pyp." An ocean of love circled the table, reflected most vividly in the depths of Amy's eyes when her gaze touched upon Pyper.

Chase responded deeply to those layers of affection. "How long since she passed?" Chase settled a freshly buttered roll on his plate then wiped his fingertips on a cheery yellow napkin before returning it to his lap.

"She's been gone a couple years now." Amy sighed. "I miss that big, generous heart of hers. She helped me settle in and find my feet when I left Michigan behind."

Interest piqued, Chase turned his attention to Tyler. "I remember reading somewhere that you stayed with her when you went through the reality competition that launched your career. Is that right?"

"I did. She opened her home to me, and it became my safe haven during all the madness that followed."

"Tell us about your family, Chase." Amy dished herself a second helping of salad. "You Tennessee born-and-bred?"

"Yes, ma'am. Murfreesboro. My folks still live there. They stood by me when I hit bottom, and they were good about raising me right. Thing is, they couldn't really take away the loneliness I felt, and they weren't overly emotional people. Still they were solid. Dependable."

"I remember reading somewhere you were an only child." Seated next to Chase, Pyper gave him a prompting smile.

"Yep. Mom was a seamstress. Dad was an accountant. Left brain, right brain—all their friends teased them about it. I suppose I inherited the creativity gene from my mama. I loved music from day one. My folks loved to joke that I was always hooked up to something listening to music."

Tyler's laughter filled the air. "I contended with that issue myself. What's your favorite?"

"I like it all, sir, truly. Rock, country, soft and sweet or driving and intense. Doesn't seem to matter. The beat, the melodies, the lyrics are what speak to me. I couldn't afford lessons or anything, so I relied on the good hearts of my music teachers in school to show me how to read notes, learn keys and timing and chords."

"They did a good job, Chase."

A silence passed; Chase studied Pyper's mom in pleased surprise. Unexpected affirmations still startled him, even after the successes he had enjoyed—especially coming from people he respected. Earning the praise of yes-men was easy, and fake. Winning the praise of people he admired was far more meaningful and hard-fought.

"Thank you, ma'am."

"I'm Amy. Please."

Chase dipped his head, his lips curving in a shy form of acknowledgement. "Don't mean to be so formal. Believe it or not, I was raised to be a southern gentleman—and always show proper respect."

"How could…" Amy stopped speaking, folded her hands beneath her chin and studied the table top.

"How could I have back-peddled so far?"

Amy's answer to that was a chagrinned look in his direction; meanwhile Chase held the undivided attention of everyone at the table.

"I was lonely and pretty quiet as a kid. I was non-descript, workin' to get by. But then came music. Then came my friendship with Shay and our band. Music. Music fueled a fire I didn't even know could rage so hot, or be so consuming—for better and for worse.

"I fell into a trap of my own creation, never realizing the harm until it was way too late. I was handed implicit acceptance, monster success, adulation."

"Scariest masters around."

Tyler's interjection earned a firm nod from Chase.

"It's a tough battle to win," Tyler continued, "But you did it, and you did it well, sir. I admire that."

Sincerity flavored every word. So did longing. Chase thought fleetingly of Zach, who polished off a roll and forked some salad greens, devouring his meal with typical teen-style gusto. During the drive home, Zach had admitted to hero worship. It occurred to Chase now that, in much the same way, he emulated Tyler Brock.

Tyler studied Chase for a long, intent moment. "Coming back strong is just as important a victory, Chase. Keep that in mind, and keep it up. You've got friends, you've got support, and you've got God. Lean on 'em all."

"That's my plan." Chase pictured himself easing into the lines and pages of Pyper's family. All of a sudden he found it tough to swallow against the lump that tightened his throat, so he hoped the large, easy smile he wore spoke volumes about the place where he now found himself.

12

After dinner, Chase made a quick dash to his truck to retrieve sheet music for "Forgiveness." Back inside, he followed Pyper to Tyler's music room where her dad had just tabled a trio of glasses filled with lemonade. The space was acoustically insulated, squared off neatly, and lined by guitars in stands. A coffee table was strewn with sheet music covered by notes and lyrics in what appeared to be Tyler's bold script. Walls were decorated by framed albums and awards. Then, there were shelves with even more awards, and a plush area rug where a group of leather seats begged a person to sink in, strap on a guitar, and go with the flow.

Chase crossed the entryway and never wanted to leave. This was where Pyper had come of age as a musician, cultivated a God-given gift under the loving and expert hand of her father. Chase twined his fingers against Pyper's, giving them a slight squeeze. The gesture drew her focus and for a second or two, he lost himself in her eyes.

Tyler handed him a guitar then sat forward on the edge of a nearby seat, strapping on a guitar of his own. "What I love are those moments when the whole writing process sort of just takes you by storm. When a simple inspiration leads to the creation of the exact melody, the words, the beat you were after in your heart."

Chase nodded and sat in the chair next to Tyler's. In unison, they began to tune their instruments. "Just enough of those moments come along to keep you satisfied, but at the same time leave you hungry for more." Chase wondered if the same kind of mind-set applied to what he felt for Pyper. She had settled cross-legged on the floor between their two chairs, a feminine delight, to be sure, yet so much more. All at once, those self-doubts he had discussed with Mark rose up like ghosts. This was a fantasy. A glimpse of the kind of joy that would keep him hungry for a long, long time…

"After the Opry event, I was so on fire I came home and started writing," Tyler said. "Everything came fast and furious and perfect. I don't think my head found a pillow 'til early morning. The words, the melody, just flowed through my mind and flew off my fingers, know what I mean?"

"I do at that." Chase strummed. He grinned, savored being able to improvise as Tyler interjected simple chords and a steady, building rhythm. "I call it heaven."

"So do I."

"You mentioned wanting to try out 'Forgiveness', so I brought the sheet music."

"Great."

"Can I take a look?"

Pyper extended a hand and for the strangest reason, he focused on her slim, creamy wrist, and long, tapered fingers that he could feel in a beckoning caress… He forced words past his lips. "Sure. Have at it."

Chase passed off the pages, and Pyper bent her head in study, twirling an errant wave of hair around her finger.

Chase shook free of the desire that licked fire against his gut. Sure the Brock's were kind-spirited and genial, but he couldn't imagine for even a quick second that they'd be pleased by any romantic intentions on his part. Forcing himself from her pull, Chase initiated a run-through of the song. They finessed the word play, worked at the refrain, and then Pyper added a batch of freshly-created words in answer to verse one of the song, which were so skilled and seamless she earned an even larger dose of Chase's respect.

Tyler kept time and added his own thoughts as the song continued to take shape from the rough cut Chase had provided to Imperion weeks ago. In the end, the blend delivered a spread of chills against his skin. Man, had he missed this kind of collaboration.

Tyler kept his fingers moving against the guitar strings, nodding in acceptance of their latest efforts. "You've definitely got a winning theme; the melody is rock solid, but I keep coming back to the words."

"Yeah. I agree." Chase's joy faded a bit. "Words were always Shay's domain."

"Not necessarily, Chase. Yours are great. All they need is an infusion of hope. What Pyper added just a bit ago was the perfect answer to your first verse. Kind of like heaven's answer as we struggle with sin, know what I mean?"

Chase and Pyper ran through the song one more time with Tyler accompanying.

Too much time wasted to be young again.
Too much time wasted to taste pure again.
To ever be worth the Father's gift…
Forgiveness…forgiveness…

The word echo blended his voice to Pyper's; it

reverberated, full of questioning, full of a battle to find self-worth and a spot in God's world despite falling down. Pyper found her way to the next verse.

Don't you dare believe that lie,
Life's too precious to let go by…
Forgiveness….forgiveness…
Reach out for forgiveness…forgiveness

From there, their voices synched into a blended harmony.

Don't cower behind a thick, brick wall.
God's determined to see it fall…
Forgiveness …forgiveness…
Reach out for…forgiveness, forgiveness.

Their voices blended once more.

I see how precious love can be…
That's what I want for you and me.
Forgiveness, forgiveness…
Let's find our way to
Forgiveness, forgiveness…forgiveness.

In the end, Tyler delivered a short, appreciative whistle. "Great back-and-forth. I almost hate to say it, Chase, but it seems to me like you have another duet on your hands with this one."

The observation was spot-on, and Chase knew exactly why the song worked so much better now. In tandem with Pyper—with the woman he longed to reach out to and pursue—the aching redemption that was so intrinsic to the song coursed through every note he sang.

"Seems there's part of me that's incomplete."

"Maybe so."

Tyler spoke, but what Chase noticed was Pyper's retreat, the way a hint of wariness tossed shutters against the natural light of her eyes.

"I dunno. Even though I've recovered"—he made a pair of air quotes—"maybe the words for my new stuff are one-sided because I'm still searching for something."

"There's nothing wrong with searching if it leads you to what's good."

Pyper's decree caused him to home in on her exclusively. He maintained her focus with nothing more than a steady, engaging look. "Let's try it one more time, OK?"

"Sure."

She added a light shrug, so obviously unintimidated and sure of herself when it came to music and performance. For some reason Chase felt compelled to throw her a slight curve ball...

"Pyper? You know this song well enough. Leave the pages behind. Look at me. Look into my eyes."

He kept the summons quiet, tender but firm. All the same, her hesitance marked each beat of the second hand on the wall clock while she visibly debated, then lifted her eyes to his.

"Now," he beckoned softly, "sing."

Their gazes never wavered. They sang to one another, lost in that intimate emotion which only shared melody and shared lyrics could bring to life. It didn't matter to Chase that Pyper's father sat just a few feet away, that her mother rustled through the kitchen just beyond the threshold. This moment, its bond, belonged to him and Pyper alone. This was good. This was pure.

His heart rocked into an unsteady, thundering beat, promise brimming, hope cresting...

We'll find the passion, find the joy.
When we get and when we give

Forgiveness…forgiveness…
All we need is forgiveness…forgiveness…

ॐ∾ऀ

The intense exchange left Pyper drained, yet in paradox, a flow of invigorating energy sailed through her system. Working with Chase was beyond incredible.

He expelled a breath and shook his head, delivering a sheepish grin. "With that I think we can ramp down the intensity a bit, maybe figure out a couple more songs for our gig at The Stage." Lightening the mood further, he stood and stretched. "I spied a grand piano in the next room. Are we allowed to put it to good use?"

Pyper tilted her head, looked way up and lost herself in the deep, dark allure of his eyes. "I think that can be arranged."

He offered his hand and lifted her to her feet with ease. "Let's sing for fun. Without all the push. Just us."

"Sounds good."

Her father stood as well. "I'm going to check in on Amy. Y'all enjoy."

Pyper led the way to the living room and took a seat on the cool, glossy bench of a black walnut grand piano. Chase settled against its far edge, hooking the guitar strap around his neck once again. His back was to her, but they remained close enough that they touched, brushing slightly as they moved. His warmth and an earthy, masculine wood-spice enveloped her at once.

"Want to hear a story?" Pyper's fingers began a timeless dance against the ebony and ivory keys. "A story about when I was little?"

"Absolutely."

"Tune up. I'll give you the pitch." Pyper struck 'E' and Chase plucked, twisted pegs, refined tone until his guitar was properly tuned. "On my first visit to Tennessee, the first time I met Tyler, I got stung by a bee. I was all alone with him because my mama had gone shopping with Aunt Ruthie. I was playing outside while Tyler gardened, and when I kicked my rubber ball, I upset a pack of bees. When I got stung, I was terrified. More so of what Tyler might do to me than the pain of the venom."

Chase had begun an improvised melody that came to an abrupt halt. "Pyp, he'd never hurt you."

"Oh, I know that now. But back then? All I knew at the age of four was a man's rage if I ever dared to cry or step out of line or interfere with his world in any way. Anyhow, after I got stung, Tyler wrapped me in hugs, in love, and he bound my wound—in more ways than I can ever express. After? We came right here, and he let me play this piano.

"This very spot is where my life began, Chase. The life I live now, the life I live in full, started that day. I was dazzled. I couldn't believe he'd let me anywhere near this gorgeous instrument." Her fingers swept along. "It was a defining moment in my life. Sealed my fate, I think. In that time, I found joy. I found music, and I found out what a father's love is really like. Right then and there I became Tyler's protégée. I knew music would be a huge part of my life."

"Pyp?" Chase leaned back just far enough to give her a fortifying nudge. "I'm so sorry for the past, for the pain it caused you."

Pyper fought to swallow against a fast-building

lump in her throat. "I am, too, but the past gave me now. I wouldn't trade the life I have with Tyler and my mama." She polished their brief piece of improv with a flourishing twinkle of the keys.

"Here's something else." Chase maintained a steady gaze. "You can't put in what God left out. Musically, you're gifted. You're blessed. God knew just how to bring that to life." He chuckled. "You know, I was just thinking. Musically, I've always been a six-string man."

"And for me, because of that moment with Tyler, the piano reigns supreme."

"Seems that way. You know what that means?"

"No."

"Together we're a great combination."

For an instant, Pyper froze. *A great combination.* Perhaps a lifelong combination? Was God tuning and blending much more than music between them? Hope—expectation—took hold as the idea burst free and glanced against her heart.

Chase continued to look over his shoulder, watching as her fingertips returned to drifting against the keys. "Whatcha feel like?"

"How about 'Better Than a Hallelujah'?" The song choice came out of nowhere, an inspiration that simply struck home. Pyper started to play; the piano intro had always been a favorite riff of hers. When Chase added his guitar, when the verse kicked in, the moment carried to her in a Spirit-filled flow Pyper could only attribute to God Himself. They ended up spontaneously alternating verses. Chase sang of a drunkard's cry; Pyper sang of beautiful messes transformed by Christ.

The mix of their voices, the connection they shared

when exploring each layer of the song, gave her tingles of elation. She wanted to do this again—and again—just jam with him, make music, create. She wanted to share moments like this—moments that were revealing and powerful.

By the end of the song, emotion nearly grabbed the best of her. Tears built and stung once the last notes faded to silence, so she caught her breath. She closed her eyes, re-finding center as Chase bumped against her shoulder, deliberately calling her attention. When she looked his way, she found herself captured within a tender, beckoning gaze.

"You. Are. Good."

Pyper rested her head against his shoulder, her smile lighting to full-beam. "Same to you. That was a lot of fun."

Only then did Pyper realize they were no longer alone. Soft applause filled the room, coming from the threshold, from her parents. Shy and awkward, Pyper moved away from Chase, fingering back the thick fall of her hair while heat seeped across her neck and cheeks. Being with him this way came so easy...and felt so beautiful. Pyper's wistful spirit yearned.

Chase cleared his throat and seemed to shake free of the moment. She appreciated his discretion and nod to propriety. After all, this was, for the most part, a professional endeavor, right? She puzzled on the topic for a moment while her dad settled an arm around her mother's shoulders. "After hearing that, and your combined take on 'Forgiveness,' I know Kellen's on the mark. The two of you are going to be great performing together."

Her mother nodded in agreement. "By the way? Dessert is ready in the kitchen if you're interested.

Peach cobbler."

"You won't have to ask me twice." Chase unstrapped the guitar and handed it to her father so it could be returned to the music room.

Pyper lifted from the bench and followed Chase to the kitchen. "Mama's recipe is the best. Her peach cobbler is one of my favorites."

Fresh from the oven, dessert went down easy, topped by just-starting-to-melt scoops of vanilla ice cream and fragrant servings of coffee. Afterward, Chase and Tyler chatted in the living room while Pyper lingered in the kitchen and helped her mom rinse and load the last of the dishes.

When she returned, Chase stood as though preparing to leave. Something about his imminent departure caused a heart lurch followed by a tinge of sadness. As though registering her reluctance, he caught her fingertips with the swing of his hand. "My truck's out front and nothing much more is going to be accomplished tonight as far as the music session is concerned. Feel like a quick drive?"

To where? For What? Didn't matter. In the end, Pyper didn't want this evening with Chase to conclude. Not quite yet.

The ride they shared was short, silent mostly. Just a few miles north of Pyper's home, he backed his pickup truck to a stop so the tailgate faced the banks of a wide, bubbling creek that sparkled and shimmered. Sunset painted the sky in vivid hues of yellow, orange, pink and blue. The mountains went all jagged and purple against the rapidly darkening sky. Pyper made ready to leave the vehicle, but Chase stayed her exit by pressing a hand against her arm.

"Let's drop the tailgate and sit in back. We can

watch the water. The lightning bugs'll be coming to life, and there's a full moon tonight. Should be beautiful."

Pyper marveled. Without any kind of roadmap, Chase knew just how to glide into her spirit and tuck in tight. How could this be so? She had never come across anyone like him. "That sounds nice."

"Wait here; I'll get your door." Chase leaped from the cab and rounded to Pyper's side of the truck. He helped her to the ground then reached behind the passenger seat to extract a stash of blankets and a pair of water bottles. "They're not cold or anything, but maybe they'll do."

"They're fine. Thanks."

Pyper smiled at him, touched all over again by his thoughtfulness. Their fingers brushed when she accepted her bottle and that increasingly familiar jolt of electricity created a need that stemmed not just from the physical but the emotional. Lightning bugs, moonbeams, the heightened emotions that swept through her soul transported Pyper to a bittersweet season of life that she wanted to share with him. She needed him to understand her, to know her, fully.

Chase unlatched the gate and they hopped into the truck bed, moving in comfortable syncopation while they spread blankets. From there they stretched out and sky-gazed for a peaceful time.

"You came prepared." Offering a teasing smile and a hand gesture, Pyper indicated the blankets and beverages. She wondered about his intent and purpose.

Chase twisted to his side and propped on an elbow. His lips quirked in a way that spoke of tenderness. "This is innocent, Pyp. I keep 'em handy because when I drive, I mull things over. I come up with ideas to explore. When that happens, I find quiet places, out of the way spots where I can just pull over, stop myself and create. This is one of my favorites. Nature is a great inspiration for songwriting."

Chase returned to lying flat on his back, arms folded beneath his head, face to the blackening bowl of a sky and its dancing pinpricks of light. He sighed deep and contented, which made Pyper feel good—the sound was so appealing.

"Sorry if I seemed a little reactionary."

"No harm, no foul. You know where I come from, so I understand—but keep your eye on who I am now, OK?"

"I'm trying, and you're succeeding."

"Thanks for that. Still, I wonder. There are times when you pull back from me. I have to believe that's because you're conflicted about me, and us. But today, especially when we sang together, you let go. That made all the difference."

"Like lightning bugs and moonbeams." Pyper whispered the words, falling headlong into moments from her past she wanted to share with Chase. She needed to trust—and display that trust via revelation. "I told you about that moment when I played the piano with Tyler."

"Yeah."

"That night, I was so happy I thought I'd burst. I'd never felt so free. I bubbled with so much joy and energy I wanted to run for miles, dance, play, sing—"

Chase laughed low. "I can just picture it, crash."

Pyper snickered, savored the cool breeze that blew against her skin. "Just after sunset, my mama and Tyler were camped out on the front porch, on that swing we all love so much, and I charged through the door and into the grass just beyond where they sat. That's when I discovered a brand new miracle. Fireflies. To me, they seemed like such happy creatures. They sparked and danced, just like I wanted to do, so I chased them. Tyler was ready to give me a capped jar, so I could catch one and keep it close by."

"Your first pet?"

Chase's teasing grin was irresistible. She drew light fingertips against the stubble of his jaw. "Not hardly. You see, I couldn't do it. I couldn't trap something so beautiful and hold it prisoner. I wanted them to be free, and happy, just like me. The past held me prisoner, Chase. In some ways it still does. I'm letting fear taint what I see in you, and just like capturing a firefly, that doesn't strike me as right, or fair." Pyper snuggled close to his lean, warm side and stared into his eyes. "To me, you're moonbeams and lightning bugs. You're warm light and sparks of life that can't be denied no matter how rough the road you've traveled. I'm trying, and I don't doubt you as much as I doubt…*me*.".

"Pyp, your honesty means more to me than I can say." He gave her a quiet, but pointed look. "Confusion is OK, but you have to get over it. Get over being afraid of me. Get over being intimidated by the call of your heart. Stop being afraid of *us*."

Just like that, appearing like sparks set against a rapidly darkening sky, the fireflies came to life. Cooling breezes continued to curve in, chasing away the last of the day's humidity, tickling her skin with goose bumps.

"No answer to that, huh?"

Pyper faced him square, ready to sputter a

defensive reply, but she stopped short. Acting from a knee-jerk response, rather than an honest assessment of her heart, wouldn't do either of them any good, so she quit while she was ahead, aiming a sassy, charm-packed grin in his direction. "It's kinda hard to refute the truth when it's thrown at your feet."

"Oh, don't worry, crash. I know how to be gentle. But I also know how to fight for what I want."

"Meaning me?"

Shimmering white moonlight intensified as darkness built, dancing like diamond dust against the surface of the creek while it bubbled and rolled. Chase's lips curved—long and full—slow as a lover's caress and equally as tempting.

"That's my dream, yes. You. Music. Redemption. Finding a pathway to self-worth that God alone would ever see fit to give me."

She looked away, overcome by such a straightforward, beautiful declaration.

He shifted to an elbow and lifted her chin until their gazes met. A song named Chase Bradington took flight in her heart. Pyper had to fight the urge to snuggle even closer and surrender fully to a heart-fall she had never seen coming.

"All of that is because of you. Because of what we create when we mix. Want to talk about that?"

So, that was the purpose of their drive. OK. She could deal with that. Sort of.

"Sure. I can be straight up. I'll tell you flat that I don't know to react to you." Her voice was no more than a wavering whisper. "I don't know what to feel."

"Actually, I think that's just the trouble. You know exactly what you feel, but you're afraid." Automatically, his thumb moved slow and light against her cheek, soothing away an instant push of agitation at being so completely revealed to a man who carried a very distinct set of emotional dangers. "I don't blame you for that. I know I'm not pristine. I know I'm not what you've been looking for, and I'm for certain nobody's role model. Still, God's using me, and He brought me to you. I want to figure out why. I want to figure out where we're meant to go. Let's find the answers, Pyper. Together."

"How?"

"By the two of us agreeing not to hold back anymore."

She stiffened; in a flash her mood turned sharp and steely, icing her like a winter storm blowing through the Smokeys. "I'm not to be had, Chase. I'm not ever going to fall headlong into a relationship just because it feels good or satisfies a physical itch. You need to know that my beliefs are—"

"Your beliefs are my beliefs, too." He cut in fast and hard. "I'm not talking about sex. I'm talking about relationship. I'm talking about discovery. Are we good together? Everything inside me says we could be, but there's only one way to find out. Take the leap. Not physically, that's the easy part. I'm talking about what's in here." He tapped the spot above her heart, eyes steady and strong, gradually creating even richer inroads of trust and understanding. "I'm talking about what we feel for each other. There's something between us. I want to explore it. Do you? Do you trust me enough for that?"

His question ignited a fire, refined a connection that came alive, sliding around them, bringing them closer and closer to a point of no return.

"Don't hurt me, Chase Bradington. Please, please

don't hurt me." She didn't know if she'd recover if he did. Cricket chirps, the swoosh of dancing long grass punctuated a silence that beat by.

Chase met her gaze without flinching. "I ask the same thing of you."

"You could hurt me. Badly."

"Ditto."

Pyper struggled against all she had known, all she had believed to be true about reformation and battles against evil. And at once she decided. He was worth it. Her answer was resounding—terrifying—because her answer was yes.

"How does all this start, Chase? What do we do?" She shifted to an elbow, looking at him as darkness became a shroud and moonlight sheened the waves of his hair, flashing through his eyes.

"Well, we can start by talking."

"Talking."

He nodded. "For starters"—he shifted to an elbow as well, so they were eye-to-eye—"I'd like you to tell me something, and I want you to answer me true."

"Always. What?"

"Is this...is us...why Darren isn't part of your picture anymore?"

She met his gaze straight on. "Yes. If it lends you any satisfaction, yes."

"Steady, angel." He went soft and careful. He gave her a moment to settle. "There's no satisfaction, just interest and curiosity so the lines between you and me stay straight. That's all. You keep trying to paint me as the bad guy, and thankfully you keep coming up short. Given your past, it's self-preservation; I get that, but I think it's time to take the cue."

Her heart thundered. Pyper cursed herself for

refusing the way he offered himself, appreciating anew the way Chase answered her tense uncertainty with a calm and reassuring attitude.

But that was just the trouble. When it came to Chase Bradington, those lines he talked about were far from straight. Instead, they dipped and curved and swirled with tantalizing appeal—like a thrill ride of sorts.

"I'm confused about Darren's place in my life...Well, I'm not confused any more, but still, two things. First, he and Anne Lucerne have grown pretty fond of each other, and I think that's great. Second, even if they hadn't found a way to each other, I'd never lead him on or be unfair if I'm...if I have...if..."

"I get the idea, sweetheart. You won't divide yourself. You're a rare spirit, Pyper Brock. You're too invested a woman to ever be cavalier about matters of the heart. That's one of the many things that keeps pulling me to you."

"You—you're pulled?"

Chase shook his head, as though marveling at her inability to see through to his truth, to the core of his emotions. "I have a pull, Pyp. A craving. A craving to be worthy, to be everything I can to you. I talked with my sponsor the other day and realized all over again that the black stains on my soul have vanished. Love painted them white. Like a miracle. God's miracle. A miracle I get to share with you."

Chase leaned back again and Pyper watched as he spent a few moments studying the sky, tracking the motion of small, hazy clouds that slipped across the face of that vivid, milky moon.

"I know my past scares you. It scares me, too, but I won't fall back into bad behavior."

Gentle winds fell alluring as a dream between them. Light and shadow framed him in a tempting silhouette that drove her heartbeat into an urgent tempo.

He turned, meeting her gaze while tender fingertips performed a gentle glide against her cheeks and neck, through the thick, tumbled waves of her hair. "I swear to you, and I promise by all that I am, I'd never...ever...raise a hand against you. Even in my worst fit of temper."

She nibbled at a tremulous lower lip. "I believe you, Chase. I know that. Really and sincerely, I do."

What scared her far more was the idea of him sliding back into self-defeating, self-destructive behavior. But by increasing and hard-earned degrees, he won her trust...and uncovered the key that would unlock her heart for good and for all.

"Chase...I...I want you to kiss me."

He moved slowly, leaning over her as he cupped her cheek; her skin flamed hot, radiant with a warmth that was stirred by desire.

"Oh, sweet girl. Be very careful what you wish for." He breathed the words and the husky decree lit fire to his eyes.

"You're in my system, Chase. I don't know how it happened. I don't know why. I just know...I know..."

She faltered, going weak against the will of her heart, the soft blankets that cushioned her back, the smell of late summer, the rustle of leaves and the glimmer of the stars. His thumbs slid soft against the underside of her jaw and she ached, releasing a soft exclamation. Chase dipped his head fast and feasted on lips that yielded to his, the flavor of him blending into the richest form of honey. Her sigh dissolved against his questing mouth.

How could she ever walk away from him now?

The kiss came nowhere near to surrender, but the connection changed everything—every foundation, every need, every wish—until the surrender happened anyway, not of body, but of heart and soul. He was leagues more delicate, more patient and seductive than she had ever imagined—and since meeting him she had imagined much. He claimed her mouth with loving reverence, feeding her spirit with an unquenchable fire. Languor rode against her limbs, leaving her weak but conversely infusing her with strength.

"I need to take you home, Pyper." He rolled away, but sheltered her in his arms, drawing her tight against his side, just as she hoped, just as she wished, so their connection would continue even as a sensually heated moment cooled. "If I don't, this time and place will spell trouble. For both of us."

"But I don't want you to leave."

He rolled her to her back once more then propped above her like a fierce and loving protector. He leaned in to gloss kisses against her cheeks, her forehead. "I'm not leaving you. Just taking us to safer ground."

Nobility layered the words, turning them into a soft caress that slid against the curves of Pyper's heart. In that moment, she realized she was falling in love—hard and true. All over again, he unlatched the gate of her heart, walking into a place she felt sure God had reserved just for him.

13

Pyper was in heaven. Absolute, unquestionable heaven. What wasn't to love? She was seated front-row-center at The Stage, with an incomparable view of the District on a Saturday night. She watched from a tall stool as a vibrant collection of bodies, street traffic, loud laughter and eager shouts clamored for attention in and around the legendary honkytonk. The life-tide became a force all its own, rolling along Broadway, weaving past the entryways of dozens of bars, storefronts and restaurants. Best of all, though, were the nightclubs, the historic locales that operated in the shadow of the mighty Ryman, catering to the best up-and-coming musical talent and welcoming home the ones who had made it big. Just beyond those golden gates, street musicians worked hard, some with talent equal to the acts that performed inside. Those hungry artists entertained tourists and locals alike with songs and performances that could stir the soul.

Neon lights flashed, illuminating the window behind a slightly elevated wooden dais where Chase currently wrapped a performance of his classic "Color of Life." Pyper's smile spread as she propped her chin in her hand and watched. He absolutely rocked the happy, enthusiastic crowd.

A tall, ponytailed waitress weaved neatly through the packed crowed. Black apron bulging with tips and straws, she approached Pyper's spot, delivered a cheery wink along with a tall, icy lemon-lime soda. Pyper responded in kind then chugged, continuing to absorb. Nothing here was left to chance. Positioning was critical. Folks on a jaunt through downtown Nashville wandered past, peeked inside, and once they heard the music, they were caught with a hook. The recipe for success here was ages old, and tonight was no different.

She snapped to proper focus when the last chords of Chase's song faded and he addressed the audience. "Ladies and gentlemen, y'all are so kind. Thank you for that wonderful welcome. It's always an honor to be able to play at The Stage. Standing here, performing at what has to be one of the greatest venues in The District, I feel like I'm at the center of Nashville's history. Nashville's heart. I don't take that lightly."

Pyper registered the delighted response of the crowd. Take him or leave him, love him or otherwise, there was no denying Chase Bradington knew how to command—and win—a venue. She rejoiced at the thought, giving him snaps of respect.

As if he could read her thoughts, he glanced her way, sent an acknowledging grin before continuing. "For now, to keep the good times going, I want you to help me greet the real star of tonight's show. Please give it up for Miss. Pyper. Brock."

Right on cue, Piper lifted from her perch and trotted the pair of steps leading to the stage. In the more private, second-level seating area that rimmed three sides of the bar, she spotted her dad and Kellen Rossiter watching while they leaned against a railing. Smile blooming, she waved to the crowd and acknowledged a few of the folks seated close by. She drifted into the applause and made her way to the spot where Chase stood at a solitary mic stand. Crossing the scarred wooden floorboards she threw another wave toward the house.

At that point she caught Chase's reaction to her entrée, and her footsteps faltered. Deep, smooth eyes never once left her face; his expression spoke clearly of the words amazement and captivation. He took hold of the mic stand and brought it into position between them, smiling warm. Pyper couldn't help but be swept straight to him.

"You know," he began, finally readdressing the crowd, "you can call me an old fashioned southern boy, but there's something incredibly attractive about the sight of a woman who strolls onstage wearing dark blue denim, a pair of worn leather boots and a cowboy hat. Pyper, you are gorgeous."

Oxygen fled her lungs. What was this all about? While she battled a sensual tremor, Chase tugged her gently to his side and kissed her cheek. His lips slid against her skin like the brushstroke of a feather, and he smelled so good…

For the benefit of the crowd, Pyper continued to smile, but somehow she needed to earn back a bit of control and assert herself. "Well, my goodness. Who here can say charm and gentility have died? Isn't he the sweetest thing? Thanks so much for the welcome. How y'all doin'? Havin' a good time tonight?" Cheers flowed in, easing that tense layer of awareness that crept along her shoulders.

Chase resumed strumming his guitar; the band followed his lead. "Folks, I want to tell you a story about the night I met this lady. It was at the Opry. The night her daddy, Tyler Brock, was awarded membership into the performance family." Cheers and applause rose up. "I was honored to be a small part of that event."

Pyper cocked a hip and initiated a playful stare-down with her colleague. "Oh, that's right. The very night you crashed into me and nearly bowled me straight over."

"Darlin'? I could only hope." In emphasis, Chase delivered a wicked grin and winked. Pyper's intellect flew away on fast feet. Meantime, Chase addressed their cat-calling, jovial crowd. "Isn't she a sassy piece of work? As I was saying, the night we met, we had a discussion about country music and its history. Its love affairs."

Where was this piece of repartee headed? Pyper's cheeks flushed scarlet beneath a blush. Where should she take this? "Yeah, we did, because Opry staff landed you in the It Takes Two dressing room. A spot at the Opry created to honor such legendary romantic pairs as Johnny Cash and June Carter, George Jones and Tammy Wynette." Applause and whistles broke out in the midst of their country music fans. Pyper's pulse thrummed. "Your point is?"

"My point is, since it seems we're going to be singing together every now and again, why not pay them homage? How about we launch into a cover of Johnny and June's classic, 'It Ain't Me, Babe' before we introduce the new song we've been working on?"

"It Ain't Me, Babe." They had horsed around with the song a time or two in recent days. The lyrics formed a spirited ode to the push and pull of relationships that, on one level, should never happen, but on another were as destined as the sunrise. Was he trying to build a bit of romantic connection to their performance?

Pyper's eyes went narrow, but playful. "I'm game. It's a great song." More applause rushed in while she accepted a tambourine from one of their backup musicians. Prompted by Chase's intro, Pyper returned to front stage center and whispered, "I'm so not afraid of you."

"And that just might be your first mistake." His quick retort and wolfish grin played havoc against her senses as the intensity of his gaze stroked her as sure as a caress.

The band lit up. Subtle percussion built followed by a harmonica intro that was joined by a thumping bass and the build of Chase's guitar.

Pyper threw herself into the song as she would any other, but this rendition was special, and she knew it. Judging by the flare of pleasure in Chase's eyes, the same held true for him.

They were a dynamic team—no mistake. The cover and their debut of "Forgiveness" and "Burning Bridges" brought down the house...

❦

Relieved to take in some cool, sweet air outside the bar, Pyper paused for a moment and closed her eyes, replenishing her body and soul for a moment following the conclusion of her set with Chase. Restored, she ambled comfortably along the still busy street, drawn as always to the corner turn off Broadway that led toward the timeless edifice of the Ryman Auditorium.

There, she came upon Chase, back propped against a nearby brick wall. An incline in the road led directly past the historic church turned iconic performance venue and he seemed to drink in the flavor of the night as well. Although he was tucked into shadow, he was in no way obscure. No man with his level of magnetism could remain invisible for long.

Pyper moved to join him, but a pair of middle-aged ladies beat her to the punch. "Mr. Bradington. Good show tonight."

"Thank you. I appreciate that. Glad you came out."

Surprisingly, they didn't stop, or ask for an autograph. They continued to walk on by. The one closest to Chase cast a sneer over her shoulder. "Too bad you fell so hard and so far. After the way you've lived your life? Sorry, I just can't remain a fan. Goes against my good conscience."

Pyper's heart broke—for, with that cavalier, uninformed judgment, they were gone, traipsing into a land of self-righteousness and up a hill that would lead them away. They never paid heed to the fact that Chase watched their retreat, or that he sank against the wall at his back. Unaware of Pyper's approach, he shook his head and focused on the ground.

Defeat rolled off him in waves she could taste.

An easy stride in place, she stepped forward, intent on pushing him away from the bleak storm clouds those women had left behind. "So...you took me by surprise with the whole June and Johnny reference, and that unexpected duet."

Chase looked up; the smile he extended was fake—she recognized the fact only because she was getting to know him better...and better.

"Hope you didn't mind. It felt good, and it segued well into 'Burning Bridges.' The audience seemed to love it."

"They did. Even those two." Lifting her chin, Pyper indicated the two women who had already vanished into the night.

His shoulders sagged just a trace. "You heard that?"

"Didn't like it, or agree with it, but, yeah, I heard that."

In a startling move, Chase bashed a booted heel against the wall where he stood. Other than that, his focus remained straight ahead, his arms folded against his chest. When she moved closer, she noticed the tight set of his jaw, the sharp flash of those coal eyes.

"It makes me sick."

"What? Them? Don't give 'em the time of—"

"It's not just them, Pyper." He ground out an angry sound. "Truth to tell, I don't know who and what I am anymore." He spoke in a harsh tone.

She felt the quaking roll of his temper unfurling, which caused her to rear back slightly. "What do you mean?"

Giving a snort, Chase shook his head as he watched the passing car traffic. "If I try to live by Christian values, folks shoot me down because of my past. On the other side of the coin, if I try to remain true to my old roots in country music, I'm labeled as a newborn, self-righteous holy roller. I don't know who I'm supposed to be."

Pyper studied him, sank into his words, and the emotion that gave them fuel. "You're supposed to be who and what you are, Chase. You're supposed to be who and what God created you to be. Nothing more, nothing less." She moved a bit closer. "Honey, don't buy into their disdain."

Chase delivered a long, pained look. "Tough

proposition when people refuse to trust me. I brought it on myself. I know that. Still, when you work hard to reform, when you hope for a clean slate, rejection stings. I'd like to be the good guy."

"Seems to me you're winning that battle. Keep it up."

More silence passed. "You and I had some fun playing around with 'It Ain't Me, Babe.' I sprang it on you for two reasons. First, I knew you'd handle it like the spirited ball of fire you are."

Pyper didn't even have time to react to that revelation before he continued.

"Second? June and Johnny had it right when it comes to the kind of feelings that run between me and you. I'd like to be the one, but I'm probably all wrong. Doesn't seem to stem the tide, though. Right or wrong, I think you're…"

The sentence dangled, but Pyper filled in the blanks with ease. He saw—he felt—that she was someone worth a heart-risk, no matter what the equation. She felt the same way about him.

"Just remember, no matter what the world ever tries to say or do, I always want to be the kind of man who's worthy of a woman like you."

"It's not about worth, Chase. You're worthy and then some, but you need to tune out all the static. Listen in here"—she settled a hand against his heart—"instead of out there. You're doing just fine."

"Fine enough for you?"

So, he wanted to push on the topic. Pyper's throat went dry. So did her lips. She decided at once to respond with nothing less than that same level of honesty and revelation he had granted. "More than fine enough. We're taking the leap, right? Finding the answers, like we talked about?"

He pulled her close and held on tight. Pyper absorbed the welcome warmth of his body, the feel of his heartbeat quickening against her cheek.

"Thanks, crash." The breath from his murmured words skimmed along her hairline, igniting heat and a tingle of happiness. "That's all I needed to hear."

That night, not even thoughts of a morning breakfast interview with the one and only Petra Goode could keep her mood from lifting high. While a spectacular night in the District transformed from reality to precious memory, while stardust and sparkles followed her to sleep, so did the image of a rugged man with soulful dark eyes and a plaintive voice full of deep, raw longing that begged for bad bridges to burn and disappear into the promise of hope.

14

Between Franklin and downtown Nashville, right off the Old Natchez Trace on Highway 100 stood a Tennessee icon, a classic restaurant catering to enthusiasts of southern comfort food. When Pyper pulled open the doorway of the Loveless Café, she spotted Petra Goode right away. The reporter was already seated, and it was tough to miss a bleached blonde dressed in a vivid red suit. Smile wide, Petra lifted her hand high to issue a fingertip wave.

Bite the bullet and get it over with, Pyper thought, answering the summons with a smile that was in no way real. The traditional air kiss ensued, along with an over solicitous gesture from the reporter inviting Pyper to claim the wooden chair opposite.

A round of idle chit chat followed while they placed breakfast orders—Pyper opted for biscuits and gravy. Their orders arrived soon after and with a mini-recorder, notebook and pen at her elbow, Petra launched the interview while she nibbled at her batch of bacon and some scrambled eggs.

"Pyper, your debut album from last year, *Anchor,* launched the single by the same name and it won you fast fan loyalty and critical acclaim as well as a Dove nomination for best debut album. Talk to me about anchors. Who and what would you define as the anchors in your life?"

"Most definitely my family and my faith in Christ

help keep me anchored. My mom and dad, my brother, they're the most important people to me; they absolutely constitute anchors in my life."

"Um…yes…Tyler and Amy…Zach. You come from a family that can be best described as Christian music royalty these days, what with your dad's induction into the Opry."

"Thanks for that, yes. Absolutely." Pyper knew her smile, and the warm glow that spread through her system, revealed authentic joy in both tone and attitude. So far, so good.

"I have a confession to make. When you and Chase entered the Monroe anniversary party together, I just had to do some nosing around. I'm such a reporter, and y'all make such an intriguing couple. I just couldn't help myself!"

Although they shared a mild laugh, Pyper's sense of ease instantly bit the dust. Petra munched on a triangle of toast, drawing out the moment. Pyper gritted her teeth.

Following a swig of coffee, Petra continued. "Come to find out, I discovered a little something about Chase's mentor, the man who helped him recover while he was at Reach."

Confused by the direction of the conversation, Pyper openly puzzled. "Oh?"

"Oh, yes. In fact, the connection might be of interest to you. Of course, as close as you and Chase have become, you might already know…"

"Know what?" Pyper was about to down a final serving of the grits that had accompanied her meal but stopped short.

"We'll get there. First off, though, does the name Mark Samuels mean anything to you?"

Pyper froze, caught in a spider's web that had been spun to perfection. "Ah…"

"Let me explain." Petra leaned in. Pyper leaned back, dizzy, hot, head suddenly pounding, an instant fever building to a rage. "Mark Samuels is Chase's sponsor. His mentor to this day. Furthermore, he's going to be heading up Reach North right here in Nashville. I'm so sorry…didn't you know? Didn't Chase tell you?"

"Ah…" Curse it all, she couldn't speak. She couldn't dance far enough away from this double-fisted bombshell to find even ground. A queasy stomach turned the world green. Mark Samuels…her biological father…was Chase's recovery sponsor? Mark Samuels was in town? Permanently? Heading up a rehab facility at which she would be performing as it opened its doors?

Questions, emotions, hurtled through Pyper's head like the ricochet of gunfire.

Relentless, Petra pushed on. "I hear you and Chase will be singing at the benefit opening of the facility next week. Did you have any idea at all the event would lead to a reunion with your natural daddy? It's fascinating to me that he's come home to Nashville, all set to emerge on the stage of your life in what seems to be a pretty big way. You must be thrilled. After all, according to his bio on the main Reach website, he's found the Lord. He's battled and defeated alcohol addiction, much like Chase. From there, of course, I was fascinated. Once I did some serious digging, I discovered he had some gambling issues as well. Is that right?" She didn't allow Pyper time to answer, or recover from shock. "After that, I came across some interesting reading material from the St. Clair Shores police department back in Michigan. Seems there are reports on file from your mama that indicate domestic abuse. Mmm, mmm, mmm. To think of the badness he's overcome." Petra's eyes narrowed to cunning, wicked slits. "You must be so very proud."

In spite of flaming heat and an overwhelming sensation of dissolving, then spinning outside of her body, Pyper found her way to a response and a purely false smile. "Yes, Mark Samuels is my father by blood, but beyond that, I don't know the man. At all. I haven't seen or heard from him since my mother divorced him some twenty years ago." How on earth did she keep the biting hatred she felt for the man packaged deep down inside and away from plain view? "I wasn't even five the last time I saw him, so my memories are hazy at best, and inconsequential. I'm afraid I can't be much help with your probing."

Was Petra Goode keen enough to register the understated barbs and pin-pokes of her reply? Lord have mercy, Pyper hoped so.

"That's so true. I've come at you by surprise, and I do apologize for that. See, I couldn't help myself. When I uncovered the truth, I knew it would make for a great story so I've been real eager to chat with you. Maybe it would be best if I give your mama a call. She'll certainly know more about the history here, and I'm sure it'll be in her best interest—and Tyler's, too—to help fill in some information before I go to print. And I am going to print on this, Pyper. No way is this story staying under wraps. From my perspective, it shouldn't."

Pyper experienced a fierce internal scrabble as she fought to claw her way out of a hole made of quick sand. What could she do? What were her options?

Petra held every card, and she knew it.

"If you would be so kind, Petra, I'd ask that you give my family the benefit of some dignity and grace."

Her eyes went wide. Her lashes fluttered. "Oh, but I think I already am. You see, it's the perfect platform and life situation for the Brock family to demonstrate what it's made of. I can see it now—so heart-warming and touching—watchin' y'all stand up for the Christian beliefs you hold so dear. The very idea gives me goose bumps. You, welcoming home your hard-working, reformed biological father. A man who's found redemption, who lives to help troubled souls? What's not to love?"

Pyper fought to keep steady, prayed for the power to remain seated when all she wanted to do was run away screaming.

Indulgent smile in place, Petra claimed their breakfast check with a smooth swipe of her hand against the linen covered table. "It's truly my pleasure to treat you today, Pyp. Out of my respect for you and your family, I'll hold off on publication until after the opening. Besides, I'm sure that event will give me even more to include in the story. I can't wait to see y'all at Reach in a few."

❧❦

Chase spent the morning completing another dynamite recording session. "Burning Bridges" and "Forgiveness" were going to be the star entries on his next album once the songs were completely finessed; but the eight subsequent tracks weren't shabby either. In addition, Zach Brock possessed mad guitar skills, which Chase loved being able to cultivate and encourage. The kid had really clicked with the other members of the band. His passion mirrored theirs, and although they were older, they took him in. Take today for example. Chase enjoyed the way they included him in an after-session lunch at Gabby's—the very spot of his first meal with Pyper.

All in all, he left the studios of Imperion feeling like tethers around his spirit were breaking free, allowing him to be uplifted...and by more than just music.

He pressed the power button for the window of his truck and breathed deep of the air that rushed in and galvanized his entire soul. His evening at the Brock farm had clinched it. The performance at The Stage had set matters in stone. He was in love—big time, and like no other instance in his life. In fact, he was in love for the first, and the last, time in his life. Pyper was that precious. That meaningful.

His fingertips danced against the steering wheel; in came the memory of laying a soft caress against her cheek—silk was nothing more than a pathetic imitation—followed by the memory of kissing her, of tasting the sweetness of soft, full lips that took, and gave, and danced in perfect time to his.

Like they were meant to be.

This was real. This was end-song. The Grand Finale. Happiness washed through him in a flood so potent it couldn't be contained. Laughing aloud, banging a fist against the steering wheel, he let out a whoop of happiness he knew carried straight to heaven, to the ears of Christ and Shayne Williams.

Traffic piled up as Chase entered downtown, so he tempered his mood, paying close attention to the road even as a commercial aired on the radio advertising jewelry. His heart skipped a few beats. Soon enough he intended to present her with a diamond ring along with a lifelong commitment encompassing the whole of his heart. It'd be a ring as breathtaking as the woman to whom it would belong, as big and fantastic as the emotion he battled to control right here and right now.

He laughed once more, spying the merge up ahead that would lead to his condo. His phone came to life. At the first stop light, he glanced at an incoming text message from Kellen Rossiter and his smile fell when he read: *Need to c u. ASAP. It's about Pyper. Can u stop by? I'm at the office. KR*

Chase had just enough time before the light went green, to type: *Just left the studio n I'm not far away—b there in ten.* An ominous shiver skirted against the fine, tickly hairs along the back of his neck.

෧෨

"Gossip mongers are the double-edged sword of the entertainment industry." Kellen paced the floor of his office. In an agitated motion, he raked back his hair. Seated on a couch that lined the far wall, Chase propped forward against his knees, watching and listening. "Petra Goode is hot on the trail of a story about Pyper."

"What could possibly be her angle? Pyper's as clean as can be."

"After catching wind of you two at the anniversary party, she's on a mission."

So that was it. Disappointment wiped away the joyful buzz that had accompanied him along Highway 65. "I see. Petra figures there's a romance brewing between the devil and an angel, so she's after—"

"Actually, no." Kellen flopped into place at the other end of the couch and scrubbed his face. "That's not her angle. She's uncovered information that's much more tantalizing—some history concerning Tyler's wife Amy and her first marriage."

"What?" Chase spat the word.

Kellen simply nodded.

"Pyper told me there was abuse involved—for her and for Amy. I never pushed her beyond that because the topic was obviously painful. What's going on?"

Kellen steepled his fingertips and rolled his head, seeming to release a few tense kinks from his neck. "I'm glad you're ahead of the curve here, because things are even more complicated than that."

"How so?"

Kellen seemed to give up trying to relax and launched to his feet, pacing to his desk. It was a large glass and chrome number free of paper and distraction except for three items: a brass framed photograph of Kellen and his wife Juliet, a phone, and a docking station where a laptop hummed.

"Did she ever tell you the name of her father?"

Chase did a memory peel and came up empty. Surprisingly, the topic had come up, but never the name. Again, by mutual design and in deference to obviously painful history, neither one of them had pushed the topic. "No, why?"

Kellen groaned and pinched the bridge of his nose while he closed his eyes. "Your sponsor. His name is Mark Samuels, right?"

"Yeah." Chase was completely and thoroughly lost. "What does he have to do with—"

"Chase...he's Pyper's father."

15

Shock, fear, rage mixed to a boil that threatened to explode through Chase's body. "Mark...Mark is what?"

"You had no idea."

Fortunately Kellen didn't phrase the words in the form of a question. With a few simple words positioned against the framework of Pyper's past, Chase experienced the sensation of watching a tidal wave bearing down, arcing toward shore in a furious curl of destruction based on nothing more than water, and sand, and the rhythm of the earth. *God, help me. Please. Right here and right now. I'm begging you.* "I had no idea, Kellen. None at all." Still, Chase went defensive. "Do you honestly think for even half a second I'd keep something like that from her?"

"No!" Kellen paced the length of the room. His footfalls were silenced by plush carpet, yet remained no less urgent or forceful.

"As for Mark's connection to Pyper, what reason would I have to know that kind of personal background information about him? I was his patient. Reach counselors are short on personal detail but long on philosophy and therapy, which is as it should be."

"Agreed, and I'm not accusing you, or him, of anything. I'm simply trying to understand the timeline so I can protect Pyper and the Brocks. And you. That's my job. I had no idea who your sponsor was, didn't care much as long as you emerged from rehab clean and sober, but around ten this morning, I got a call from Petra Goode. She sprung this on Pyper at breakfast and wanted to know if I had an official comment to offer on behalf of my clients Tyler Brock and Chase Bradington. I wanted to throttle the woman for ambush."

"Get in line." Chase's voice was a rough growl. Walls closed in, caging him tight. His senses thrummed.

"Once I got the call from Petra, I knew I had to get you involved, especially since everyone will be coming together at the Reach event next week. Worlds are about to collide, Chase, and like it or not, you're the guy standing in the middle of the blast zone. I want you to be prepared. You know and care for them all, so you're going to have to help them get through whatever happens next. You're the only one who can."

"How, Kellen? How can I possibly be there for her when I'm a mess myself? Mentor or not, all I want to do right now is plant my fist in his jaw for ever—ever—hurting her."

And who knew, really, what Mark's intentions were in returning to Nashville. The man was far from stupid. He was far from uninformed. He was on Pyper's trail just as surely as Petra Goode. Chase thought about the gossip rag he had found buried in Mark's groceries. He thought about the standoffish behavior his mentor…his *mentor*…had exhibited when Chase helped him move in. Fog cleared, revealing an uneven, treacherous pathway ahead. Chase's trust disintegrated.

Mark Samuels, abusing Pyper. Mark, one of Chase's most treasured confidantes, had lashed out at an innocent child with words and hands while in the grip of an alcoholic stupor. Pyper had hinted at it all along, in cryptic descriptions of her life with Amy in Michigan. She seemed unwilling to revisit anything having to do with her father, or the first five years of her life; Chase had respected that measure of distance, knowing the best and truest revelation of her past would come to the fore when the time was right.

Now, truth struck home like a lightning bolt to the center of his chest. This was Mark. The man who had taken hold of his hand and, with God's help, yanked him out of an abyss. A man he respected and admired. Cared about.

A caldron of mixed emotions continued to explode into hot bursts of fear and uncertainty. Chase's world went into a freefall, spinning downward until he couldn't think straight any longer, because this was also the man who had nearly ruined Pyper's life.

"I've got to talk to him. And I've got to talk to Pyper."

He stumbled to a stand, reaching blindly for an exit from Kellen's office. This meeting was over.

❧❦

Chase sped from the business district. A headache twitched behind his eyes. An unholy, rip-your-guts-out level of thirst built to a dance that slipped and slid against his taste-buds, prompting temptation, eliciting that familiar need toward a cooling, numbing dose of alcohol.

His mind raced—weakness quirked its dastardly finger in his direction. He craved a shot of whiskey. An easy taste. Just this once. Just enough to help him push through the smog and the fear that shrouded his mind. It'd be OK. Really.

Chase pulled his pickup to a fast stop in front of a low-slung, non-descript retail center. When he threw the vehicle into park, when he came eye-to-eye with what he was about to do, his chest began to heave.

But that didn't stop him.

The third shop from the left sold liquor. That's all that mattered. He yanked on a baseball cap and marched inside the store like he owned the joint. He hunched his shoulders beneath a light windbreaker he had nabbed from the back of his cab and slid into place as an added bit of camouflage. Not making eye contact with anyone, he stepped straight to the counter, tossed a twenty across its faded, chipped surface. "Need a bottle of Jack. A pint."

The store clerk didn't pay him any mind; bored, visibly eager to move on, the guy bagged the bottle, handed it over, and Chase booked from the shop without even gathering his change.

A raging battle didn't stop—not even when he landed in the kitchen of his condo. Stuttered breaths caused his entire body to tremble. God help him, he craved this shot of whiskey. A couple fingers would ease his nerves, clear his mind. It would provide such relief. It would soothe, and fortify...

No, son. The answer is no. Heed Me. Trust Me in better things—even now. Trust.

Chase braced, squeezed his eyes shut against the pull of God's call versus the pull of temptation. The facts ripped him apart all over again. Mark Samuels. Pyper Brock. Father and daughter with a white-water river of pain flowing between them. And here he stood, strapped between the two with nothing and no one to blame but fate. Temper blasted through his system in pyrotechnic explosions. Chase whacked at the right hand water spigot, the one etched by a bold, cursive 'C.' He slammed the whiskey bottle onto the counter to his left and leaned over the sink, breathing hard, waiting for the temp to turn bracing cold before dipping his hands beneath the stream and splashing water across his face.

Over and over he threw the clear liquid against his skin, gasping and trembling. Before long, the water would go no colder and the shock value wore off.

Only then did he look up to meet his own ghosts and demons. He stared at his reflection in a small, oval mirror positioned on the wall above the sink, shocked into sickness by the naked display of need he discovered. On one side of the sink rested the fresh bottle of whiskey, seal not yet broken, its familiar promise sending his pulse pumping. One sip. Maybe two…or three. A finger. A double, maybe.

On the other side of the sink there was nothing. Empty space. A clean slate.

Pyper.

He shook to the core within the hammerlock of a choice that loomed, a choice only he could make. Good or bad. Angel or devil. Victory or ruination.

He looked into the mirror once more and his stomach rolled, nearly rebelling. Was this really him? Was this what he wanted? Was this what would bring him peace? Fulfillment?

No. An inner voice all but screamed at him. *Don't do it. Honor Pyper. Think about Crash. Think of all the ways she's touched you, and think about what you want and what you can have. For once in your sorry life make the smart choice. Help her through this. She's going to need you. Make the Godly choice. The choice that stems not from a black, ashen past but from the heart in all its sweetness and all its vivid, sometimes turbulent hues.*

The revelation struck him hard. That was the kind of poetry Shayne would have created once upon a time.

A black, ashen past—a heart in all its vivid hues…The words were like lyrics, a forever anthem. He was being given the chance to craft, perform and memorialize a life of music with the woman of his heart. Verses. Melody. Harmony. Peace.

Forgiveness was no longer just a catchy album name, or winsome song title. Forgiveness was now his reality, an ideal that called through his mind while the internal light of his soul switched from off to on.

Chase wasted no time. He grabbed the neck of the whiskey bottle and carried it with him to the commercial-grade dumpster located behind his condo complex. There he treated himself to the satisfaction of taking that bottle and smashing it hard as he could into the depths of that rank, wide-mouthed trash receptacle.

Stillness came at once. His breath went even. Panic subsided. A grin spread slow and sure, because for the briefest instant, the aroma of spilled liquor wafted through the air, stirring revulsion instead of the much more familiar, bone-rattling ache of need. He turned from the garbage bin and escaped, accompanied by bird-song and a sweet combination of floral scents that formed the essence of a late summer day kissed by warm earth.

Determination pushed him forward—a mission in need of completion. He had work to do, and that work would begin with Mark Samuels.

16

The steady rumble of the truck engine soothed Chase's troubled mind. The rhythm and jostle of the ride from Kellen's office to the soon-to-be inaugurated Reach branch just a couple miles away afforded him the opportunity to pray. When he angled to a stop and parked to the left of the building, it occurred to Chase that his appeals to heaven centered not so much on Mark, or Pyper, or even the will of his own heart. Rather, he dug as deep as he could, begging God to take his upcoming actions, meager though they might be, and make good use of them.

The rehab center was housed in a flat, squat facility wedged between a pair of taller office buildings. Chase strode through a set of double glass doors. Behind a frosted glass reception desk emblazoned with the words *Reach North*, a stout, middle-aged woman with weathered features busied herself unpacking supplies from a banker-box on the floor at her feet. Her kind-eyed gaze earned Chase's nod of greeting and a smile.

"G'afternoon. I'm here to see Mark Samuels."

"Mr. Bradington, right? He told me to expect you. He's in the first office to the right, straight ahead."

"Great. Thank you, ma'am."

At the threshold of Mark's office, Chase stopped and shored up his strength. Mark's back was to the door as he dropped a few squares of sticky notes, some paper clips and pens into an open desk drawer, whistling quietly.

Now...or never.

Chase walked inside. "Hey, Mark."

"Chase." Focused on the task of assembling his office, Mark hardly broke stride, but he tossed Chase a glance accompanied by a lopsided grin. "Your call couldn't have come at a better time. Heaven knows I could use some muscle." Mark tossed legal pads and a batch of manila folders into a side drawer then turned in full. "Or, if you'd rather, you can help me put a few nails in the wall and make this place look a little less antiseptic—"

Their eyes met and Mark's conversational track came to a halt. He went still. It didn't surprise Chase any that his sponsor could read the meaning behind tense shoulders and a stiff, edgy attitude. Chase also didn't bother to acknowledge Mark's opening comments, which was just about unheard of.

A split second passed between them, silent yet full of unspoken recognitions that Chase sensed in full— sorrow, guilt, regret, leagues of sadness. He watched Mark pull himself together, and wondered if there were times like this when even battle-hardened life counselors needed to pause and remember the fundamental truth that no one entered eternity without being tested.

The idea left Chase with much to think about.

Mark cleared vulnerability and any form of personal emotion from his features by relaxing his stance and the tight line of his jaw. He looked steady into Chase's eyes, but a tell-tale throb against the base of Mark's throat told Chase everything he needed to know.

"You seem out of sorts. Everything OK?"

"No. Not really. I need to talk to you."

"That's what I'm here for."

Rule one, Chase? Face life square. Same goes for what you feel. Face it and deal. Untended emotions are like weeds. They overwhelm, then consume. Be open, be true to who you are, then hold fast and withstand the storm.

With no difficulty whatsoever, Chase called on the memory of those words from Mark—his most trusted ally. It took only seconds for Chase to be swept into the hours upon hours they had spent together in therapy while Mark taught, molded, uplifted, and helped Chase emerge from ruin.

At one point, Chase had thought his exit from recovery would be the end of the battle. He knew now that wasn't the case—at all. He didn't want to feel sympathy for what was about to happen, but all the same an ache built at the center of his chest. He needed to catch his breath before he launched into a confrontation. He needed to tread lightly, do the Christian thing and give Mark time to explain, but he refused to flinch from Mark's unyielding gaze.

Chase finally broke their stare-down and took in the small, bright space Mark would call home at Reach. "The place is shaping up."

"It's a work in progress."

"Like all of life."

"Now, that's a profound statement." Mark guffawed, forcing a wedge of humor into the stilted moment.

Chase bypassed the banter and hefted a framed picture of a dangerous looking precipice painted by golden sunlight that featured the words: *'Take the leap.*

When you do, one of two things will happen – you'll either fly on God's wind, or He'll catch you if you fall. The irony left him somewhat dazed.

"That piece of artwork seems to have caught your attention." Mark cut in. "Hammer and nails are in the corner, on top of that stack of boxes. Hang it wherever you want. What did you want to talk about?"

Silence held sway while Chase gauged hanging spots for the photograph. "I've been thinking."

"About?"

"About how little I really know about you."

When Chase glanced his way, Mark offered nothing but a shrug.

"Do I remember you saying once you came from Michigan?" Chase turned his back, angled toward the supplies Mark had indicated.

"Yeah, but that was a long time ago. I grew up there. That's quite a conversation starter. Why do you ask?"

"Just curious. Suburban Detroit, right? St. Clair Shores?" Chase eyeballed a spot on the wall, hammered a nail into place.

Mark moved in, surrendering pretense. His brows furrowed, he tapped a ruler against the palm of his hand. "That's right. Why the sudden interest in my past? I'm the one who's supposed to be looking out for you, not the other way around, right?"

"Like I said, I'm curious about your background. I got to wondering what'd prompt you to move from South Carolina to Tennessee. To Nashville in particular." Chase hung and finessed the angle of the picture then refocused his attention on Mark. A dangerous circuit of energy, sizzling and electric, surged through the atmosphere. Chase combated the current by leaning against the wall, waiting a couple of beats, but all the while he stepped closer and closer to the edge of that canyon and made ready to fly—or fall—into the hands of God. Diplomacy ruptured into directness. "Did you come back for Pyper? And Amy?"

Mark dropped the ruler on his desk; its clatter vibrated through the atmosphere like gunshots. He hefted his chin and looked Chase straight in the eyes. Then he nodded. "You found out. I wondered when you would."

"Do you like hiding?"

"Actually, I don't like it at all. And I don't like being judged, Chase. You don't know the half of what I'm all about, so you best be careful. Let's keep that straight from the get-go. Hear?"

"Don't counsel me, Mark. Not now. Not after what you've done. Not after the way you're sliding into town like a snake, not even announcing yourself or allowing the people who'll be most affected by your presence to have a chance to brace and deal with the upcoming implosion."

Mark's features fell, emphasizing the tired groves around his eyes. "How did you find out?"

"From my agent, if that matters. Evidently a reporter corralled Pyper today with all kinds of questions and innuendo about you and your daughter and your ex-wife."

"So, they know I'm here."

"I don't know about the rest of her family, but Pyper sure does, and I would imagine she's filled them in."

"Chase, I don't intend to hurt her. I don't intend to hurt any of them. Just the opposite. All I want is—"

"Well, you're too late on that count." A surge of

adrenaline crested through Chase's body. "The hurt already happened. That nosey little ink slinger blindsided Pyper during a breakfast interview because she uncovered the sordid family history along with a connection between you and me and my stint at Reach. She wants fodder for her scandal sheet—the juicier the better—and she found just what she was after, a life-rocking story she can twist and spin into dirt about a good, decent family."

"A good, decent group of *people*, Chase. I'm not the villain here."

"From where I sit, that's exactly what you are!"

"Step back and think about what you're saying. I haven't done anything wrong coming to Nashville. In spite of my past, I have the right to live my life as I see fit. I've got some goodness and decency to me, too. We all do. You haven't lost sight of that fact, have you?"

Diving his fingers through his hair, Chase met Mark's gaze. "So, the truth is Amy Brock was your wife. She married you and together you had Pyper."

"That almost covers it, but life is never that cut-and-dry, now is it?"

"All right then. Explain it to me. Help me understand."

Mark squeezed his eyes shut, and Chase could almost see the man tumble into the realm of an ugly past. "Amy was pregnant with my child when we came to the tail end of high school. Those were the days, Chase. Once upon a time, I was a gifted basketball player. I was the team captain in high school aiming for some kind of scholarship and the means to a better life, the means to keep some kind of adulation going. I know now that basketball was secondary to what I really craved. Acceptance. Acclaim.

Affirmation. All those 'A' words that mess with your head in such big ways."

Like fame as a singer. Of course, Mark didn't say the words, but Chase sensed that warning in Mark's an otherwise steady tone. Chase firmed his lips, tightened his shoulders and delivered a narrow-eyed stare. He waited and bristled.

"Amy was the sweetest thing." Mark propped a hip against the edge of an aged but sturdy wooden desk. "Gorgeous, innocent, a conquest worth the battle—and she was mine. Completely. I looked at her like a possession and worked my way past every one of her morals. Every one of her beliefs. We made love, and my every intention was to wish her well at the end of summer and move on to a life of bliss."

Like so many high-school romances, Chase figured, if you could even refer to them as such.

"Anyway, late spring came to life. Graduation—freedom—lay just around the corner. That's when she met me at my house. She could barely talk, but somehow she got the words out. She told me she was pregnant."

"So, you married her."

"Yep. Not out of love. Out of duty. I had no choice. It was what I felt I had to do. At first, marriage was OK. A friend of mine hooked me up with a job on an assembly line at an auto plant. I earned enough money to land us in an apartment, and Amy worked part-time for as long as she could."

"Then?"

"Then Pyper was born, and Amy wanted to be a mother. Everything was up to me. The responsibility weighed heavy. I had dreams back then. I had big goals and ambitions. But instead of dreams, I woke up every day to a wife and a daughter and a home to maintain. Shackles and chains. Day in and day out I was forced to deal with the fact that their welfare depended on me. Resentment didn't just grow, it took me over. I hated everything about my life. Liquor became a crutch. It helped me escape. It soothed the rage, or so I thought. As you know full well, the numbness wears off and before long, you're looking for more. For different. For relief."

"But—"

"No buts. Hear me out." Spinning away, Mark basically collapsed onto the rolling chair behind his desk. Squeaks filled space for a moment. "Liquor didn't work anymore. Not all by itself. Everything escalated. I was out of control. I needed more. I needed escape. That's when I discovered gambling. I hit it lucky a few times at the local casino and like a fool I figured I could beat the system. That led to debt, to more stress, to more resentment. Once that piled up, all these hot, angry pin-pricks came alive, eating at me, making me think things, feel things, do things, I'd never dream of had I been functioning in a sane state of mind." He paused, peered at Chase while he leaned forward on his knees. "Do you know that tune?"

Chase answered that forthright question with a glower; he brimmed with revulsion. "No. That tune isn't familiar to me at all. Never—ever—did I hit a child, or a woman. Nor would I. As you know better than most, I was content to ruin myself instead."

"Oh. I see. So, you think your actions haven't hurt those around you? Those who care about you? Think again. Voice of experience here. You don't need fists and hands and shouts and temper to cause severe damage, Chase. Think that over."

Think it over? How flippant, bordering on self-righteous. This was the man from whom Pyper had escaped as a child with angry scars bubbled across her heart and distrust simmering through her spirit. That was wrong, a sin in need of punishment, yet Mark returned, as though bent on wreaking more havoc.

"So what you're trying to tell me is this arrival of yours is some kind of an attempted do-over? Some kind of make good? Do you honestly believe they'll grant you a fresh start like that?"

Mark flexed his jaw and glared. "I'm praying for *grace*. I owe myself, and Pyper, nothing less than the effort of trying to rebuild what's been broken. I'll make something else clear, since you're involved directly. It doesn't matter to me if I retain your trust or not. I'm going to do what I need to do. You won't stop me."

"Hurt her, and I will, and you'll need a whole lot more than a fresh start if you do, Mark." Chase growled the words. "Pyper is scarred by you, but she's bright, and beautiful. She's vibrant. Passionate. You missed all that. You messed it up. You hit a defenseless child. How could you, and why? What'd she *ever* do to you? I can't get my head around such a thing."

Chase designed his words to hurt. He knew they painted pictures that would ram home the damage Mark had done. His words also lashed wicked gouges across the terrain of their friendship—and the layers of trust Mark had mentioned. Right now, he didn't even care.

"You're right. And, God alone knows what I've missed."

"No. Not just God. Pyper does, too. And so do Tyler and Amy."

Mark straightened and squared his shoulders.

"Which is why I'm here. Which is why I left South Carolina. I want to lay down permanent roots in Tennessee. I want to make amends. That's been my hope, my solitary prayer, for close to two decades. Believe it. Don't believe it. I couldn't care less. I know what's true."

Chase clenched his jaw, remained silent for a time behind a flinty-eyed stare. "Those are pretty words, Mark, but I still can't believe this. The only thing that keeps me from knocking you into tomorrow is the fact that you're not the same man you were then."

"No, I'm not. I changed. I received a new life by nothing more than God's hand. That change is *real*. Just like yours. Consider *that* before you spend too much time condemning me. That's all I ask. I left Michigan for South Carolina where I found a job and the means to clean myself up. I landed at a facility where I could disappear and heal and grow. I found my truest self in the heart of the mountains. I forced myself clean and found my way home. I didn't end up in your pathway because I'm some kind of angel, Chase. That's been clear from the start. I'm just the opposite. I wrecked lives with careless abandon because I valued the power of amber fuel, freedom and power above everything else—even the love of my family—the love of my child, and a good woman."

"So when exactly were you going to spring this on her? At the benefit? In front of TV cameras and media types with microphones and recorders? Were you going to out yourself as her father then?"

"Would you please trust me on this? I wouldn't think of disgracing her that way. I plan to see her before the start of the event. That way we can have a few private words, and, yeah, the venue might force her to be still for just a few minutes and simply listen to me. I don't want to reveal myself publicly before we have a chance to talk, but the details are up to God alone."

Chase rested in a silence that calmed the air between them. "Why didn't you tell me about her? That day at your apartment—when I found that tabloid—why didn't you come clean?"

"Why would I? What business would it be of yours what I choose to do with regard to my daughter and my desire to make amends?"

Chase gestured widely, astounded. "Gee, I dunno...maybe because you're the one who's always professed an interest in social feeds and keeping up on my career. What an error of evasion! What a lie! You're like Adam and Eve hiding in the tall grass, cowering in a space between knowledge and guilt and shame, thinking God won't see you."

Mark's eyes glinted, and turned hard as stone. "God sees everything about me, Chase, the good and the bad. I'm warning you once more not to judge."

"But you knew from the start I was involved with Pyper. We even talked about her. You knew I had feelings for her. All along, you couldn't find ten seconds in a day to tell me she was your daughter?"

"That's right. Like I said, this has nothing to do with you, Chase. This is between me and Pyper."

Chase snarled and shook his head. "That's where you're wrong. Your connection to Pyper became my business the minute I found my way into her life." He clenched his jaw then shook his head all over again. "Finally my dreams were sweet. Finally life was good. Full. Because of her. Because Pyper looked at me with trust. With belief. She let go of what you put her through and allowed herself to be open with me in spite of all my mistakes. I treasure that gift more than I can ever say. I want her to love me freely. Now, I'm not so sure that can happen."

"Because of me?"

"Because I'm trapped between the two of you, and I share your history of addiction. But know this. I vow to be there, at her side, holding her up, no matter what. If it's a choice between you and her, she wins. End of story."

"Or maybe the beginning, depending on your point of view. Regardless, what the two of you share doesn't change a thing about me and what I need to do. So, do what you promise. Be there for her. Love her. Love that girl well." His chin quaked. Chase watched as Mark clenched his jaw in rebellion to that reaction.

Chase paced the narrow confines of the office then rounded on him. "You know what? Don't speak rehab lingo to me anymore. I'm finding it intolerable coming from you right now. Furthermore, I will *not* let you rip the carpet from under her feet again."

"Understood, but I meant what I said. I don't intend to hurt her."

Chase let out a sound that crossed between a growl and a roar. "If I were a different man, I swear—" he balled his hands into fists, barely controlling the rage that burst through his body. "I want to flatten you, but at the same time, I want to honor the person I loved and trusted for months during the worst episode of my life. How do I handle that contradiction, Mark?"

Emotions pouring free, he rushed on. "You struck that beautiful girl in anger, in misguided fits of drunken temper. You stole irreplaceable pieces of her innocence and trust by shoving her and her mama out of their home for no other reason than meanness and spite. I had no control over any of this, but the ramifications are killing me. Through no fault of my own, I'm going to have to do something I swore up and down I'd never do."

"Which is?"

Chase looked him in the eyes and absorbed a fresh eruption of pain and turmoil. "The fact that she's involved with me is going to throw her into the middle of her worst nightmare—an unavoidable confrontation with her estranged biological father. Because of my ties to you, her heart is about to get broken."

17

The hushed serenity of a royal blue nightfall blanketed the undulations of land that comprised Pyper's home. Birdsong quieted while insect chatter built, vibrating through the air in a steady cadence that lent comfort to her soul. She sat next to Chase on a padded wooden swing that was suspended from the roof of the wraparound porch. Resting her head on his shoulder, she forced herself to relax and find some measure of contentment. Cradled within the palm of this timeless spot, her heart mingled with his, searching for rest. Chase kept the swing in motion by pushing a booted toe against the wooden floorboards. The answering squeak of metal chains became a musical rhythm as comforting as sunset to her troubled spirit. She wanted nothing more than to snuggle into Chase's embrace and drift into peace.

Instead, Mark Samuels encroached, seeping through her mind like a form of slow-acting poison. His reemergence snatched away her happiness and the passionate vigor that had coated every beat of her life since leaving Michigan, and his nightmares, behind.

"I'm so sorry, Pyper."

"Chase, none of this is on you. Honest, and from the depths, that's what I feel and what I know to be true."

"I believe you, Pyp, and I appreciate it, too. I know that doesn't come easy."

"No, it doesn't." She swallowed hard, overcome on so many levels. She battled rage and bitterness toward Mark and an equally powerful sense of compassion and acceptance of Chase's emotions and loyalty to the man who had obviously done well by him in rehab.

Chase squeezed her shoulder then leaned in to brush his lips against her cheek and nuzzle her neck. "I know you've been knocked sideways."

"Not really. Mark means nothing to me. At. All." Pyper clenched her hands, channeling tension away from already tight muscles. The veracity of her reaction instantly disproved that statement. Chase seemed to realize the fact because he initiated a soothing caress against her arm. "Tyler Brock is the first man of my heart—the man I consider to be my dad in every way but blood."

"And that's exactly as it should be."

Buttery light bathed the space all around them. Beyond a railed set of stairs, darkness encroached, much like the darkness of her turbulent heart. Pyper nestled against his side like a life-sized puzzle piece, as though they had been grooved into alignment by the blessing of God's hand. To her mind, that's precisely what they were—the coming together of God's will.

Except when it came to a slime bag named Mark Samuels.

She had to surrender the obvious. "Still, Chase, I know you're torn."

"In a way, but I'll tell you what I told Mark. Your place in my life outweighs my gratitude and affection for him. I confronted him, and I listened to his explanations with a stone-cold heart. But when I left his office, and thought things through, it occurred to me that something important rang through his words. Authenticity. Regret."

Pyper stiffened all over again. Sure, these first stumbling steps needed to happen, no matter how treacherous and rocky the terrain. That didn't mean she had to like them. So, she bristled. "Authenticity. Regret. Let me give you *my* version of what's authentic and what I regret." She bit the words then sighed, sliding her fingertips against his arms in assurance. "I'm so sorry, Chase. Really. Please bear with me. I'm snapping at the wrong person."

"Don't worry about that—just talk to me."

Pyper tilted her head, smoothing her hair to the side while moonlight drifted against the planes and hollows of his squared jaw and rugged face. Heat flicked, lit and built strong enough to burn away her fears about being vulnerable to the deepest, most lasting pain she had ever known.

"Let me tell you my side of the story."

"That's what I want most, crash." He paused, angling her chin with a fingertip, which sweetly and effectively captured her full attention. "Not because of Mark, but because of you. Because of us."

Tears sprang; her chin quivered, but she fought on. After nodding resolutely, following a fast, hard kiss to Chase's lips, a determined stride carried Pyper inside and up the stairwell of the farmhouse. "Mama, are my scrapbooks still in the wooden secretary upstairs?"

"Yep." The reply came from somewhere near the heart of the kitchen. "You'll see 'em right behind the glass doors."

"Thanks."

She retrieved the two cloth-bound items she

sought, the ones covered by flowers, crafty do-dads and her name in press-on script. Back on the porch swing, she settled in.

"These scrapbooks were a gift to me from my mama when I graduated high school. I've always thought of them as a roadmap of my life, full of memorabilia crafted by a woman who lost her connection all such precious and irreplaceable things. Because of him. For the longest time, my life was a wreck. Because of him."

For nearly an hour she led Chase through page-by-age of her life, leaving nothing out—for now—except the missing puzzle piece that included her years between the ages of one and five.

The missing years, as she had always thought of them.

But, missing years or not, a messy recollection grabbed hold, poking at a piece of Pyper's spirit she would have preferred to stay dead and buried. Instead, she surrendered to the path before her and took a dive into the rank, oily waters of her four-year-old self, praying for strength while a dark aisle of her heart opened to Chase's care…

"Get out of my sight!"

Pyper's daddy screamed the words and she quaked in terror. His face was all red; his eyes were big and bulgy with hate. Hate—toward her. Why didn't he love her? Why couldn't she find a way to make him treat her gentle and sweet like she saw with so many other daddies?

Actually, Pyper knew the answer. He acted this way because she was bad. Very, very bad. The realization struck her down, made her knees all wobbly and weak. Pyper tried to be strong, and not cry—daddy yelled even louder when she cried—but he was so mad that her face crumpled and her eyes stung. Tears rolled down her cheeks, big and wet and hot.

"Quit it, Pyper! Right now! Stop it!" The words were followed by a growl so loud and rough it vibrated in the air all around her and made the insides of her ears tickle. The growl scared her. The growl made her heart pound. Her tummy bounced and jiggled all of a sudden because just like a mean dog, when her daddy growled, he'd strike out. He'd bite and hurt.

What had she done wrong? How could she make it right? It felt like she was being chased by a monster from a scary story. Pyper scrambled when he moved closer and her widened eyes moved from spot to spot in the main room of her house. How could she keep him from getting so mad that he'd hit her?

That's when she saw it. Of course it was her doll house. There were lots and lots of little parts strewn across the carpet. He'd call her sloppy, and a messy slob. He had done so before, and she always felt sick in her tummy, and so dizzy and awful when she let him down. Before Daddy started yelling, Pyper had been putting furniture in the bedrooms; she'd set tables and chairs in a dining room with walls covered by sunny decorations. Pyper loved to imagine a happy mommy and daddy and kids living in this beautiful house. Her mommy had given it to her for her birthday this year. She wanted that kind of life so very much.

Sure enough, he kicked the bed, and the whole house, into a busted, toppled-over mess on the carpet in the middle of the living room. Pyper's sobs burst free—and she knew she would be in big trouble for crying and making sad noises—but that didn't keep her from crying hard.

"Daddy…no…please! I love my house!"

"Shut! Up!"

His voice roared, mad and awful. All she wanted to do

was make him feel better. This was her daddy. "Daddy, I sorry! I love you. I won't be bad. I won't be bad!" She spoke in earnest, falling to her knees to pick up lamps and couches and stoves. In desperation she grabbed doll house furniture as fast as she could and tossed it inside so it was out of his way. More tears rolled down her cheeks, they burst from her eyes like the streams of rain that pounded on the windows when storms hit.

"Stop it! Cut it out! Stop your crying and be quiet!"

Pyper hiccupped on dry air, trying with all her might to obey his command. She couldn't. She continued to cry, knowing she had messed up all over again. She turned to look at him, wanting to be big and brave, wanting to tell him again that she was sorry. Her daddy erupted with another loud growl. He slapped her across the face and shoved her to the floor so hard her head banged against thin carpet and the wood floor beneath. Terrified, Pyper squealed and charged away, running for the safe-zone of her bedroom. She slammed the door in a hurry, continually gasping for enough air to fill her heaving chest.

Jesus, *she pleaded,* why did he have to come home early from work? Why did he have to wreck her daydreams of a family full of smiles and laughs and happiness? *These days, Pyper only felt really safe when her mommy was near.*

She heard her daddy stumble against a nearby wall and she jumped away from the noise. Her daddy didn't seem to hear or notice. He cursed and she heard him pull open the doors of a cabinet in the next room. Trembling, she pressed her body against the door when she heard the clang and bang of glass on glass, the gurgle and splash of something being poured.

It had to be even more of that evil, awful gold stuff. Liquor. Oh, how she hated liquor, and oh, how she hated her daddy...

Pyper released the long-ago years when she realized she'd sunk against Chase's side, when she realized she was crying in a way she hadn't cried in close to decades. She released the rush of emotion that wrapped her in a vise. "That's *my* side of the story." Hard-edged and gravelly, her tone made her conviction clear. "Nothing will ever change it. Nothing will bring me, or him, back to what could have been. Ever. I want him gone. I want him out of my life. I want nothing from him but to be left alone. That's the end, Chase, and that will not change. Ever. So don't ask it of me."

18

An awkward two-step led Pyper to the day of the Reach North opening. By then, she had pretty much adjusted to the shock of Mark Samuels's arrival in Nashville, but as the hour of their unavoidable meeting drew close, her nerve endings vibrated and stabbed. Nothing, Amy and Tyler told her, would be gained by stewing, but that hadn't eased Pyper's anxiety about the day to come. Yes, this was out of her control. No, this entire situation was in no way Chase's fault. Still, a layer of discomfort had distorted everything between them in the days that followed the interview with Petra. Doubts—real and imagined—crept through her mind and stole her peace. Yes, Chase seemed sincere in his convictions as well as his loyalty to her. Yes, she believed in him. But wasn't she usually wrong about men?

Late that morning, she sat next to Chase, riding shotgun as he navigated the quarter-mile stretch of gravel that led from her family's farm to the main road that would take them downtown.

She propped an elbow against the window frame of the vehicle, closing her eyes as a warm flow of air caressed her cheeks. "When we first decided to sing at this event, I remember telling my folks how excited I was to meet your sponsor, and thank him for everything he's done to help you. Now, I'm not so sure."

She delivered a quirked grin and tried to be easy-spirited, even a bit cheeky; no surprise, Chase saw right through the acting job. She knew he registered the flatness in her tone, the hesitance that betrayed her solid tangle of emotions. At the next stoplight, Chase reached forward, just far enough to trace a fingertip against the tight, achy spot between her brows. His touch felt cool and gentle. Heavenly. Pyper's eyes fluttered closed and a whisper of air passed her lips.

"You still could, you know. The facts remain true, even if the player isn't who you expected."

How she wished she could refute that solid, if thoroughly unappealing piece of logic. Instead, she kept quiet. Stewing.

"Crash, I'm so sorry...I..."

Her eyes popped open. "We've talked about this. It's not your fault. You had no idea. This doesn't change..." She dipped her head, shy, tucking a tumbled curl of hair behind her ear. "It doesn't change me and you." She pushed back that sliver of uncertainty that prodded her to think she might be wrong about her feelings toward Chase.

She closed her eyes once more when Chase cupped her chin and tilted her head just enough to press a light, bone-melting kiss against her lips. Seconds later the light went green, and he surrendered to the drive. "Then have some faith. We'll get through what comes."

"But what about my mom? My dad? What about Zach? He's been confused about everything lately. This isn't going to help."

"I repeat. We'll get through. All of us. Together."

The idea, the ideal, was appealing. Pyper made an agreeable sound, aiming to reassure him more than anything else, but she couldn't find her way to his level of confidence.

Chase navigated his vehicle to a stop in a parking lot already packed with cars. The presence of several media trucks paid testimony to the interest to be found in a celebrity-endorsed life recovery center.

Pyper straightened and firmed her jaw. The mission, the objectives of Reach North were important. Lives and hope were on the line here. Healing. That's what today was all about. Eyes on the prize, she coached herself. Eyes on the prize.

All the same, she clung to Chase's hand like a lifeline when they walked through the entrance of the facility. Media personnel gathered fast and furious. Photographers captured the moment; they smiled and waved, but she spotted Petra Goode almost immediately, and Pyper's nerves threatened to shatter.

A second later, her searching gaze came to rest on Mark Samuels.

When she saw him, Pyper experienced the strangest sense of transformation. In a blink, she froze, terrified. In a blink, she trembled and nearly ran. In a blink, she became that desperate, broken child, taken under by an ingrained, instinctive quest for self-preservation.

God, please help me. Please be with me.

Mark sat on the dais meant for speakers and board members of the facility, and he fidgeted nervously with a rolled up program, tapping it against his knee. His eyes roamed the crowd. As in her youth, Pyper wanted only to vanish from his sight. She ached to disappear into oblivion, into a time and place far away from this man and everything he represented.

A pair of guitars rested in position to the left of the

raised platform, ready for her upcoming performance with Chase.

The performance of "Forgiveness".

How in the world was she supposed to sing an anthem to extending God's mercy when a slab of granite rested on her heart, preventing her from doing just that? She wavered to such a degree that Chase started to reach out, but she stepped away from his touch. Her skin was icy. The devastating sweep of a mental tidal wave thundered and roared within the darkness of her horrorstricken mind.

"Crash? You OK?"

Chase had leaned close enough to whisper in her ear. Still transfixed, Pyper managed nothing more than a faint nod, but she noticed now that she pulled slightly against Chase's hold, resisting when he tried to move them forward and through the building onslaught of reporters, paparazzi, and fans.

Pyper squeezed his hand tight and fought for control, for the kind of poise everyone expected. Like Chase, she smiled and waved, greeting the enthusiastic crowd as would be expected of country-Christian music's newly crowned "it" couple. But her motions were stilted, and though her smile spread wide, it didn't reach deep. It pulled at her skin, made her feel waxen and posed.

"Remember, this is a different time, and a different place. You're different people now. Stay strong, Pyp." Chase kept close, his body a welcome source of warmth against her side. His whispered words were gentle. She tried to absorb the truth he offered, but failed.

Pyper's mom and dad arrived, slipping in behind them with her brother on their heels.

"I'm going to check in with the musicians; catch up with you guys in a little while." Eager and unaware of the drama set to unfold, Zach moved away to join band members who set up equipment on the dais.

People continued to crowd in, filling space until the room became claustrophobic. During the commotion of her arrival with Chase, Pyper noticed the way Mark's attention fell on them and stayed put for a beat. He stood slowly and started to walk their way. Pyper craved an exit route, but none could be found.

When it became clear Mark was about to step into her path, Pyper decided to work an immediate preemptive strike.

"Hello, Pyper. I—"

Three tentative words were all she allowed him to say before cutting in with a low, discreet hiss. "Understand something clearly, and let there be no mistake. I do not want to talk to you. I do not want to hear anything you have to say. I want nothing to do with you. I'm going to sing, and I'm going to give my support to this facility. Beyond that, you stay away from me. And unlike before, I have the means to fight back if you cross the line. Now, step aside."

"Pyp."

Chase's quiet admonishment held no weight. Neither did the way Mark reared his head and wordlessly backed off. But when she elbowed past him, blood simmering with hostility, their eyes met. Blue on blue. The sadness she detected slowed her steps some but didn't keep her from walking away.

Once seated, she crossed her legs. Outwardly demure, she donned an attentive mask, one of politically correct behavior and interest. The crowd assembled and staff members prepared to kick off proceedings. Out of view, knowing the long flounce of her jean skirt masked things from view, she latched a booted ankle around the leg of her chair. Such was the only way she'd remain in place and properly grounded.

Petra Goode glided past delivering a plastic smile and wearing a too-snug powder blue suit. Silent screams pushed and beat against Pyper's chest, her throat, her temples. She looked straight ahead, extending courteous glances toward the audience. Once she unclenched her tightly laced fingertips, she offered a wave of acknowledgment to a few members of the staff who were seated in the front row and encouraging smiles to the teens sitting close by. The kids had been working with Zach and Chase over the past few days and represented Chase's freshly established music therapy program. The group would be joining them on stage shortly.

Soon she'd have to sing. Perform.

For a centering moment, Pyper bowed her head and prayed.

Father, on Your strength alone will I get through this.

❧

The DJ of the Christian radio station's morning drive stood at a wooden podium, addressing the assemblage about midway through the event.

"Before we enjoy a musical interlude and some refreshments, I'd like you to meet the director of Reach North, the man who'll be managing the corporation's new outreach center. He's already staffed the facility and will both counsel and head up operations here in

Nashville when it opens in a couple weeks. In fact, he's the one responsible for recruiting the talents of Chase Bradington and Pyper Brock to lend support to today's event. Please help me welcome Mark Samuels."

Pyper was used to being in the public eye, used to controlling her physical and mental responses no matter what the outward pressure. Nothing could have prepared her for this moment.

Mark moved slowly to the podium, visibly uncomfortable. He withdrew a short stack of papers from a cubby in the lectern, smoothing them into place so he could read. He cleared his throat, adjusted the mic.

"Hey, everyone. Thank you so much for coming out and for lending your support. I want you to know you're looking at one of the thousands of reasons why Reach North is necessary." He cleared his throat again. "They say the best form of witness is the story of your life, so, if you'll be kind enough to spare me a few minutes, I'd like to share mine. I hope it'll demonstrate the ways recovery, rehabilitation, and the support of community outreach centers like this one can turn death into life."

He shuffled his feet. When he cast a quick, telling glance toward Pyper, she ducked her head promptly and focused on tightly clenched hands folded neatly in her lap.

"It was a sticky, humid day. The kind of day you see maybe half a dozen times during the course of a Michigan summer. The heat amplified my mood. My hate. My raging sense of injustice at the world. Sound familiar?"

Pyper focused on the crowd, anywhere but the podium. Some uncomfortable, understanding glances ran through the room like a circuit. Her attention returned to Mark. Visibly centered now, he no longer looked left or right. Instead, he re-smoothed the crumpled pages. Pyper steeled her back against the kind of care and effort of handwritten pages being crafted by him.

"I lost my job," he went on to say. "I got fired that day, and instead of acknowledging the shame, the fault that was mine alone, I stopped at a liquor store on my way home. I pulled out a twenty and bought a pint of whiskey. I came home to my four-year-old daughter. Happy as could be, she sat cross-legged in the middle of the living room next to our sitter, Marcey. They played dolls, or house or some such thing. None of that mattered to me."

His voice caught. Pyper gulped and simmered and seared him with a look he didn't even see. He was traveling to the past? Oh, she'd love to shove him down its battered and broken pathway to reveal precisely what hell he had wrought. She itched to leave him somehow bruised and beaten the same way he had done to her and her mother. Monster. Sure, she couldn't shout the word like she wanted, but releasing that toxic cloud of anger into the recesses of her mind helped steady her overly-frayed nerves.

"I screamed at them." His fingertips brushed the pages from which he read. "I carried a bottle in my hand, wrapped in a brown paper bag, and I had one focus alone. One goal. Drunken oblivion. So, I shoved Marcey out the door with a handful of bucks and sent my daughter to her room for no reason at all other than the fact that I didn't want to see her, and I didn't want her to see me. She fought me. She wanted to play. In answer to that, I shoved her to the ground and when she cried, I slapped her across the face. I wanted her out of my sight. I wanted her gone. I didn't want her kind of sweetness and innocence to interfere with me and a full-on quest to destroy myself, so I terrified her into submission."

Desperate to maintain control, Pyper relived the moments he described, that backhanded slap across her face when she stubbornly, willfully refused to obey him. Odd how she could still feel the giant, rolling tears that had crested her lashes and worked soothing dew against the burn of a fast-swelling cheek.

In the here and now, Pyper realized, her tears weren't phantom, they tracked down her face, silent and choking.

"I beat her."

Pyper dashed shaky fingertips beneath her lashes.

"I beat that unsuspecting child. I yelled at her. I cursed at her, and I locked her in her in a room—"

Pyper gave a subtle jump when she absorbed the warm touch of Chase's roughened hand settling atop hers. His tender caress caused a fresh push of tears, but she swallowed hard, she blinked, she battled the beasts and fought back discomfort as best she could, struggling to remain composed.

At the podium, Mark swiped a kerchief beneath his reddened nose. He squared his shoulders. "My wife came home." His gaze darted to Amy, who clung fast to Tyler. "We argued with words. We battled physically. I shoved at her. I beat her and yelled at her and locked her out of our home. That moment, my blackest moment, paved the road to this podium, to the promise of this facility and everything good that can be accomplished within its walls."

All over again Mark danced nervous fingers across

battered notebook pages. He shifted from the top page to the one beneath. "I had lost my job, but that was no excuse. I was a drunk. I was an out-of-control alcoholic, but that was no excuse. Let me tell you about the end of that day. While I thought I had won, while I strutted, guzzled, fumed and stormed through the house like some kind of self-righteous fool, while I thought full-well that I had won the battle, I lost a war. A war for my happiness and peace of mind. I went to my daughter's bedroom, intending to make sure I had her right where I wanted — imprisoned. I wanted control. I wanted her restrained like a possession. Squashed beneath my thumb."

Mark's tears rolled into a flood, dotting the paper. That's when Pyper stopped to consider the words he had crafted. Did those sentiments come from tears? From regret? She stared at him now, brows puckered, head pounding as her stomach rolled and her heart turned over and over again while bile rose in her throat.

"I opened the bedroom door and found the window screen had been torn away. My wife refused to leave our daughter. She had climbed through shrubs and she had ripped metal netting from its frame on the window with her bare hands. She had hauled our baby over the sill to keep her protected. To get her away from a man who had already done serious damage." Mark ignored the pages, looking straight ahead.

Pyper could barely breathe.

"My wife had nothing to her name. I saw to that. She had no purse, no money, no phone, only a church, a pastor, a group of friends and renewed bonds with her family to bring her back to God and to life again. And she did so with my daughter in her care. That's my shame. That's the sorrow I've fought to overcome, and even though I know I'm forgiven and redeemed by the grace of God, it eats at me every day. That's why I'm here. That's why I've become a counselor, and that's why I've completely changed the direction of my life. I know I can never atone for what I did. I can only rely on God for forgiveness, for mercy, and the second chance that places like Reach North can provide to others in need.

"My wife, my daughter, they found salvation and happiness with a man much better than the one I was back then, but the message I want to convey today is this: I also found salvation. I found a way back to goodness, to God's love. You can, too."

Mark's passion, his power of conviction, drew Pyper's reluctant focus until she broke away briefly to glance at her mom. Her mama's chin trembled and her eyes sparkled against what Pyper could only assume was the shattered crystal of broken dreams.

"Don't walk the same road I did. If you do, you'll suffer the same way I did. You'll lose the same way I did. Don't let it happen. Please. Hold on to your soul. Live, don't destroy. Let us help you find the miracle you need right here, in this haven for battered souls looking for redemption. You'll find help here. You'll find safety here. You'll find a second chance here. All you have to do is surrender the darkness. Thank you for letting me share my story."

Pyper's ears rang. Accompanied by crashing applause, Mark returned to his seat and the emcee claimed the podium.

"Thank you, Mark, for a powerful sharing of what can, and will, be accomplished through the work of Reach North. Now, we'd like to welcome Chase

Bradington, Pyper Brock, and a wonderful mix of their bandmates along with some gifted musicians who are part of the recovery program here at Reach. Chase, come on up!"

Chase stood right away and Pyper blinked when she heard their names. Zach slid a pair of stools into position while a stage tech moved mic stands into place. Somehow she stood. She sank onto the closest stool and Chase took over from there, slinging on his guitar, addressing the crowd with a warm smile and those clear, vibrant eyes.

"Hey, y'all. Thanks for the warm welcome. You know, I'm a lot more comfortable on a tall stool, with a guitar in my hands than I am talking to folks at the head of a reception room so I hope it's OK for me to talk to you from here."

Whistles and applause rang out. Pyper settled, gripped her microphone stand and made a height adjustment. All the while, she trembled to the core.

"Reach North, like other Reach facilities across the south, will be about reclaiming a life that's good," Chase continued. "It'll be about community outreach and community service projects for young people. We need to catch problems at the start, through referrals from schools, from churches, through family intervention. We need to do whatever it takes to break the cycle of addiction. I'm another witness to the power that can be found in recovering from the war that destructive choices can cause, and I appreciate your support here today."

Chase stopped there and his eyes sparkled, sheened by moisture. Pyper was a confused mess at the moment, but nothing diminished the empathy that swept through her, the love and gratitude for Chase's rebound.

Why couldn't she feel the same way about Mark Samuels?

There was no time for analysis.

Chase strummed the opening chords of "Forgiveness". "I'd like to share the best piece of advice I ever received in therapy, and it came from the man sitting directly to my right, the one who just spoke, my sponsor Mark Samuels. He once told me, 'The past is the past and nothing can be done to change it. The future can never be fully known, but readiness depends entirely on what we do in the here and now.' Heed those words. Take them to heart and let them change your life like they changed mine. They'll bring you to God's hand, and they just might save you. Thanks."

On cue, fighting for control, Pyper picked it up from there. "In honor of those who fight the good fight, who push hard for healing, promise, and hope, Chase and I would like to dedicate the following song. It's called 'Forgiveness'. We hope you enjoy it."

Applause became a warm vibration that worked around all the turbulence and gave her strength enough to sing. She started out OK, but for some reason she kept glancing toward Mark. When she did, her throat and heart would squeeze and her pulse would race. The melody built, the song hit an impassioned crescendo and the words jammed in Pyper's throat, tears building against her lashes as she closed her eyes, fighting desperately to keep going as the song took her under and carried her away.

Chase, bless him forever, covered strong on the last verse when her voice went weak and began to fade. She hit the closing harmony, and they ended fine, but she had nearly lost it. When they took a bow and acknowledged the response of the crowd, Pyper knew Chase tracked her carefully, but her response couldn't be helped. Stiff shoulders and edginess were punctuated by numbness, by a deadness of sensation that caused her to fold her arms against her mid-section.

Chase leaned in and whispered, "You gonna be OK?"

His breath brushed against her ear, skimmed her neck, warm and lush enough to chase off a building chill. Her heart fluttered through her chest, so many ribbons sliced and torn. She turned just far enough to catch the light of his eyes and longed to lean into him. Pyper shook her head and literally bit her tongue.

"Hang tight, crash. We're in the homestretch."

Not by a long shot, she thought, but she delivered an agreeing smile.

࿐

After the bulk of the audience disbursed, an informal press conference took place. Board members of Reach North were joined by key staff members, by Chase, Pyper, and a few of the more prominent financial contributors. Most of the questions had to do with specifics about Reach North—how many employees, how many patients were expected to cross the threshold, a bevy of supporters were mentioned and thanked.

After that, Petra Goode stepped to the forefront, and Pyper's blood flowed to a bone-chilling standstill.

"Mark, this question is directed to you. First off, I want to congratulate you for not only an inspiring turn around in your life, but your mission to help rehabilitate troubled individuals and help them find a way home."

"Thank you."

"I'm a little surprised, given the roadway of success you established, that you didn't acknowledge your daughter by name." She hesitated, but Mark offered no comment.

Petra plowed ahead. "Especially since she sat not more than a few feet from the podium."

Pyper's skin flamed. Mark glanced her way, lines carved deep against his mouth and eyes. She braced.

"The story you shared left a good many of us in tears—your daughter included. Isn't that right, Pyper? You seemed genuinely moved by your father's story, and who could blame you."

She dropped the explosive information so casually a few seconds of stunned silence beat by. But then, chaos erupted and nearly two dozen reporters launched into a feeding frenzy.

"Pyper...Pyper Brock is Mark Samuel's daughter?"

"Pyper, over here!

"Tyler, any comment? Pyper? Amy? Zach?"

Zach—poor Zach! Pyper turned toward her brother, reached desperately for his hand. He held on fast, but looked like the clichéd deer caught in headlights. Their physical connection was instinctive, but leagues away from soothing.

"Mark, have you seen Pyper before today? What have you said to her? Are you reestablishing contact?"

"What's next for y'all?" Smug as could be, Petra positioned herself toward the front of the pack and dragged her photographer along with her. "Let's get everyone together for a photo."

A hungry band of photographers maneuvered Pyper and her family—Mark and Chase included—into alignment in front of the podium which bore the logo of Reach, the spot where Mark had stood and plead his case for understanding, for love and mercy. The thought launched, then dissolved like a crushed skeet target as questions continued to be lobbed.

"Pyper, how does it feel to be reunited with your father? Is this the start of a new chapter for the two of you? Tyler, are you pleased by Mark's arrival in Nashville?"

Petra pushed sideways, deliberately blocking the reporter who had just spoken. "Pyper, your biological father, a remade, rededicated man who helps others conquer addiction, and the one who took Chase Bradington under his care at Reach. How much of a thrill is this? Hollywood couldn't script a more eloquent storyline. How do you feel right now?"

Flashbulbs split Pyper's vision into strobes. Overly-bright camera lights left her blinking, causing her adrenaline to push and rush at high octane.

Smile, she told herself. *Don't say a word, just smile, turn away, and vanish into private space ASAP.*

"Thanks for coming out, y'all." Tyler stepped to the front line of the battle zone, giving a wave, a smile full of easy warmth that Pyper knew masked a thousand shades of emotion. "We'll have a formal statement later. For now, please keep spreading the word about Reach North—these folks are going to work miracles for troubled souls all over Nashville. That's the newsworthy and important thing here."

Space cleared fast as reporters chased deadlines with an incredible story to tell. Meanwhile, Pyper and her family were taken under the wing of Reach board members who led them to an empty conference room mercifully free of windows.

Tyler closed the door and rounded on Mark. "Quite the debut, Samuels."

"Tyler...please, listen to what I have to say."

"No, you listen to me. I'll smooth this mess over with the press, but hear me loud, and hear me strong. Your story featured a pretty message about moving on in life, and I'm all for it. But I have a story of my own to tell. A story about two beautiful women you shamelessly battered. Twenty years ago, I spent a summer afternoon on a boat with Amy, Pyper, and my pastor, Ken Lucerne. We paid a visit to Lake St. Clair. It's a spot I think you know well, right? That day is set in my mind with concrete because that's when Amy told me everything. She told me all about the wretched way you treated her and an innocent girl. Your *daughter*, Samuels. It was evil, and for the first time in my life I couldn't find strength enough to pray for a fellow human being. Didn't even want to. I've come a ways since then, because Amy and Pyper have bloomed. But don't expect me to welcome you in any way, shape or form. I said to Amy then, and I say to you now, eye-to-eye, you don't deserve one precious second of the time God gave you with them. Steer clear of my family, Samuels. *Steer. Clear.*"

Pyper's entire body quaked. She glared at Mark and couldn't repress a closing shot of her own. She motioned to Tyler—her daddy. "Protection. Unconditional love. Absolute conviction of spirit. That's what a father's love looks like."

She burned to reached up and strike Mark with a resounding slap; she stilled that impulse. What would change if she inked a red splotch of anger and recrimination against his skin? Nothing. She'd be lowering herself to his level. Curse it all.

All the same, she was on fire. Pyper's chin wobbled; her eyes filled with hot, stingy tears. Spinning on a booted toe, she escaped the room with nothing but her dignity intact. The rest of her massacred heart scattered as dust across the ground upon which she fled.

19

"Tyler. Wait. Amy, Tyler...can I have a quick word?" Chase bounded after them, making fast tracks down a private hallway that led to the parking lot.

Tyler stopped. "Yeah. I think we should. Not here, though. Come on back to the house."

Chase nodded, looked at Pyper. She didn't meet his eyes. Her small frame pulsed with tension. "Pyp, can I give you a ride?"

"I'm gonna go with my folks. See you at the farm."

That gave Chase the entire half-hour ride to Franklin to stew, for steam to build. He loved the Brocks, but this was wrong. The flat-out rejection offered by each and every one of them felt in no way to Chase like the kind of thing Jesus would preach in the face of heartfelt reform. Plus, if they found it so easy to shun Mark, what kept them from shunning him? How could he ever be trusted and welcomed without reservation to the heart of their family and Pyper's life?

He drove, steady at the wheel yet wracked by turmoil as door after door slammed shut in his face.

His emotional temperature skyrocketed right up to the moment he turned onto the gravel drive leading to the Brock's home. He tailed Tyler's vehicle to a graceful curve that angled directly in front of the entrance.

He parked his truck, bowed his head, and prayed with all his might because temper threatened to overwhelm, and that wouldn't do. Pyper's agony wrecked him. Completely and totally wrecked him. Evidently she could forgive him for his role in the reckless, shameful death of a human being as wonderful as Shayne Williams, yet she refused to acknowledge any form of hope for change within the life of her biological father. How could that possibly be the case? His mental spin increased.

No doubt Pyper was a beautiful soul, instinctively giving and kind and spirited. Certainly he understood why her fear and anger ran so deep. Despite his allegiance to Mark, he had given Pyper the necessary leeway to release twenty-years of pent-up hostility so she could come through it renewed and then release it forever.

Chase thought things over and shored his courage. The battle would be one of the toughest he had ever faced, but two pain-wracked lives—two strong-willed hearts on opposite sides of a jagged, barbed-wire fence had collided.

Maybe God could help him intercede. Perhaps God's purpose here was to use him to help smooth the storm-tossed waters between the people he had come to love. Suddenly, instead of feeling trapped, Chase sensed a mission building.

But could he remain steady enough to see it through?

They convened in the great room. When Amy crossed the threshold, Chase watched her run gentle fingertips against the edge of the fireplace mantle, where silver-framed photos rested. For a time she lost herself in family snapshots, formal portraits of Zach, Pyper...

And within her eyes crested an ocean of sadness

that twisted his stomach, because he didn't think they were going to like what he had to say.

"Excuse me for being torn between two sides here, but I don't think you should have treated him so harshly. Why are you painting him with the lines of a brush that's decades old? What right do you have to do that? It's not fair, and it's not worthy of the people standing in this room—the one's I've come to know and care for so much."

Pyper crossed the room, headed for her mother's side, but she drew up short and stared at Chase. Zach stood not far away, brows furrowed, arms crossed, gaze pinging from one person to the next as he visibly attempted to sort things through.

Tyler stepped into the tense and building void. "Chase, you're right to be loyal to him. I don't discount the ways he helped you find your way, but I need you to hear us out on this. You need to understand that—"

"No. There's no need for an explanation. I get it. You're all about second chances; you're all about redemption; you're all about that feel-good, all-encompassing word forgiveness, right up to the point when it involves someone who's hurt you deep. Well, I know Mark far better than you, and I respect him. He worked hard to overcome. I can relate to that struggle because life forced me to walk his same walk. He's a troubled, flawed man who tells me he's working hard to be what he needs to be, what he wants to be. I had my doubts about his arrival, and I know how he hurt y'all. But after his witness today, after the way he accepted his cross with grace and humility, I feel he deserves a chance. Why did you lash out at him without knowing thing-one about the demons he's slain?"

"Demons!" Pyper rounded on him. "The demons he's slain? Chase, that man is a wrecking ball! Any demons he faced, he brought on himself!"

"Absolutely, and those demons will lurk over you as well, Pyper—over all of you—if you storm off and refuse to give him the time of day. That kind of judgment I don't want or need. It's toxic, unfair, and it certainly isn't Christian."

"Chase!"

Pyper's cry mixed pain and anger; the realization registered then evaporated.

Temper erupting, he pressed forward through lightning strikes and storm clouds he could taste in the air. "The man you hate so much—and don't even try to hide from that truth—is the man who helped me, and nothing but God led Mark Samuels to Nashville. If you can't see that, then you don't understand all the words you use about seeing His hand in our lives, and recognizing His actions, His interventions."

Pyper's eyes filled, and Chase rebuked the resulting stab of pain.

"That damaged man found healing; that damaged man repented and worked hard to restore himself. I've learned a lot from his journey, and he pulled me scratching and clawing from a black hole. I'm sorry for what he did. Truly I am." His gaze roved Pyper's precious face, then moved to Amy. "What he did to you and your mama is reprehensible, but you should look at who he is now." Chase focused on Tyler and Zach as well. "All of you need to see his redemption rather than his past. He's covered by grace. He's loved. He's forgiven. Right?" His gaze landed square on Pyper's bewildered face. "Just. Like. Me." He invaded her space. Fire burned in his chest, stirring an all-over ache as he strove to drive home his point. "Or do you believe Jesus would leave an honestly repentant man cowering in the sand, covered by sin?"

Zach launched away from the wall and stormed across the room. "You know, for all the preaching and singing we do about Christian values and living, this family is"—Zach shook his head, lips curled in disgust, green eyes dark and stormy—"completely messed up. I'm sick of trying to be perfect. I'm sick of trying to be something I'm not! I'm sick of everything. Hear?" He stormed through the front door, slamming it in vivid punctuation of his exit.

Tyler rubbed his forehead, groaning. Pyper tucked next to her mother. "You'll never understand the damage he inflicted, Chase," she remarked in a choked, quiet voice.

"Does that mean he can't be transformed? Does that mean he can't move through the wounds he bears, and the wounds he caused, to become something better? Pyper, if that's the case, then how could you possibly believe it of me? What are we basing our relationship on exactly?"

"Chase, I'm not talking about you, and you know it."

"But you're being double-sided, Pyper. Don't profess forgiveness if you don't mean it." Pyper was about to argue, but he cut her off. "I'm not just talking about him. I'm talking about me. Us. How can you say you forgive me the sins of my past but not even give him the time of day when he's making a solid effort? How do you explain that?"

A laden silence snapped and crackled as dangerously as a downed electrical wire.

"I can't believe you, you of all people, would side

with him in this—and judge me to boot!"

"Once that boil of yours cools to a simmer, I want you to think about something. In what way did I ever make you feel I was judging you? I'm nowhere near qualified. Furthermore, I wouldn't ever want the responsibility. All I wanted to do was share some wisdom I had to absorb the hard way. Take it. Or leave it." He turned, forcing himself to disengage, even as it put a blade-tip to his heart. "I've overstayed my welcome, and for that I apologize. Pyper, call me when you feel like talking."

☙❧

The next morning, Pyper sat at the eat-in kitchen table, staring out the large, bay window. A golden sun just crested the distant tips of the mountains, spreading vivid rays through soft mists as it lifted into a sky of powder blue. The aroma of toasting bread—a homemade gift from Kellen's wife, Juliet—warmed the air. Pyper stood, her mouth watering, her bare feet padding against cool ceramic tile. She crossed from the fridge to the toaster, butter tub in hand, knife at the ready.

"Something smells great."

Her mom approached and Pyper turned in welcome. "Aunt Juliet rocks at making bread. Seriously. I'm in awe, and I'm hungry." The toast popped, all golden and crispy. Pyper nabbed the steaming slices, dancing to the island to finish preps after she dropped two more pieces in the toaster. "Carbs are bad, but carbs are so good."

"Preaching to the choir. Where's the loaf? I think I'll make some, too."

Pyper went to work buttering. "I already have you covered. They're toasting right now. I figured you'd want some when you smelled it. It's like a siren call or something."

Laughing, Amy ran gentle fingertips along the drifts of Pyper's hair. In passing, she kissed Pyper's cheek. "You're the best, snug-a-bug."

Though she'd never admit it aloud—to anyone— Pyper adored that childhood nickname, especially today, when she needed all the comfort and TLC she could find. Memories of yesterday's explosion crowded in and she sighed, refusing delivery, returning to the table with bread in hand. "Has anybody heard from Zach?"

A crease appeared instantly across her mother's brow. "He's not in his room?"

"Not that I could tell. I'll double check when I go back upstairs. I thought I heard him take off around nine o'clock or so. Maybe he went for a run or something. He stormed into the house pretty late last night."

Her mother's shoulders bent beneath an invisible weight. Pyper's bitter mood hit the skids. How many times, and in how many ways, had her mother been forced to endure episodes like this and remain steady? And poor Zach was an innocent caught in the crosshairs. Pyper knew just how that felt, and she softened at once.

"Mama, I'm sure he's OK."

"I'm sure he is, too. Still, I need to check on him. I need to talk to him about everything that's happened."

With that, a figurative elephant entered the room. Straining to ignore the topic to come, Pyper devoured her toast. Out of the corner of her eye, though, she saw the way her mother steeled her spine before pulling bread slices from the toaster. "Have you talked to Chase since he left?"

"Nope." Pyper looked out the window, craving avoidance. Confusion swept in from all sides. So did anger and sadness and love. Lots of love…

Silence held sway while her mom squeezed a plastic honey bottle in the shape of a bear; she added a dollop to the top of her toast. Before her mom could comment, Pyper latched on to some courage and picked up the ball.

"Mama, I'm furious at him."

"Why, honey?"

Aghast, Pyper dropped her bread and stared. "Oh, my word. You need to ask?"

"Yeah. I want your take on all this."

"He behaved horribly toward you and dad."

"You knew he had a temper."

"Maybe, but that's the first time I've ever seen it in full color."

"He spoke from love. Remember that."

"So, you're on his side. You think I'm awful for not running into Mark Samuels's waiting arms and rejoicing to be reunited with a father I've never known, never cared to know, and spent the bulk of my life despising. Is that it?"

"Oh, Pyper, please. It's more complicated than that, and we both know it."

The sharp, parental tone left Pyper to wilt. She expelled a wavering breath. "I hate this, Mama. I hate having all these doubts, all this turmoil. Nothing is quite right—not with Chase, not with Mark, even my family. What am I supposed to do next? I'm at a loss right now." She gave her mom a plaintive look. "Why couldn't God leave well enough alone?"

"Maybe because He wants us to grow into something better than 'well enough.'" Her mom sank onto the chair directly across the table. Reaching across the blonde pine wood, she linked their fingertips. "And all I want is for my daughter to be happy."

The show of empathy brought a lump to her throat. "I'm trying, Mama. Promise. I'm trying to find the road ahead. The *right* road ahead."

"For now, snug-a-bug, that's enough. Trust in that. Believe in that. And, maybe this will help. As much as Mark did that was wrong, the one thing Mark and I did right was welcome you into this world. Without Mark, I wouldn't have you. You are not a mistake. Even in that messy, sordid chapter of life, God had his hand on everything." She leaned forward in emphasis. "He took my and Mark's sin, forgave us, and turned it into something wonderful—you. And let me take that point one step further." Her mom kept hold of Pyper's hand and gave it an assuring squeeze. "At the end of the day, you don't belong to me, you don't belong to Tyler, you don't belong to Mark...or even Chase. You belong to God, Pyper. So, pray. Pray hard, and ask God what He wants from all of this. Believe me, that's what'll bring you the most peace, and the greatest joy. Once again, voice of experience talking here."

"Why do I get the feeling that's not all you want to say?" Pyper frowned.

"Because you're smart." Her mother attempted a smile, but trouble formed a backlight to her eyes. "You need to talk to your dad."

Pyper inhaled sharply through her nose. "He isn't here right now, so I can't, but I'll certainly do so when we have our weekly dinner date at the Franklin Chop

House tonight."

Her flip answer was greeted by an arched brow and tight lips. All over again, Pyper dissolved into an emotional mess. "Mama, you're not making this any easier."

"Then maybe this will. I think you're right to love Chase, past history and all."

The comment caused Pyper to go still, and attentive.

"I have to admit, I had my doubts at first, but I've been forced to look at a lot of things since he entered our lives. Just like you, I've done a lot of thinking about what he's dealt with in his life. You're stung right now, Pyp, and that's to be expected. But Chase loves you. He loves Mark, too. That leaves him split into pieces over this whole situation. Have respect for that. Maybe the end of a twenty-year-old horror story has God's grace written all over it. Maybe God's saying all of this needs to be laid to rest. You owe it to yourself to find out. You need to put this behind you, for once and for all. Talk to Mark, and talk to Chase, OK?"

The sliding glass doors in the family room came open and Zach burst across the threshold, ending their conversation. Dressed in shorts and a sweat-stained t-shirt, he had obviously taken out his frustrations on a run along the green trail not far from their home. Pyper gave him a wan smile that he acknowledged with nothing more than a brief nod.

Breathing hard, he paused for a few seconds to shake out his arms and stretch his legs. When he crossed through the kitchen he nabbed an apple and a banana from the wire fruit holder.

"Hey." He grunted the word, never missing a stride as he strode out of the room.

Pyper's heart ached. Zach needed reinforcement coping with the dramatic residue from yesterday. A disease crept its way through the fabric of the relationships she held most dear. She could heap the blame on Mark Samuels, of course. She'd even have enough left over to dish some over Chase and his hot-headed reaction after yesterday's fiasco.

But Pyper knew her mom was right. She needed to take some ownership of the situation and move forward before matters turned worse.

20

That afternoon, Pyper reported to Imperion for a recording session meant to finalize the studio rendition of "Forgiveness". Seeing Chase, sharing small, overly-warm booth space with him, was only the start of her inner battle. While she sang, thoughts of Mark swirled and fought against her beliefs as a Christian, choking her freedom of expression, shackling her emotions.

Two takes in, Pyper was miserable, struggling for control and the means by which to sing the blasted song. At that point, Chase pushed the headset pad away from his right ear. "Let's take a break."

"No. We need to lay this down. I'm ready now. Promise." She tried hard for an encouraging smile.

Chase didn't move on right away, but when he did, it was with a sigh passing his lips and a head-nod to the team in the control booth. "OK, then. We're ready."

Music played. Pyper closed her eyes, relaxed into the flow of the melody. Chase chimed in on the opening verse and she sank into the beauty of his voice, the words he sang.

And completely missed her entry cue.

Pyper hung her head as the recording stopped and tension pulsed through the air. She groaned, but a gentle caress skimmed the back of her hand. Long fingers laced through hers, curved in and held on tight. Chase. Her soul all but breathed his name, savored it…

"I need to grab some water." He drew her gaze with a touch to the cheek. "Come with me?"

Time off would be for the best. Through the headset she wore, techs could be heard in the background as they cued up for a fresh take. Pyper surrendered her gear and stepped away from the mic. Hard, taut lines formed through her back and shoulders.

Meanwhile, Chase addressed the crew. "We're going to take fifteen, gang. Let's gather again at three o'clock."

There was a utilitarian cafeteria on site and Chase led the way. Treating herself to a container of fresh fruit, Pyper followed him to a table toward the back of the room. Employees were sparse this time of day; the seclusion was welcome.

"First off, a question since we didn't have much of a chance to talk before the session started."

"What's that?"

His lips tipped. He slid his hand across the table and took hold of her drumming fingertips. "Are we past the cooling off period, because I've missed you like crazy, crash."

Chase's opening established instant ease and charmed the weight straight off her body. Pyper even laughed, leaning forward just far enough to brush his lips with hers then softly and quickly claim his mouth. "Yeah. We're past it. I missed you, too, and I'm so sorry about today. I don't mean to be such a mess, but I can't focus."

"No worries. 'Forgiveness' is a work in progress. It'll get there."

Pyper wondered if there wasn't a level of double meaning behind that observation. "I know you must think I'm a horrible person for the way I treated Mark, but I'm scrambled on the inside. I hope you can understand that."

"I do, and actually, that's part of the issue, Pyp. The scramble. Your emotions. The past. All those issues you're dealing with? All the leftover chaos that's going on inside you toward Mark? They belong to you, not him. They're your responsibility, not his. He's reaching out and asking you to hear him out, one-on-one. That puts the next move directly on you."

"Well, I hope you'll excuse my reluctance."

"Pyper, stop."

"No, hear me out. When you're a terrified four-year-old, struggling to find a way to your father's love, trying everything you can to make that man love and understand you, the emotions you talk about can't be so easily dismissed, and until you've lived them, you can't ever really understand them."

"That's true. But that's also what *was*. Confront it. Get rid of it. Together the two of you can move forward. Until you find a way to deal with that fact, you're no good to anybody, because you're no good to yourself."

Pyper wanted to find a way to argue the point, but came up empty. He was spot on, and that crawled under her skin like an irritant. "I wanted his love so much. I fought so hard to make him love me. No matter what I did, no matter what I tried, all I remember of him, all I really knew of him was violence. Anger. You know what that did to me."

Chase edged forward and captured her hands in a tight squeeze. "And for real and for true, there's not much that could turn me against the man except that." He paused as though to let that sink in. "What he did was reprehensible. Never, ever doubt that I'm on your side here, Pyp. But he's coming to you on his knees. What does your heart, and your life as a Christian, tell you to do with that?"

Again, Pyper had no answer, no ready refute.

"All I ask is that you take a look at what's real in the here and now, because that's what matters. That's why you're willing to give me a chance, right? Because of authentic reform, because of grace?"

Again he paused, and arched that thick, dark brow in challenge. Pyper didn't know whether to drag him close and sink into his arms forever or flat-out strangle him. Agonized, she pulled a paper napkin from the silver dispenser, wringing it tight.

"I'm not so sure I can live up to God's ideals this time around, Chase." She unwound the napkin and systematically shredded it to bits.

"I think you can. You're too good a person not to, Pyp. I know it'll take a huge leap, but you can do it. And maybe, after that, you'll find a way to live up to, and sing, the words of our song. The one we created together. The one I believe, to the depths of my heart, came about because God wanted you and me to look at forgiveness and accept it—and give it—on His terms."

For certain the equation came together with ease and made perfect sense. Reform, reclamation, forgiveness and renewal. In the cold, stark weather of reality, however, Pyper continued to struggle.

"I'll forgive him, but I don't want a relationship with him. I won't give him anything of who and what I am."

"Then your forgiveness is superficial, and unworthy of the woman I admire and care for so deeply. Not to mention, you're squandering a luxury."

"What luxury? What squandering?"

"The luxury is redemption. The squandering is that of second chances. Think about Christ. Is what you just described the means by which he's forgiven us for the wrongs we've done? The pains we've caused? The sin? No. He welcomes us freely and loves us. We've been called to do the same."

He ignored Pyper's affronted gasp, and she realized anew that Chase had emerged from battle as a man of deep, strong conviction.

"Seems to me you're being pretty tight fisted and stubborn toward a person who wants to do nothing more than apologize, begin a new chapter of his story and give you love." At last Chase uncapped his water bottle and guzzled. "Know what else?"

"What?" Pyper seethed, but only because his words were truth, and they struck through her pliant heart like perfectly aimed arrows.

"I know you well enough to recognize the fact that you're fighting it all the way."

"Fighting what?"

"Mark's offering. As a Christian, as his daughter, it looks to me like you want to start over, but as a human being, you're refusing delivery. It'll be interesting to see where God takes that. You can be a victim, or you can be an overcomer. The choice, the control, is now all yours, and it's time to decide." He took another long swallow, his eyes never drifting from hers. "Talk to him, Pyp. Just talk to him."

❧❦

The longest emotional walk of Pyper's life began the moment she exited her car in the parking lot of

Reach North and strode past the reception desk inside. She had no appointment with Mark. She didn't want to be announced. What she craved was the element of surprise. Most of all she wanted to run away.

But she didn't.

Driven by purpose, she stood her ground and breezed right past the kind-featured lady who stood guard. The woman lifted to her feet and sputtered but didn't get in Pyper's way.

Jesus, Pyper prayed in silent fervor, *the request I'm about to make isn't a test. Honest. I know better than to test Your goodness—but whatever comes next is all on You. If he's here, if he's available, if he can give me the time of day that everyone seems to believe he's after, then fine. Now is the time, and this is the moment. I'll listen. It'll be You, and me, and Mark. If not, then that's fine, too. At least I'll have tried. At least, then, I'll be able to turn my back on this whole wretched mess and—*

At the threshold of Mark's office, she froze. Pent up air clogged lungs and panic set in, because for better or worse, there he sat. Folded into a chair behind his desk, he typed on a keyboard, focused on the monitor just ahead. Pyper's lips twisted into a wry smirk.

As if God would let either one of them off the hook that easily, she mused.

Pyper, My precious child. Rest.

The Spirit breeze worked through her body and soul. She calmed, though not entirely. Since Mark remained unaware of her arrival, she stayed put to observe and absorb. Attitude skeptical, she stood ramrod straight and clutched the doorframe so tight the skin along her knuckles turned white. Open file folders were strewn next to the keyboard. Hunt-and-peck keystrokes filled the air with stuttered clicks until her tentative knock announced a summons.

Mark spotted her and lurched to his feet so fast he upended a cup of coffee across a nearby stack of papers. He yelped a surprised curse then flushed beet red. "Pyper, I...I'm...ah...sorry. I'm a klutz."

Pyper didn't say a word but stepped cautiously into the office. Mark yanked a stash of napkins from his desk drawer. Bent on rescuing files, she helped him mop, dry, and clean.

"I'm sorry about this. You kinda startled me. Wasn't expecting...you know...a visit or anything." Mark stuttered, but all of a sudden his motions came to a stop. "I suppose this is ironic. You helping me clean up a mess."

Pyper's head came up as she set folders aside to dry. Her demeanor iced in an instant. "Don't expect this to turn into a greeting card moment."

"Fair enough. I won't."

What was with that gentle tone, she wondered. The calm he displayed was at complete odds with the man of her memory. Together, they repaired his desk, and his somber sense of resignation stirred guilt. Tremors hit, sending her nerves into a hot-wire dance against her skin. Soon the silence became unwieldy. "I know we need to talk...and so...I stopped by...to—"

Groaning, Pyper surrendered the stilted and worthless attempt at civility. She tossed ruined napkins into the trash while Mark shrugged, avoiding her eyes as he repositioned desk items. "I have no doubt your efforts are instinctive rather than affectionate. All the same, they're appreciated."

"I...I know I reacted like some kind of gunslinger at the benefit. That was wrong. I just...I don't know how to take this in. There's a lot of baggage inside of me when it comes to you. Plus, your tie to Chase certainly knocked me over...but...I guess...I suppose...we should deal. Right?" She didn't call him dad. She didn't call him Mark, either, or refer to him in any way personal. Instead, she bungled forward as best she knew how.

"I realize it's early yet, but do you have time for a quick lunch? I found a deli nearby that serves good sandwiches."

Pyper straightened her purse strap, clutched it tight. "Yeah...I suppose we could."

Reaching out, Mark smoothed a comforting hand against Pyper's arm. The motion might have been an automatic response from his heart, but she flinched as though burned and moved back a pair of generous steps. Mark retreated as well and grabbed his wallet from the desk drawer.

"Ready?"

All Pyper offered was a silent nod.

The short walk to the retro-style deli was silent, painful in its tension. They ordered and Pyper settled stiffly across from him at a scarred Formica table. They stared at each other for agonizing moments.

"I've said it to so many patients, so many times," Mark said. "Dissolve the muck and the mire with the power of your convictions. Work through the trials a step at a time until the water runs clean and you can start swimming free again." Mark leaned on his forearms, dusting his fingers across the laminated surface of the table.

Pyper folded her arms across her midsection in tight protection.

"The words are therapy-speak, sure, but they're

true, and it seems they're relevant to the moment."

The dissolving process to which Mark referred was much more difficult than she could readily imagine. Pyper lifted her corned beef sandwich from the tray he had collected at the order counter and placed between them. She took a bite. When their gazes met again, she swallowed and firmed her resolve.

"I'm here because of Chase. You helped him, and he cares for you. I told him not long after we met that I looked forward to meeting his sponsor one day, and saying thank you. He's come back to life as a wonderful, solid man. You had a hand in that, and I'm grateful. He means the world to me."

"And I know the same holds true for him toward you." During an eloquent silence, his gaze bore into hers, as if words, and feelings and regrets rolled through him, pushing to burst free. "My point in wanting to see you, to talk, is to let you know that I've come back to life as well. I've battled to find a path home, too."

"I listened to what you said at the benefit. Like everyone else in the room, I was moved by your story. How could I not be? You're telling me and the world that you've changed."

"I have. I met Christ when I landed in South Carolina, and I've never once looked back."

"Yep. Not once. Not even long enough to look us up. See how we were doing. Find out if we were dead or alive." Doubt and hesitance formed a backdrop when she realized how mean and condemning her words sounded. What if he meant all of this? What if, in some small way, she needed to come to terms with his reform and take his journey to heart? Pyper's muscles went tight. She couldn't allow him to step through that kind of an opening. Not yet.

"Your mom married Tyler Brock. That was kind of big news, Pyper. I kept up, and I know you took his name when he adopted you." Mark's brows furrowed. "What more did I need to know? Amy was where she should have been in the first place; you were well loved. In the meantime, I worked as hard as I could to rebuild a life that had turned out nothing like I ever intended."

He ate a few bites of his sandwich; Pyper figured he might be trying to find words, so she followed suit, but the food tasted like sawdust and didn't land well in her roiling stomach.

"I had to find my way. I was in no position to approach either one of you. At that point, why would I? Why would I interfere? Why would I mess up the life the two of you had made?"

"Spite. Scandal. Monetary gain. Bitterness. And that's just for starters."

His nose flared. His eyes sparked with flashes of temper. This version of Mark Samuels was painfully familiar to Pyper, and she realized at once she stepped close to a boundary line best not crossed. Fear instantly set in and she nearly bolted from her wobbly metal chair. As fast as that flood of terror washed in, she watched him bank the flare of anger by going still, folding his hands into a tight clench.

"And in spite of those temptations, I stayed away. What does that tell you?"

"I don't know the answer to that. What I will say is this. You hurt me deeper than anyone I've ever known. I'm not sure I even want you to be part of my life. I know you realize that fact, so why are you pushing at me so hard for something I don't think I'm going to be able to give?"

The questions forced her to confront the worst of herself and attempt to smooth a scar that had formed over the deepest—and softest—reach of her heart.

"You're part of me, Pyper. Whether you like it or not, whether we can ever move forward or not, you don't just belong to your mom, or Tyler. You belong to me, too. If not for me, you wouldn't be who and what you are. You need to come to terms with those facts just as much as I need to come to terms with what I did to you. The choice is yours now, I've already made my decisions, and I'm acting on them. Now it's your turn."

"So, you expect a fresh start? Unreal. As it stands right here, right now, the answer is no. It's like you have no clue how terrified I was of adult men when I was little. Men scared me to a degree that I couldn't even be around ones I didn't know unless my mama took me by the hand and led the way. That's because of you. I could barely find my way into a relationship with Tyler until I realized he was so loving, so kind, so trustworthy, that I had no choice but to give him my heart. That's because of you, so you're right. I am who I am because of you."

Mark leaned back, visibly absorbing the sting of her indictment. He clenched his jaw. "Well, I wanted you to have your say. I didn't figure it'd be easy to tolerate, but I owe you nothing less." Following a hard beat of silence, he looked straight into Pyper's eyes. "That said, I want you to tell me something. Do you trust Chase?"

Pyper blinked, taken out of the moment entirely by his unexpected question. "Of course I do."

"Makes sense. After all, you've said it to me

yourself, he's a changed man. A solid man. A man made new by the power of God and authentic reform."

"That's absolutely correct."

"Then why can't the same be said for me, or anyone else who's battled back from an evil pattern of life?"

His words acted as the equivalent of a mic drop. She fought to challenge the truth he presented so succinctly; a scramble of words formed and poured out of her in a mighty push. "Chase has willingly and completely humbled himself. He earned my trust and respect by not just talking the talk, but walking the walk."

"What do you think I'm trying to do right now, Pyper?" Mark heaved a quiet but heavy sigh and closed his eyes for a moment before focusing on Pyper once more. "I suppose I deserve no less than recrimination after the hell I put you through. Nonetheless, I'm holding on to the promise that Jesus knows my heart. I've gotta believe He knows how hard I'm tryin' here, and how much it means to me."

She withstood the barrage of emotional shrapnel, the confusion, the heartache and turmoil, still, her chin wobbled. Tears filled her eyes, one or two cresting over her lashes.

"I'm asking for a second chance. I'm asking for an opportunity to show you a life can change over the course of twenty-plus years. I'm hoping for the chance to show you who and what I am now."

"Why?"

"Because I love you, Pyper, and I always will, no matter what comes to be. I've prayed long and hard for the chance to earn something I know I don't deserve."

"Which is?"

"Forgiveness."

The word—his bold, emphatic use of it—caused Pyper to quake. All through her mind spun the lyrics of the song she had created and struggled with at Chase's side. Assailed by overpowering vulnerability, her defenses rose hot and strong. "Don't you dare try to go all Dad on me at this point. It's way too late and you lost the privilege long ago."

"Being your dad isn't what I asked for, now is it?" He paused, obviously letting that set in. "And if rejection is your final answer then you're not behaving at all like a Christian. If you don't believe I can change—that I *have* changed—then how can you possibly believe it of the man you've fallen in love with? What interest would you have in a man the likes of Chase Bradington? A drunken, immoral singer who wasted years of his life and destroyed people he loved?"

Horrified, Pyper reared back. Gasped.

Mark forged ahead. "I had hopes and dreams. I gave up on every one of 'em after I graduated high school because—"

"Because of me. Because of adulthood. Because of life. You're not in high school anymore, Mark." Sharp and dismissive, her interruption came wrapped in tight shoulders, a taut set to her jaw.

"And neither are you."

"You were my father. I trusted you, and you destroyed that trust. You say you had hopes and dreams? Well so did I! So did my mama! You ruined them." Sorrow built—pressure beneath a volcano. "I couldn't even defend myself. Well, I can now, and the way I'm going to do it is by saying this: I want you to stay away from me."

Something in the unyielding tone of her edict must have caused Mark's determination to crumble. He flexed his jaw, nodded, and gathered himself straight even as she sensed his surrender.

"Thank you for letting me say what I needed to say." Again he spoke with a sense of calm that was all but foreign to her experience. "I'd like you to keep something in mind. Look at where your life ended up compared to mine. Who ended up on the right side of the road? Who ended up moving into blessings instead of pain and regret and rebuilding a life that was busted to pieces?"

He stood and took the meal ticket with him, leaving Pyper with more tears brimming over already wet lashes.

21

After chasing his way through yet another episode of fitful sleep, the last thing Chase wanted to be greeted by in the early morning hours was an incessant electronic buzzing sound. It wasn't the alarm clock, he realized, raking back his hair and rolling from his stomach to his back. The annoyance stemmed from his stinking cellphone.

He grabbed the device and punched it into silence before realizing the reason for the alerts. Zach Brock had sent him a text.

Hope u get this fast. Need u to pick me up. No questions, K? Plez just help me out ASAP.

Cobwebs of sleep cleared from Chase's head in a big hurry. Before launching to his feet, he fast-typed a reply.

On my way. Where u at? You hurt? Safe?

I'm at Kim Monroe's. I'm OK. Please, just come.

Fourteen-year-old Zach was with Kim Monroe at—Chase rolled to check the bedside clock—just after one in the morning? That was more than enough to thicken Chase's pulse to a hot throb and prompt him quickly from bed.

And Zach, Chase discovered, was totally wasted. Drunk to the point of nausea. Zach tumbled into Chase's truck and they barely made it down the driveway before the kid passed out, groaning in misery. For the time being, Chase asked no questions, exerted no pressure. He stored it all up for later, because he fully intended to give the kid a swift shake to the soul. For now, though, he needed to get Zach on his feet and find out exactly what had happened.

They landed at his condo and Zach tumbled into the bathroom. Chase followed, relentless and torn between the idea of lending comfort and giving the kid the chewing out of his life.

Zach moaned, leaning over the commode, stomach emptying.

"What happened?"

"Kim invited me over. We hung out."

"Yeah, I can see that. Now, tell me the rest of the story."

"Her folks were gone."

"And did you know that before you went over?"

"No."

"Don't lie to me."

Clutching his stomach, crumpling to the floor, Zach closed his eyes and let out a quiet wail. Chase felt no pity whatsoever.

"She said she wanted to see me. That's all I knew. And I'll admit, I didn't mind a bit finding out they were gone. I'm into her. I like how she makes me feel. That honest enough for you?"

Where was this defiance coming from? The hostile attitude?

"What is *up* with you?"

"Nothing much other than the fact that I'm getting a clear picture of my life and the people in it, and I've decided to do what I want to do. Why can everyone else live however they want except me? Even my supposedly perfect family is far from perfect. Why should I be held to a standard even they can't uphold?

I wanna be what I wanna be."

"Well there's foolish mistake number one."

"Shut up. You have no right to be my judge and jury. You've done the same thing. Besides, what do you care? All you're in it for is Pyper."

OK, that one stunned Chase speechless...for a moment. "What on earth do you mean by that statement?"

Zach snorted. "Oh, come on. Get real, and don't *you* lie to *me*. Hanging out, bringing me into your band, asking for my help in the studio, none of that is about being friends, or helping me find a way, it's about Pyper. You like having the inroads to her and my family."

Struck wordless again, Chase stared, open mouthed. "That is without a doubt the craziest thing I've ever heard. I wish I didn't even have to dignify it with a response, but I will anyway. What I did, I did for you, Zach. Out of my affection for you and out of wanting to right the ways I did Shayne Williams wrong. It had nothing to do with Pyper or your family. I didn't want to see you make the kind of mistake you went ahead and made anyway, so I guess I'm no kind of a mentor. Talk to me about the booze. How'd you get it?"

"What does it matter?"

"Want to get kicked out of here on your backside? Keep it up."

Zach wilted. "It started out as no big deal. We were just going to have a mixed drink, like her parents and everyone else does."

"Please tell me all you had was liquor. Please." Though, for a fourteen-year-old, that was more than bad enough. He had sensed from the start that Kim

Monroe lived and moved within a faster, less moral circle of friends. Not a good mix when it came to a hormonal, crushing kid like Zach.

"We had rum and cola. The drinks went down so easy that one or two became...well...more."

Zach threw up all over again. Close to rabid with disgust and anger, Chase growled beneath his breath and prepped a couple cold wash cloths. He squeezed off the excess water then spun back to Zach who had recovered enough to lurch to his feet and glower as he staggered and righted himself against the edge of the bathroom sink.

"So I slipped and had too much. What's the big deal? How's it any different from what everyone else does, including you?"

"The big deal is you're hammered, and you're under age. Is this what you want? Early morning rescue missions and sickness? Over a girl who'd drop you like garbage for a bigger, better deal? Well answer me this, pal, how's that workin' for ya? Does it feel good? Was it worth it?"

Zach shoved past, staggered against the doorframe of the bathroom. "I'm sick, all right. Sick of everyone acting like I'm a baby, protecting me from truths like, oh, say, Pyper's bio-dad has come calling, bent on accomplishing who knows what, and we sure can't have the little baby boy being exposed to such a thing."

"And what you've done just now? It proves their judgment on that point is right on the money. You've acted out like the immature fourteen-year-old you are instead of the adult you profess to be. This stunt was a monumental fail. Think that over, Zach! As soon as she opened the liquor cabinet—no, as soon as you found out you were home alone with a sixteen-year-old girl bent on trouble—you should have hauled yourself away from that place as fast as possible." Thunder and wind built to a storm requiring immediate release. "Grow up, Zach! I've lived the road you're traveling, and when you get to the end, I don't want you blaming jealousy of your sister, or living up to your dad's expectations or anything else for where you end up. You'll have no one to blame but yourself, and just like me you'll be forced to face the truth that you had to try every form of stupid until the right thing came along. Don't be an idiot. You've had every advantage and you're shoving that fact right back into God's face like an ingrate. If that's who and what you are, if that's the person you told me you wanted to discover, then let me tell you right now, you're making the mistake of your life and wasting the only gift worth having. Your life, Zach. Your *life*."

Silence worked a small measure of calm through crackling levels of tension.

"What are you going to do?"

"I'm not keeping this from them. I'm not covering for you, and I'm certainly not gonna lie. Got that?"

Zach's fear danced through the atmosphere. Chase knocked it aside with ease. This kid needed to learn. Fast.

"I'm going to let them know you're safe; then I'm going to caffeinate you 'til you're sober. After that, I'm taking you home. The rest is up to you, but you're coming clean."

Zach's stubborn bravado faded. "They're going to ground me 'til I'm forty."

"Maybe so. Wouldn't blame 'em if they did."

"Yeah? Well, they're probably going to force me out of your band, too."

If Zach expected that statement to be a trump card, he was woefully mistaken. Chase just shrugged. "Guess I'll have to make do, won't I? Good thing for me Music City is bustin' with great guitarists. You broke the only rule I laid out to you. All I asked was for you to stay straight and focused. Now, answer me true. Did anything else happen with Kim?"

"Since you're not being much of a friend, I guess that's none of your business."

"You made it my business the minute you asked me to come get you. Now, I want an answer. Did you do two stupid things tonight?"

Still green-skinned and wobbly, Zach lurched toward the living room couch and sank onto the cushions, burying his face in the towel Chase handed him. "No. OK? It got pretty heavy, but I pulled back because I didn't feel good."

Well, thank God for a weak stomach, Chase thought, rejoicing at the way the kid's system had bucked against alcohol intake. After consuming an ocean of black coffee, after a couple hours of recuperation, Chase returned Zach to the Brock farm.

The sky was just beginning to lighten from ink black to pearly blue when Tyler met them at the front door. Once Zach saw his dad, he reverted almost instantly to the child he truly was, and Chase wondered how the return home would play out. The Brock family had been through the wringer of late.

Slow but purposeful, Zach exited the truck and met his dad's steady, waiting gaze. A heartbeat of time elapsed between father and son, powered by a bond Chase recognized and revered.

"Dad, I'm so sorry."

Tyler didn't say a word. He tugged Zach into a

long, hard hug, visibly moved.

"I promise you can yell at me all you want later on." Zach's words were patterned by tears and a husky voice. "Please, for now, just know I was an idiot, and I won't ever be this stupid again."

Tyler didn't release his hold. "Fair enough—for now—but we're going to talk this over when you're rested. I'm just grateful you're OK."

"I am. Promise."

Chase made ready to leave. He turned, but Tyler caught his eye and mouthed, "Thank you." Chase's tiredness warmed into affection and he smiled, giving Tyler a nod.

He accepted Tyler's final wave and left as quick as he could. The last thing he wanted right now was to see Pyper. Seeing her would shatter what little control he could wrangle into place. Had he failed as a mentor? Had his well-intentioned influence on Zach backfired?

With this episode riding on top of everything she had endured with respect to Mark's arrival, Chase didn't want to look into her eyes and see disappointment, or doubt.

❧

The day following Zach's stumble with Kim, Pyper tossed restlessly beneath a light layer of blankets, stretching and reaching for her phone where it rested on the nightstand. A wavering mist sifted and danced across the dips and flats of land outside her window. Sunlight formed a warm block of gold against her body.

Pyper scrolled to Chase's name on her phone and

tapped out a text message.

Have I mentioned lately how much u mean 2 me? Thanks for helping Z. I have so much to say, so much to tell u. There's no sessions 2day, just free time and R&R. Have you got time enough for a picnic?

Rather than babysit her cellphone, begging and pleading for a reply, Pyper prepped for the day by showering, changing into soft, well-worn jeans and a white tank top, which she paired with a waist-tied button down shirt in deep pink. While she combed her hair and worked it into a ponytail, a music alert sounded from her phone.

She ran to her bed stand.

I'd love it, crash. Name the time.

Pyper couldn't quell the tingles of relief and happiness that spread through her body. Smile wide, she replied: *How soon can you get here? Seriously. XO.*

See you around eleven, sweet thing.

An hour later, mood ebullient, Pyper moved through the kitchen with her mom, helping to put the finishing touches on a batch of potato salad.

"You're not putting onions in it, are you?"

"Yeah, I am. I always do."

"Oh. Yeah. Umm. OK."

Her mom turned in question, but Pyper neatly avoided eye contact and initiated a stream of warm water. She started rinsing a stack of pots and pans, loading them in the dishwasher.

"Pyper?"

"Well, Chase isn't a fan of onions. Umm…"

Seemed to Pyper like her mom fought to keep a straight face.

"Want me to separate a serving for him?"

Pyper flashed damp fingers in a gesture of

dismissal. "Oh, no…I mean…yeah. I mean, if you don't mind. If it isn't any trouble."

"Pyper you're tongue tied."

"Am not."

Yeah, she was, but her mom's grin, her sparkling eyes, made her defensive. Once mixing was complete, after the diced, sliced and cooked ingredients had been combined—except for the onions—Pyper breathed deep and released a contented sigh of pleasure. "Mmm…summer picnics wouldn't be the same without your prized offering, Mama. It's so good."

"You're so easy."

"Don't let it get around." Pyper grabbed a spoon from the nearby drawer and sampled a spoonful of the creamy concoction. Promptly she felt the sting of a light slap against the back of her hand.

"You mooch."

"Guilty." *Worth it*, she added in silence, licking the spoon and then depositing it in the sink. Pyper watched from the corner of her eye, noticing her mom bend to retrieve a plastic tub and a lid from a cabinet next to the stove. Next, she scooped a large portion inside and sealed it tight…only then did she add the onions and mix the remainder of the salad.

Pyper blushed, and tingled, thinking only of Chase, of how eager she was to see him, touch him, share her heart with him…

"One time," she said to her mom, "we went to Gabby's for burgers and fries, and I noticed he opted for no onion, no tomato. Just trying to be nice and all. I was pretty hard on him, and he refuses to give up. He's helped us, and I know he's as confused about everything as I am. We need today to get things square and figure out what comes next. Know what I mean?

I'm really looking forward to it."

"Um-hum." Amy settled the container in a small sack stationed on the counter and tweaked Pyper's cheek. "I hope it all works out, Pyp. He's good stuff. We owe him."

৵৵

The impromptu date with Chase began with one of Pyper's favorite things to do in the world: ride free on horseback through the valley surrounding her home. With Chase next to her, she let her mare take the lead. Briar proceeded at a gentle trot and Pyper found herself lulled by the soothing sway and bounce of balancing herself as the animal moved through a wild meadow dotted by colorful flowers that dipped and lifted in gentle rolls of plush green grass.

Warm animal flesh met the stroke of her fingertips; a thick, coarse mane fell through the caressing fingertips of Pyper's free hand. The other hand held firm to the reins of the light brown Tennessee walking horse.

Briar's step was a bit brisk as she instinctively kept pace with the longer strides of Chase's stallion, Shepard. Shepard was her dad's horse from way back, dark brown, satiny and solid in color but for a striking white star on his forehead. Shepard was gentle, but loved to cut loose at a run when given free rein.

Somehow, that idea and image brought Pyper's focus back to Chase. She looked at him over her shoulder, tipping the rim of her cowboy hat to shade her eyes from the sun. Struck by inspiration, she flung her hair and crouched low over Briar's head, murmuring the "run" command into perked ears. The mare took flight and Pyper whooped. "Race you to the stream!"

Chase's laughter exploded through the air, and he kicked Shepard into a run. Naturally Briar was no match for the speed and size of the stallion; Chase beat her by a long-shot and slowed near an ancient willow bursting with tremulous green leaves, its curving branches trailing against the bubbling surface of a ribbon of water that curved, and tossed and sparkled across the land. Near the bank, Chase directed his horse with a gentle nicker and clicks of the tongue. Long ago, Pyper's dad had erected a roughhewn post designed to blend into the landscape and meant to tether a horse or two. Chase secured his animal while Pyper joined him and prepared to do the same.

"Hard to believe this simple little stream leads to a tributary of the Cumberland." She was out of breath. Exhilarated. "It has no name, but when my dad and I discovered it, for some unknown reason, I called it Ogonquin. Probably because I was like seven-years-old and at the time I was totally fascinated by anything having to do with Indians." Chase took the reins from her grip and secured Briar on her behalf, which charmed Pyper deep and true. "Since the name sounded Indian, and tickled my fancy, we let it stick."

"Your very own myth, shared with family." Chase chuckled and watched her with a level of intent that sizzled, yet his eyes were soft as a breeze, and just as provocative. Then, as though remembering himself, he cleared his throat and turned away, loosening the straps of a small leather carry-all that contained their lunch. Pyper retrieved a big plaid blanket and small stash of plastic ware from the pack that rested against Briar's sweat-glistened flank.

In another nod to chivalry, Chase took custody of her supplies and spread their blanket, positioning food parcels and serving items. Pyper laid out napkins, water bottles, chips, and rolls, continuing to set up their picnic.

"I love your story about the river. I love thinking about you as a little girl. The scrapbooks you showed me a while back, they give me such a vivid picture of you back then."

The statement filled her with a bittersweet taste. "I wish the road were easier. For all of us."

Chase's gaze lifted from the layout of their spread. "How's Zach holding up? Mind my asking?"

"I don't mind at all." Pyper sat on the blanket and stretched her legs, leaning back on her hands. Sunlight kissed her face and she loved the warmth so she lifted her hat away and set it next to her. "He's busted, royal, but we're all keeping tabs, and we all care. Deeply. He'll get through."

"I hope, in the light of day, your folks don't think my influence on him was bad, with the music and recordings and such. I never meant for him to start down a bad road."

Pyper surrendered her sunbath and stared at him. "Just the opposite. You helped more than you'll ever know. On a number of levels."

If he expected her to elaborate on that, he'd have to wait a while, because she just wasn't ready. Best to ease into things.

"Evidently your dad has seen the way clear to let him stay in my studio band. I'm glad for that."

"It's constructive, it plays to what Zach loves, and it connects him to a world outside of his family. That's important right now. Smart decision, I think."

"Me, too." Chase brushed an open palm against the tips of some nearby wild flowers that carpeted the tall grass. Then he plucked a few of the more colorful blooms and gathered them into a bouquet. He looked up, his eyes a dark, rich ocean. He offered Pyper the flowers then brushed his knuckles against her cheek. Charmed all over again, she lifted the flowers to her nose and captured an instant of spicy fragrance.

"You said you had a lot to tell me. A lot to discuss…"

"Yeah." Pyper braced, studied the lovely, vibrant blooms rather than his eyes…eyes she fell into without reservation.

"I'd like to go first. Especially given what happened with Zach. I have something to tell you, too."

The words came in a flat delivery devoid of the emotion Pyper knew…just knew…lurked scant millimeters beneath the surface. She rested her hand against his strong, sinewy forearm, a forearm she had admired many times as he strummed a guitar on stage, or worked his fingertips against carefully divided frets.

Or when he held her close…

She gave herself a firm internal shake. "What's wrong?"

His chest rose and fell at her quiet prod. "I have to tell you something that happened." The words were a whisper. His chest rose and fell once more.

Pyper respected the interlude of restful silence that fell into a sun-kissed moment filled with insect music, whispering grass and bird song. Oddly enough, she didn't feel fear. Instead, she wanted only to know him. Fully.

"It begins with church the other day. The sermon.

My pastor talked about the parable of the laborers in the vineyard. You know, that story always kind of ticked me off, until he explained something."

"What's that?"

"Well, as you know, there were laborers who were hired right away, who worked the field properly all day long for a fair day's wage. Through the course of the day, the land owner continued to send workers into his field. Afternoon. Early Evening. All the laborers were paid the same amount. The workers who were hired last, who only worked maybe an hour or so in the blazing hot sun, received goodness and grace based solely on the vintners generosity and goodness."

Pyper nodded readily. "It seems so unfair on the surface. The poor workers who did what was expected, worked hard the entire day, must have felt cheated."

"Exactly—but that's not the point. The story is an illustration of God's love. God gives love based solely on generosity and goodness...and our willingness to accept that love and share it in return. An excess of love. That's the point of the parable, not the idea of people being slighted, but the idea of everyone being included, and given equal mercy. That idea has such a big place in my heart."

"Why that one in particular?"

"Because I don't deserve it. Mercy. At all. I messed up in so many ways, lingering on the outside, waiting, hoping, just like the laborers in Jesus' parable. And look what God's done...he sent me you, Pyper. He sent me love, and music, and second chances."

Pyper didn't take that fact a step further. After what she had experienced with Mark, she couldn't quite bring it around to that connection.

"I know you were riled up and trying to just

survive the moment, but do you remember the way Mark described the day he lost his job, the day he kicked you out? He talked about buying a pint of whiskey."

"Kind of tough to forget." She did her best to keep the bite from her words. After all, Chase didn't deserve recrimination for trying to stand between his friend and mentor and the woman he loved.

"I did the same thing."

"Yeah, I know."

"No, you don't. I'm not talking about the past. It happened just recently."

Pyper froze. Blinked. "What?"

"When Kellen told me you were Mark's daughter, I fell apart, Pyp. On my way home from that meeting, I stopped at the nearest liquor store. I called for a bottle. The clerk wrapped it in a brown paper bag, and I left the store without a backward glance. I was so eaten up. So raw. I lived exactly what Mark described in his testimony, and I did it following recovery. I intended to break a vow I made to myself and to so many others."

"Chase...what...what happened?" Her throat closed on the words.

"I came this close." With finger and thumb Chase delineated a scant sliver of space. "I wanted that drink so bad."

"Did you?" She held her breath, waited within a world held in suspense.

"No. I ended up chucking that bottle into the bottom of a dumpster."

At once, her shoulders relaxed; a coil of tension released. "What stopped you?"

"You, Pyper. You."

"Me?" She watched him, captivated, shocked all over again. This wasn't how she had expected this conversation to go at all.

"I wanted to honor you, and I knew I had to be there for you once the storm hit. I knew I had to make the right choice or lose you forever." He paused. "You gave me a second chance. You believed in me."

"I believe in you still."

"But the heart is, without question, the most vulnerable organ in the human body."

"I'll never argue the point." Emotions escalated, heightening Pyper's senses. She folded her legs and leaned forward.

"I've never hated myself more. I was so wrapped up in telling you about me, in spilling all my baggage so you'd understand me, and care about me in spite of it all, that I didn't pay close enough attention to you, to your pain and your battles. I apologize for that, Pyper. I never even asked you his name. He tried to wreck you and your mom, and I never even knew his name."

She ignored that for the time being. "Chase Bradington, don't ever—and I mean ever—say the words you hate yourself in my presence again."

Her words weren't angry or bitter. She hoped the loving reprimand would bear ten-times the impact as a result. When he looked into her eyes and absorbed the moment, and its meaning, she sensed nothing but his love and gratitude.

The benediction seemed to cause a crumbling. He drew her in tight, buried his face against her neck, against the tumble of her hair. "I don't deserve you," he murmured.

"I'd say the same to you, but evidently, God's decided otherwise...for both of us." She held him tight, warm and tender, letting her care pour over him like a balm.

Chase finished setting up their picnic, not looking at her. Pyper kept quiet and unwrapped a pair of sandwiches, opening containers with potato salad, fruit and crackers. Chase ripped into a bag of potato chips, but his hands weren't steady.

"I was such a cocky, prideful, overly confident jerk, Pyper."

He looked up at the sky and Pyper followed suit. Huge cotton-ball clouds drifted across a wide expanse of blue. Birds swooped and cawed, the cadence of the stream caressed her soul like the gentle touch of God—reassuring, grounding.

"It honored me that Zach wanted my friendship. I looked at it like a sign from God that I could help someone who was confused and trying to find his way. When he called me from Kim's place, my heart broke as if he were my very own brother. Just like Shay. Shay was such a good guy, and he had everything to live for. He's in a better place and I know it—but there's part of me that wonders if losing him wasn't some form of punishment for all the wrongs I've done."

"God doesn't work that way, Chase."

"I learned that. It took a long time, but I learned that."

"You learned it, but do you believe it? Do you truly believe it and know it through and through? If you don't, then the learning isn't very worthwhile, no matter how well-intentioned."

"You don't hold back, crash, do you?"

"Nope." Her lips twitched; humor tickled her senses. "Should I apologize?"

"No. You should keep it up."

The admission was quiet, accompanied by a boyish smile that reflected nothing but honest humility. "Then let me return the favor when it comes to Mark."

Pyper went stiff. "Yeah. Mark. Not much to say at this point. Really."

Her too easy, too pat, reply died a necessary death, especially as she noticed the way Chase's eyes darkened, and his intensity ratcheted upward. She clenched her jaw and tears pooled to blur her vision. She blinked away the vulnerability, made it vanish like smoke. Such was how she coped these days.

"One of his favorite adages is to say that a yoke forms a team. I like to think that's the type of yoke Jesus talks about in the Bible. Jesus isn't saying He'll take away the burdens we face; because of our sinfulness He can't. But out of love and mercy, He's not letting us carry the load alone, either. His life, his love, is about helping us deal with our fall as a team. That's the kind of man, the kind of attitude and truth your father has embraced. I wish...I really wish...you'd give yourself the chance to know him as he is now."

Stoney silence met that request.

"He wants your love, Pyper. He wants so badly to set things right."

An instant of panic sang through the air, coursing from her soul like an aura. "Oh, how I wish you'd leave well enough alone, Chase. I know this must seem so simple to you. So easy, and—"

"Nothing about this is simple, crash, or easy. Nothing at all."

"I may not seem to be behaving like a good Christian, resisting your very sound and reasonable advice to just move beyond it all. Let him be a part of my life. But I can't contain what bubbles up inside me whenever I'm near him. I found that out this week when I talked to him."

"You did it."

Pyper nodded.

Chase's gaze never strayed from her face. "I care about you so deeply. I want to know you. All of you." He edged close, touched her cheek in an effort to soften her tension.

She was determined to push away from the topic. Chase seemed equally determined to achieve just the opposite.

"Don't worry about emotions—good or bad, Pyp. I'm going to get mad at you. You're going to get mad at me. We're going to fight and we're going to make up, but I'm not going to harm you, and I don't turn away from the people I love. I stick. Your faith, your trust, is what I'm after. Talk to me."

There was no way Pyper could withhold her heart. She surrendered, and cued up the bare-bones honesty he sought. "It didn't go well. In fairness, it didn't go well for either one of us. I didn't like seeing him. At all." Resentment returned, sliding just beneath her outward show of resolve. "I wanted to hurt him. I wanted to lash out and make him feel pain. I know that's not healthy, but I couldn't keep my head on straight."

Chase waited patiently and watched, drawing her ever further into that place of trust and truest revelation.

"I knew his abuse left scars, but for the most part, I thought I had left them behind. I never thought about him much, so I fooled myself into thinking I had grown past the anger and the pain because of the love of my family. I know now that I'm wrong in that assumption. I'm still a sore, angry, scarred mess, and I don't know what to do next."

"What happened?"

"He took me to lunch. He sparred with me; I sparred with him. We traded some ugly comments, most of them on my end, I admit. I couldn't help it. Maybe it was about vindication. If a couple verbal slap-downs accomplished the task of inflicting even a tenth of the pain I endured at his hands that might be fine enough. But in the end, my heart shattered all over again."

"The path to goodness never comes about through fury."

Tear glitter returned and Chase stroked tender fingertips against her damp cheek all over again.

"Rest easy, and know this, whatever you say, or don't say, Pyper, I'm with you."

She softened, craving that reassurance and solidarity, the port in a storm. She knew he was torn. She knew he battled conflicted emotions, but he had asked her to be real, and she owed that to him. So, a halting smile returned, and she did as he asked. She rested, she breathed, she swept up a few more wildflowers to add to her bouquet. Meanwhile, he captured another tear bud against the pad of his thumb as it tumbled over her lashes.

"The best answer I have for now is this: Tyler Brock is my dad."

"And that's as it should be. Is Mark asking to replace him? Is he asking to step into the role of being your dad, because it doesn't sound to me like that's the case."

A breeze brushed against his shirt, rippling the fabric against his arms and chest. Pyper watched the material dance against his skin, tried to absorb the momentary kiss of cool before heavy waves of humidity rolled in once more.

"No. He's not."

"I think…maybe…what he wants most to do is just…I don't know…wipe the slate clean. Do you think you could start again?"

She bristled instantly, all set to offer a stinging refute of the idea. Chase preempted that battle by pressing a fingertip lightly against her lips.

"Not from what came before but from someplace new. You're right; he'll never be your dad in the truest sense of the word, but he can still be worthy of your heart and care, just like me."

"Like you?"

Chase nodded. "I ruined good things, Pyper. I battled the bottle. I have a troubled past. I have a temper, but here you are. You're with me. You took the leap. I think you're capable of doing it again."

"Actually, I'm not so sure."

"How so?"

"I've made a decision, Chase. I…I don't think I can sing 'Forgiveness' with you on the album. The way things stand, I just can't see my way through it any longer. With everything that's been going on, it rips me apart, and I just…I can't do it."

"No. 'Forgiveness' is a song you sing beautifully, Pyper. It's partly your creation." He paused, forced her to confront that truth. "Give it a chance. Don't you see? God's taking you to a place where you're not just singing words, you're living them. You mean them. That makes it real."

"Too real. That's the problem. I feel like a hypocrite."

She tried to keep it together, to control and suppress like she had always done, but that's when her mother's words came back to her—amplified.

Maybe God wants us to grow into something better than 'well enough.'

Soon, Pyper was overcome by the cries of a broken soul. In comfort, Chase settled his hands on her shoulders and inched her gently forward so she could rest against him, circled by his arms.

"You're not entirely in the wrong, Pyper. That's not my point, and I don't mean to hurt you. You're right. I don't know the man you had to deal with…the one you and your mama had to run from to save your very lives. If I met that man in the here and now, I wouldn't allow him anywhere near you. Instead, I came to know the new man. The man who reformed. He's the kind of man I wish you knew."

"But I don't." Her words were a firm, stern refusal.

"True, but take a look at the wide-screen. You have that opportunity. By the grace of God you're being given the chance. No matter what comes next, you need to let go of the negative emotions. Not for his sake, but for yours, and if for no other reason than to end a painful and bitter season of your life. Even if you start small. Just hear him out. Forgive him. Then treat him like a stranger. You'd never shun a stranger, Pyper. You'd never let a stranger steal a part of your soul the way you're letting this resentment toward Mark's ancient mistakes."

He didn't allow her to answer. "Think about it. Don't answer right now. Don't answer from emotion. Instead, answer from the silence. Answer after you've prayed, and thought it over, in stillness. You might not be ready to give Mark all of yourself. I get that, but the anger and hostility you're holding onto will eat you up if you don't let it go."

He rested his chin against the top of her head. She trembled against his hold; the damp stain of her tears moistened the front of his shirt. At last she turned away, silently pushing to her feet. Walking to Briar, she loosened the horse's reins. Chase followed her lead, but she could have sworn she heard him sigh.

"See beyond the past," he urged. "See the potential. He saw it in me, and that changed my life. He knows he did wrong. Consider that helping him just might help you turn a page in your history book. Do it, Pyper. Live up to your beliefs, and the power of your heart, because your heart is beautiful. Don't allow anything—ever—to leave it marred by bitterness."

22

The thing Chase wanted to do more than anything in the world was make a difference in the war that was taking place in Pyper's heart—a war between the past and present, between battle scars and fresh beginnings. The revelations they had shared, those precious, rustic moments beneath blue skies and earth-spiced air had left him with a burning fire at his core that called him to a solitary purpose—reconciliation. Trapped between two people of tremendous impact in his life, Chase needed to let them both know—no matter what—how much he cared.

That goal had been accomplished with Pyper. Time now, he figured, to extend that same gesture of faith and care to the one who had dredged hope from the ashes. It was time to face Mark once again.

Chase set up an appointment, so he'd be sure to have Mark's undivided focus. He had nearly requested this meeting at Mark's apartment, but Chase had worked through recovery of his own, and figured the solid ground of professionalism might serve them best for now.

After the receptionist announced his arrival, Chase moved at a brisk clip to the threshold of Mark's office. When he stepped inside, Mark pushed away from his desk and welcomed Chase with a tentative grin. The old wooden chair in which he rested squeaked comfortably when he moved back and pointed to the chair across in invitation. "Come on in. Everything OK?"

"I'm good, thanks—no worries."

That was always Mark's first question, and first concern. Chase appreciated the fact that, no matter how complicated the undercurrents, Mark demonstrated faultless concern for his welfare. He needed to lean on that bottom line today more than ever.

"Glad to hear it."

Chase refused an offer of coffee, and Mark heaved from his chair and rounded the desk. He claimed a chair next to Chase's, and the meaning behind that gesture of equality didn't go unnoticed. "So, what's up?"

"I'm wondering if you'd mind me acting as a bit of an intercessor."

Mark's brow went up. "Depends. Are the two of us still on solid footing?"

Chase regarded the man. "Yeah. Absolutely."

"Thanks for that. I need it."

"And so do I. Never doubt it."

At once, Mark relaxed; relief painted soothing colors against his softened features. Light. Affirmation. Goodness. Maybe that's what it would take to wipe away decades of decay.

The realization gave Chase added courage. "You don't need to thank me for anything. There's more hard work to come. That's why I'm here." Chase edged forward against his chair. "I know I was rough on you, but it's important that I look out for Pyper—not just important, *necessary*. Like breathing."

"Yeah. I get that."

"But I need you to realize I'm looking out for you, too." Chase sucked in a deep breath. "I need you to know that I completely understand the transformation that's taken place in your life. You know I do. And I believe Pyper should hear you out, give you a chance."

Mark seemed to visibly relax a little more at that, but Chase knew the comfort wouldn't last long once he'd said his piece. "Understand, though, that I think she should give you a chance for her own good, not for yours."

"Ouch."

Chase shrugged. "I'm being straight with you here. It's what you taught me, after all. I'm going to support you—as my sponsor, as my friend, as a man I know is changed. I'm going to do what I can to ease the tension between you and Pyper, but you need to understand that she's hurting right now. She's scarred, and that's a hundred percent on you. You need to give her time. You need to let her vent and get out her resentment. It's the only way you have a shot at a relationship with her. Be gentle."

"I was gentle, Chase. I held my tongue and let her have her say. She doesn't want to hear anything from me at all. Am I even gonna have the chance to try again?"

Chase shook his head, sensing Mark's frustration—and yearning. "I hope so. I believe so." In the end, he expressed the same conclusion to his mentor that he had with the woman who owned his heart. "If you keep at it, we'll all come to terms, OK? Persist. Don't expect her trust after one attempt. Let her know you're not going to just...vanish...if things don't go the way you want. Know what I mean?"

"I do—but this is a whole lot easier with you than

with Pyper, that's for sure."

Chase couldn't suppress an agreeing chuckle. "She's a spitfire, but she's also an incredibly warm, loving person."

"I saw that, the other day, between flashes of hostility. Chase, I wish things were different. I wish I hadn't hurt her so badly. I owe you an apology, too, for that sin of evasion you talked about a while back."

Chase shook his head, lifting a pen and twiddling it between his fingers. "Mark, you weren't alone in all this. I know that. You weren't the only one who stepped back from God." He tossed the pen aside as his restrained growl vibrated through the air. How could he properly express himself? "I've done a lot of thinking lately, and I found I can really relate to Pyper's mama. Pyper told me all about her, and their history. Like Amy, I pushed through life figuring I was immune from anything bad. I was the successful lead singer, just like she was the cheerleader, the head of the youth group at her church. Like her, I felt like the golden child. God would take care of me no matter what I did. Amy's stumble came in the form of an ill-advised physical follow-through on a high school crush. For me it was fame, women, and the bottle."

Mark squeezed the bridge of his nose and shook his head. "Don't do that, Chase. To any of us. There's been enough recrimination and blame and sadness to cover any number of lifetimes. God made goodness out of the mistakes we made. He gave this world our daughter. She's part mine, no matter what she chooses to do about it."

"Hang on to the knowledge—the privilege—that you're her father as you fight back, and earn a place in her life, but don't consider that she's yours at all. She's

His." Chase motioned upwards and let that tidbit sink into the silence that stretched between them.

"You honestly think I should keep fighting? After the way she—"

"Yeah, I do." The fire in his belly burned hotter than ever. "She wouldn't be in my life without you. I'll never, ever stop being grateful for that." He swallowed over a hard, thick lump. "God's given me more than I deserve. Keep at it. He'll do the same thing for you."

"No matter what, we'll end up where God means for us to be."

"That's right. Like you, Mark, right here and right now. You're helping people. You're reconstructing lives based on the life God gave you, and that's a blessing that will move into eternity for the people you counsel—and for you, too. You're not the man she knew. Give her time, and she'll realize that. You chose the path to life, even when circumstances went bad. When you found out Amy was pregnant, you could have just dropped her, or pushed at her to get an abortion. You didn't. Instead, you tried."

"And failed."

"And came out refined by the fire." It felt strange, assuming a mentor role with Mark, but Chase refused to budge on his convictions. He wanted to embrace this moment for all it was worth.

"It was either that or end up dead."

"Which leads me back to the one thing I know to be true. God's will is perfect, even when we fall and make mistakes, even when we mess up His plan and leave Him to pick up the pieces and reassemble them into something good. Just like you, Pyper has brought so many people to the core of God's joy and goodness. That's all His doing."

Mark's eyes went red and he sagged through the shoulders, leaning heavily against his knees. "I want to find a way back so badly."

"Then see it through. Let it propel you past all of those fears she's hanging on to so tight. If she didn't want this as much as you do, she wouldn't be fighting against it so hard. If she didn't care, she'd blow you off and walk away. She can't. She's injured, but she wants the daddy of her youth to love her the way he should have in the first place. You're ready for that opportunity, but she doesn't quite believe it can happen. Underneath that tough, sassy exterior of hers is the little girl who's been hurt. If you can make your way through, you'll earn her trust and her love. I have no doubt. So, don't give up. Keep treading lightly. You're fighting the good fight, and she's worth that battle. That's what I wanted to say to you today."

⊱◈⊰

Puckett's in downtown Franklin was jumping. The hostess weaved through tight space, directing Pyper and her dad to a tall table with stools positioned right by the window overlooking Fourth Avenue. A realization came to life, a memory that tightened Pyper's throat and stirred a glaze of moisture across her eyes. The voice of her five-year-old self drifted through time and spirit. And heart.

"I decided something. Something important. I'm gonna be a singer when I grow up. Just like Tyler."

Tyler took her hand loosely and gave it a gentle shake as they sat across from one another. "I remember, too, sugar beet. This is the exact spot we shared the first time you and I and your mom spent time together in Nashville. You were, what? Five?"

Pyper rolled her lips in and bit down. The effort at stemming tears failed. A pair of them trickled down her cheeks anyway. As always, Tyler offered comfort, smoothing them away with the brush of his fingertips beneath her lashes. In an instant, Pyper was that little girl once again, loving this man like the father he had become.

Confusion nearly overwhelmed her. Because of Mark Samuels. Uncertainty simmered and prickled beneath her skin. "You'll always be my daddy. Always. No matter what."

"That's a given, sugar beet."

Tyler seemed to gather his breath and his thoughts all at once. He ran his thumbnail across a scar on the time-worn wooden tabletop, the after effects of someone else's cuts. So much like the genesis of their relationship, and the turmoil she now faced with Mark.

"Pyp, establishing solid ground, spending time with him, won't change any of that." Mischief danced through his eyes, lent a teasing curve to his lips. "And you know what? I'm about to go all 'Dad' on you, twenty-something or not."

"Oh, boy. I'm in trouble."

"Not at all." Still, Tyler's tone and expression turned serious. "I want you to think about something. You need to forgive him, Pyper. You need to get rid of the baggage and the pain he caused. Meet him halfway. It'll make all the difference. I promise you that. He eats at your peace. Don't let him. Don't let him rob you twice, OK? That's all I want to say. Maybe you'd find a way past all of it if you gave him the chance to—"

"No. I don't need him in my life." Strong,

stubborn and hurt most of all, Pyper's denial came in a low growl, but packed as much impact as a roar. Hostility etched its fine, cutting line against each word she spoke. "It's too late."

At that point, she opted out of the conversation, studying the people around her. She loved doing that on stage, too, connecting with as many smiling faces as possible. Like when she had sung alongside Chase. Lord help her she was confused...by everything.

That's when something caught her eye, a vignette playing out at a nearby table presently occupied by a large family. "Hey, dad, look at her!" Pyper reached out and squeezed his hand, drawing his attention to a little girl decked out in a blue denim skirt fluffed out by thick layers of pink tulle and topped by a white T-shirt. Best of all, she absolutely rocked a pair of shiny, spanking new, pink leather cowboy boots.

"I remember when you and mom got married, and I moved down here for good. You got me a pair just like those for my birthday."

"Every Southern woman should have 'em. That and a horse. It took you maybe a week on the farm before you batted those lashes at me and asked for a pony."

Pyper released a joyful laugh as the beautiful perfume of nostalgia swept in. "Briar was in our meadow by the next sunrise. Mom pretended to have a fit, mockingly accused you of spoiling me." Pyper's chin quivered. This man had erased so much of the horror in her life, and she was grateful. But was she grateful enough to take that last, terrifying step to reconciliation with the blood-related father who had acted like an emotional wrecking ball? Could she extend true forgiveness? She knew she *should*...but she didn't feel able. She met Tyler's gaze and gave him a tremulous smile. "I love you."

"I love you, too, sugar beet. Always and forever and take it to the bank."

The ages old reply soothed the rough patches on her soul. "You've always been so good to me. You were always there. You showed me a father's love. Nothing and no one can take away the fact that *you* are my dad."

"True. But, if he's sincere, if he's trying, I think you owe him a chance."

"I. Owe. Him. Nothing."

"Don't disappoint me, Pyper Marie." The admonishment was tender, but unyielding. "If nothing else your Christian faith tells you as much. To do anything less dishonors everything we stand for and makes us nothing more than self-righteous, judgmental and wrong."

"Dad." The word was a one-time warning shot.

He ignored it. "Don't cast stones. I know when he first showed up I told him to steer clear, and I promise you, Pyper, he won't hurt you physically ever again. I won't let him. But I can't stop him from hurting you emotionally, spiritually, if you allow the hurt to fester inside you, and that's tearing me up. Open your heart wide enough to give him a chance, Pyper. Let him know how you feel. He's after that as well, and you have the right to express your pain. But you need to listen, too. That's all I'm asking."

That was all he asked, sure, but to Pyper, it felt like everything and more. She just wasn't ready, or able, to push through.

23

"I dunno, Chase. Singing 'Forgiveness' still grates on me. It's just not coming together the way I want." Pyper sighed, resting her head against his chest.

"The recording session went fine. Stop overthinking it." Chase moved close—positioning himself into a neat, perfect snuggle against Pyper's side. They sat on the Brocks' front porch swing as dusk crept in. He breathed his fill of rapidly cooling air and sweet floral scent while pushing a heel against the floorboards to set their world in gentle motion.

Relaxing against the support of his arm, Pyper cast him a grateful look. "You're being way too nice. I'm still questioning whether or not I should be part of—"

"Pyp, you're doing what you should. Leave it at that, OK? The rest'll come." Chase cut her off deliberately, with somewhat of a hard edge because he wanted her to stop berating herself. The Spirit prompted her forward; an ache pounded through him for Pyper to recognize the fact and see a way through the heavy, thick veil of her doubts.

A silence stretched, full of chirping insects and the song of a breeze whistling through the brush. "I have a question for you."

"Yep."

"Are you...OK with things? With dating the way we are?"

"What do you mean?" The conversation shift was

unexpected. He angled toward her, loving the way she tucked her legs and propped against the side of the porch swing to face him. Somehow, someway, he knew he'd never tire of looking at her, or simply resting at her side.

"I'm sure I seem pretty tame."

His grin spread. "Tame is hardly the word I'd use to describe you. You have more fire in your spirit than most anyone I know."

He rested his arm against the back of the swing and twirled a curl of her hair around his finger, let it spring free, repeated. "Pyper, you have nothing to worry about. I want to know you. I want your trust, your confidence. If I took you to my condo, even for an innocent dinner, the temptation would be too great to press for more. I like these moments. I love being with you. That's enough, and I mean it. Like everything else, the rest will come when it's supposed to. When it's right."

"Like when we're married."

All at once, her eyes went wide. She gasped, realizing what she had just said. Meanwhile, Chase couldn't help but want to tease her, especially since laughter bubbled through his chest and filled him with delight. "Aww…darlin'…are you askin'? This is so unexpected…"

Even in semi-darkness, with only the hazy overhead light from the porch to see by, he could tell that a blush painted her cheeks. Adorably flustered, Pyper ducked her head and her hair fell in a curtain against her cheeks. Their blended laughter moved through the yard, full and spontaneous—music, Chase thought. Great music.

"You're three shades of black soot, Chase

Bradington."

The words were a sassy tease, but she was charmingly undone—disarmed. He'd bet that didn't happen to this lady often. So, he laughed all the more, drawing her into his arms for a long, warm hug and nuzzle against her neck that filled his soul.

"That I am, crash. That I am."

She giggled; Chase sighed with pleasure while she snuggled all the closer.

Pyper tilted her head to look into his eyes and she drew the back of her fingertips against his cheek and jaw. Her eyes tracked the caress and Chase's senses came alive and tingled with need. Yep. Being alone with her put him in tricky terrain to be sure. But, as he had said, it was better to be safe, and God honoring, than to be sorry.

All the same, an inspiration struck. "Know what? I've got an even better answer to that question for you. C'mon. Let's go into downtown Franklin real quick before I leave for home."

❧❦

They ended up at Sweet CeCe's on Main Street, a shop that featured the best handmade frozen yogurt in all of Tennessee from Pyper's point of view. Chase treated and they sat across from one another at a quaint metal bistro table crafted of elaborate curlicues. They both carried generously appointed Styrofoam cups stuffed with one of the shop's specialties: Old Fashioned Fudge Sorbet.

Pyper promptly dug in. Heaven. But between licks and nibbles, she kept an eye on Chase. "This is wonderful, but it doesn't answer my question about dating."

"Well it should."

"How so?"

"It's symbolic. A parable, maybe."

Pyper frowned in confusion, but the frown didn't last long. Creamy, sweet deliciousness melted against her tongue, providing welcome refreshment from the day's oppressive heat. Summer days wouldn't last much longer, but oh, while they did...

"I want to court you, Pyper. I want to win much more than your body. I want it all. I want to talk to you, hold you, know you—everything—good and bad, and I want you to know me. From there, we'll keep on building. That's my dream."

As he spoke, as his words trickled into her mind, her heart, Pyper's world came to a standstill. He finished a few bites then lifted his spoon, blooping the bottom of the utensil against the tip of her nose, which caused Pyper to jump, and issue a short squeal.

Ignoring the trickle of yogurt that inched down her nose, she dabbed a healthy dot on Chase's nose in payback. The laughter they shared, the silly, precious moment engraved his words on her heart and she came to understand exactly what Chase had accomplished in this moment. Purity. Innocence. The joy of discovery. The thrill of tumbling heart-first into love.

Recovered, he sealed her gaze with his. "Pyper, I'm not going to lie to you. Once upon a Chase, my answer to kissing you, to sharing with you physically would have been yes, yes, and more yes. Excess. Stupidity. Greed. Sin. I'd enjoy the conquest, then walk away unencumbered and unrepentant, relishing a steamy physical memory. What I know now is that

that's no way to live. It's gutless, rotten, and while I thought I was sliding through life in feel-good-mode without a care to be had, the consequences caught up to me. Not anymore. Not ever again. I want a woman like you, Pyper. I could never disrespect you like that, and truth to tell? I doubt you'd ever let me in the first place."

"Seems you've caught on to me pretty quick."

"I hope." Chase finished off his treat, visibly savoring this influx of good, of right.

Pyper joined in that melody and rested her hand on top of his, smiling into his eyes.

A short time later they climbed back into his truck for the return home. Chase turned the key in the ignition and as soon as the radio came to life, the song "People Change" by For King and Country hit the airwaves. It was like God decided to ride along with them, and that fact wasn't lost on Pyper. She froze for a minute or two, lost in the music; she turned her head, shoulders shaking as he engaged the vehicle and allowed her to cry in a silence broken only by the strains of poignant music that spoke directly to the battle she fought.

But she wasn't alone now, and she knew it. Chase settled his free hand against her arm in a comforting squeeze but focused on the road ahead as though wanting to spare her from added discomfort.

"Sometimes," he said quietly, "all the words in the world won't accomplish what a well-written song can."

"I just don't know what to do anymore."

"Let the pain in, and don't be afraid of it. Don't be afraid to break, Pyper. It'll be OK. I'm here, and so are all the people who love you. God will put you back together again, and you'll move forward as He intends."

The authenticity of those words, the passion that crafted them into being, calmed her at once.

They arrived at Pyper's home and, as always, Chase rounded his truck to open the door and accompany her to the front entrance. There on the porch, he cupped her face in his hands and she wrapped her arms around his waist, leaning into him. His expression was intent, almost somber; Pyper was about to question him when Chase stroked his thumbs against her cheeks. "I don't want one more day to pass me by, Pyper. Life's too short, and life's too precious." A steady gaze never wavered from hers. "I love you. Plain and simple. I love you." His voice, usually a faultless tool, turned to a husky whisper. "I'm not dodging it anymore. I'm allowing myself the freedom of saying it, and expressing how I feel in full. Being at your side is a privilege. Touching you is a gift. I love you."

The reverence, the bare honesty of his words, unfastened the last string holding back her heart. She breathed deep and leapt across a whole new sky. "Chase...I love you, too."

The words rocked him—she saw that clearly in the way he blinked in slow motion.

"Say it again," he murmured.

Pyper melted, restraints rippling to useless debris while her spirit soared free. "I love you."

He inched in closer, his full, waiting mouth just millimeters from hers, his breath warm against her lips. "Just...one more time."

"I love you, Chase." Melting, she pulled him in for a kiss that sealed her heart. Radiance, a soul shimmer, swept through her body. Love—a love unlike anything she had ever known or expected—left her clinging to him. "I had no idea so much love lived inside of me…and you…just searching for an outlet."

"And I've found it," Chase replied. "For real and forever I've found it in you."

Night wrapped its arms around them, filled with cricket song, the dance of fireflies, and the gentle whisper of tall grass. He searched her eyes and she caught the way he trembled. A strong man crumbled, all because of the exchange of three precious words.

"My every intention is to marry you, crash. Sooner rather than later. With all that I am I want to give you my life. My entire heart." He puffed a breath and squeezed her hands tight. "Pyp, just before this nightmare came to life, I imagined the moment of putting my ring on your finger. Forever. My world— our world—turned sideways that day, but the truth stayed rock solid, and true." All at once, a flash of loving fire came to life in his eyes. "This time I'm the one askin'. Will ya' take me on, crash? Are you brave enough? Do you love me enough to marry—"

"I accept."

Love had been set free, released into her care. All at once, Pyper recognized the gift Chase offered; she absorbed its weight, its power and beauty. She launched into his arms and he caught her waist, nuzzling her neck. Chase had delivered those sacred words along with a vow of his commitment, his reverence for what they had found together. *I love you*. They had spoken them to one another three times strong—like a benediction. There had to be something ordained in that fact, something holy and God-Spirited. Flooded by contentment, she knew she couldn't—shouldn't—keep that feeling inside. She wanted to share it. She wanted to celebrate it.

Would it hurt her—the release, the second chance, the opportunity to grow into something new, something even better than she was before?

No, it wouldn't. Like Chase, she was tired of holding back. Love was real. Love was healing, and love worked miracles. Why shouldn't it prompt her to rediscovery?

To rebirth?

24

Pyper kept her eye on the clock and on the doorway to the control booth of the studio where she stood next to Chase. At two o'clock sharp, the door came open. Mark Samuels walked in, and tension snaked across the muscles of her back and shoulders, but she closed her eyes for a moment and prayed. Tightness promptly eased. Pyper saw Chase go still with shock, his eyes full of questions.

He seemed about ready to leave the performance area, as though intent upon confronting Mark and pushing for explanation. Pyper intercepted him by resting a hand against his forearm. "I invited him. Hope that's OK. "

Chase's eyes went wide and his jaw dropped, but not a word escaped that full and beautiful mouth.

Pyper nodded, doing her best to quell jangling nerves by taking a deep, soothing dive into his eyes. "He's done so much for you; he deserves a chance to see you record, to see where his help and influence have taken you. And...and I want...I wanted to try singing 'Forgiveness' while he was around to hear it." Now her throat clogged tight, and she wondered, fleetingly, if she'd be able to sing at all. "I thought maybe he'd like the message."

For a long instant Chase simply stared. Then his eyes filled. "You're the most remarkable woman in the world. I want you to know that."

"No, I'm not. I'm just trying is all. Stay with me. Help me, OK?"

He caught her hand and gave it a squeeze. "Always, Pyp."

"I want perfection today. Your song, this journey, deserves nothing less."

She gave Mark a nod and a short wave of greeting; Chase smiled at his friend as well, and then addressed the techs through the headset, asking them to cue up for the next take of the song.

Pyper ignored the process, the flow, the trappings. Her eyes drifted closed and she fell into every note of the music, lost completely to words, melody, and a shaky, battered heart reaching out in faith.

At the end of the session, a cloud of recording-induced euphoria covered the whole of Pyper's world.

"Where exactly has *that* performance been hiding these last couple weeks?"

"Just needed to grow into it, I guess. It's good then?" Pyper spoke to the sound tech but exchanged a meaningful glance with Chase while they hunkered into empty space behind the console of the recording booth where producer Tony Edwards sat, a smile filling his face.

"Try platinum good. For real. You and Chase crushed it. Amazing job."

They listened to the most recent cut all over again, and a spray of goosebumps danced against Pyper's arms and neck. Mark hung back as techs conducted some final recording speak about layering in instrument levels, tone equalization—all the fine tuning and tweaks that would turn the recording into a post-production masterpiece. Pyper met Mark's gaze and held it. He nodded; his pride and a disbelieving joy added flavor to the private moment they shared.

After that, there was nothing left for her to do except call it a day and cross the next jittery bridge in this move toward reclamation. Pyper retrieved her purse. New time. New place. New chance. The words crossed her mind, eased her soul. "Thanks again, guys. Y'all are the best." In a discreet manner, she addressed Chase. "I'm going to have Mark take me home. That OK?"

Chase kissed her softly, rested his forehead against hers. "Completely. See you tonight?"

"Absolutely." She stayed in his arms, encircled within the safety of his love for a beat or two longer. Kissing him one last time she prepared to leave, but stopped short. "You know? You said it yourself, Chase. Few things speak louder than a well-written song. This was an amazing session. Thanks for that." The words ran much deeper than surface value, and she hoped he knew it.

"That's because of the ones who brought it to be. We're a pretty great team, crash. You. Me. God."

"I can't argue with that." Following a quick caress to Chase's cheek, Pyper turned to face Mark. Steady, resolute, she lifted her chin. "Ready to head out?"

"Sure. You did a great job." He shook hands with Chase. "Both of you did. It was a real treat to be able to see this. Thanks."

The end note he directed toward Pyper. She received the gratitude with a nod, but when she exited Imperion, walking side-by-side with Mark, her nerves came back to life in a fervent dance.

㘨❧

The basketball hoop seemed to call Mark's focus as soon as they parked in front of Pyper's home. Aside from the times she'd battle for the ball with Zach when they were kids, she had almost forgotten the thing remained on a cemented pole to the left of the family garage.

Mark, however, homed in on the netted hoop instantly, and grinned. "Do you happen to have a basketball?"

Laughing quietly, Pyper shrugged. "I'd have to check. Might be flat by now."

"Let's find out."

Tyler's treasured Mustang—a classic 1965 model and ode to his Michigan roots—and a bevy of landscaping tools filled the space inside the garage. Following a brief hunt, they uncovered a serviceable round ball. Mark palmed it like a pro and started to dribble.

"Mind if I shoot a few baskets?"

Activity would probably alleviate some of the nervous energy, so Pyper nodded and followed him outside, away from the inherently dank, dimly-lit space of the garage.

Shading her eyes, she watched Mark shoot, dribble, and unwind. As hoped, the repetitive motions and activity soothed her rough edges, lent enough bravery for her to step slightly forward on an emotional level as she sat on a nearby garden bench. "When we had lunch a while back, at the end of the meal you asked me a question."

"Yeah?" After a net swish, he looked over his shoulder in question. "Which one?"

"You asked me who had come out on the right end of the deal. When you think about it, I suppose we all did. I ended up with my mom and dad. That was a blessing. You seem to have turned your life around, and now you're doing good things. You help people who are troubled, who face battles like addiction find their lives and a way to God. Your life ended up on the right end of the deal as well. All of us ended up where we were meant to be. And it occurred to me after our lunch that we all ended up on a blessing path from God. This isn't going to be easy, and there are probably going to be a lot of fits and starts along the way, but if you mean what you say, I'm willing to give this a try." By now Mark had stopped shooting and stood stock still, staring.

"Is that why you called? Why you asked me to the studio?" He gestured wide. "To your home?"

"Yeah. It is. It has to start somewhere, right?"

"Not without my story, OK? I want you to understand something that's probably incomprehensible to you. I want to start over again. Clean slate. In order to do that, I need to explain what I can."

"I'll listen this time. I promise I'll listen."

Mark propped the ball on his hip and walked slowly to her bench seat. He sat, but didn't crowd. Pyper appreciated the fact.

"Liquor was an escape. It distorted everything, twisted my life into a cycle of anger, abuse, but that mess wasn't ever...ever about you. You were a sweet child. I loved you, but I wasn't ready for you. Not at all. I was eighteen, and in no shape to be a husband or a father. I'd drink every once in a while, but every once in a while turned into a habit. The habit turned into an addiction, and before I even realized it, the addiction overwhelmed my world."

Pyper remained silent, watching and intent.

"This isn't the life I would have ever chosen—"

"It's all my fault." Pyper folded her arms across her chest; wind tossed the waves of her hair, rippling a few strands against her face. The tears of her youth, of the fear and nightmares that had tracked her for two decades, rose and spilled free.

"What?"

"It's all my fault."

"What is?"

Her lips started to tremble. Here she sat, in the front yard of the home she had grown up in, felt safe in, where she had always felt both precious and cherished—reacting to a man she had sworn would never crawl under her skin and hurt her again. But, like Chase had said, she needed to break, to let the pain in, so it could be released forevermore no matter what came next for her and Mark.

"You didn't want me. I came along and I messed up everything for you. It's understandable you hated me. Resented me. You raged at me no matter what I did, and I couldn't find a way to make you love me."

An anguished, guttural moan rose from Mark's chest, releasing on a sob that heaved his chest. "Pyper. No. No."

His pain didn't hold her back. "It's true. You didn't want me, and that killed me inside."

Mark covered his face with his hands, tipped his head to the sky and sank against the back of the bench. When he dug his fingers through thick, shaggy brown hair, she got a good look at his face. Wetness covered his cheeks. His eyes were bright red, emphasized by a spray of lines that paid testimony to his struggles, and a sadness that ran bone deep. She couldn't ignore that truth, or the compassion it raised.

"That's why I need to set the record straight." He seemed to struggle for steadiness. "It's not that I didn't want you or your mom. It's that I wanted a life I could live on my terms. In my way. Not Godly, by any means, but selfish and free of commitment."

"Instead, you had to focus on an unwanted obligation. Me." Emotions built into a roll that pressed against her—inside and out.

"I was too pigheaded and immature to see beyond my own selfishness and ambitions. What I know and understand now is that what I did—the drinking, the yelling, the times I lashed out at you with words and hands, the times I banished you from my sight and ruined anything that brought you joy—was a battle against how angry I was at *me*. How much I hated *me*. You were a helpless bystander. So was your mom. You had no fault whatsoever in any of that. If you take nothing else from my presence in your life, from here on out, please, I beg you, let that be it. I'm to blame. Not you."

Pyper crumpled. "I tried so hard."

"I know you did. And the loss is mine."

Mark moved cautiously into her space and drew her toward him with a gentle pull against her hands. Pyper was too weak to resist. She sobbed, overwhelmed by the release of twenty years' worth of pent up emotion.

"I'll never have the moments Tyler and your mom have been given. They nurtured you and shared in every milestone of your life. Not me. I'm the one who messed it all up. I was lost, but I've worked so hard to get found. I gotta believe God steps in and makes all things good. It's the only truth that keeps me moving forward."

Pyper continued to dissolve, falling headlong into a world of forgiveness she never would have dreamed possible.

"You accused me of ruining things, and I can't deny that fact. I'd never try. I took your things, your mom's things, and I tossed them into a dumpster. Literally threw away the best part of a life I could have known."

Pyper didn't accept or reject his words. Rather, she remained still, rooted to this time, this spot they shared. The child inside her had waited for this moment for so long...

"You endured hell. No question. But please rejoice in what God delivered to your life. Tyler. Amy. Chase. That man adores you. He loves you the way a good man needs to love a woman."

"I love him so much it scares me sometimes."

"Love is like that."

"He holds the power to rip me apart. He could hurt me even worse than...than..." *You.* The word burned against her skin, and she was pretty sure he knew exactly where she was headed.

"To this very day, have a hole in my heart with your name on it, Mark." She stalled for one second— then another. "But...I'll try to forgive you."

The surrender left her so shaken, she couldn't say anything else. Fat, rolling tears cascaded down her cheeks, weakening the fortress she had created around her heart.

Silence fell between them. Peace settled. At length, Mark brushed his thumbs against the back of her hands. Only then did she realize, they had remained connected almost the entire time...

"Pyper, I kept something. I kept something that I want to show you now." Mark moved just far enough away to shift and pull a worn, brown leather wallet from the back pocket of his jeans. He cleared his throat as he extracted something small from the inside. "Here."

Curious, Pyper took custody of a small photograph that was worn along the edges, a bit faded by time. The picture elicited an instant, stunned gasp. "It's...it's me."

"You were four." His voice was husky, rough. "It was taken at your preschool the year you and your mom had to leave me." He jutted his chin, steeled himself, and took ownership of his actions in a visible way Pyper could sense in the air around them. "The year I shoved you out the door."

Pyper bit her lips together, buffeted now by much more than the wind that whistled through the trees and curved in through the valley. "Why...why on earth...why would you keep it?"

His eyes filled fast; his jaw clenched for a second before he answered. "Because it's the last picture I have of you when you were still mine."

Pyper wept openly, breaking and healing, and she found herself wrapped snug in Mark's arms. He cradled her against his chest and she found she didn't want to pull away. She rested against him, coming gradually aware of the fact that he gently stroked her hair.

Over and over again he murmured, "I'm sorry, Pyper. I am so, so sorry."

Epilogue

Through a gauzy fall of tulle that shielded her face from clear view, Pyper tingled and beamed, overjoyed by the path that stretched before her.

"You ready for this, sugar beet?"

"Oh…Dad…you bet I am." She trembled, and happy tears tracked down her cheeks as she nodded firm.

Tyler understood without another word being spoken. He drew her left hand through the fold of his arm, settled it snug. The twinkling, several-carat diamond engagement ring Chase had installed on her ring finger six months ago was temporarily housed on her right hand, because for now her ring finger awaited a much more important circle of love—a simple, platinum wedding band from the man of her dreams.

Together they walked down the church aisle, side-by-side, heart-to-heart, her cathedral-style gown an ocean of white lace and satin that trailed against a pale pink runner—her chosen color for the bridesmaids—though a slightly darker, more vibrant hue was worn by her maid of honor, Anne Lucerne. The ceremony, at a small stone church in Franklin, was an intimate affair. The upcoming reception, however, would be much larger and splashy—a necessary ode to the public life she would share with Chase including a veritable who's-who list from the Nashville music industry.

At the end of the aisle stood her mother, in the head pew, waiting. Pale blue silk flowed over the form of the woman Pyper could only pray one day to become. Strong. Vibrant. Understanding. Loving to the highest power.

And next to her mother stood Mark Samuels, eyes moist but never wavering as she neared the front of the church. Six months had passed, with moments of tears, moments of laughter, with bonds continually strengthened by love and the embrace of second chances.

Amy stepped from the pew, lifted Pyper's veil, kissed both cheeks and pressed a trembling hand against Pyper's arm. "I love you, sweet angel."

All Pyper could manage was a nod.

Mark also stepped forward, clearing his throat, a few stray tears breaking free. Pyper surrendered her bouquet to Anne Lucerne and then linked her free arm with Mark. As a trio, she, Tyler, and Mark faced Pastor Ken Lucerne.

And Chase.

God, thank you for Chase. Thank you from the depths of my soul. I know You so much better because of him. I love You so much more because of the love he gives me. Please know how grateful I am. How my heart fills and overflows.

He wore black-tie to utter perfection, and next to him stood Zach as best man.

"Who gives this woman to be married?" Ken asked solemnly.

"We do."

Pyper absorbed a thrill as both her fathers answered in perfect unison. Mark kissed her forehead in a warm, lingering manner before transferring one of her hands to Chase.

"He's waiting for you, Pyper. He's been waiting for you his whole life." Mark stepped back with a nod of surrender, of love from the ashes.

Pyper hoped her loving gaze spoke to the pain they had come through and now worked resolutely to defeat. Together.

Next came Tyler who still held her other hand. He looked into Chase's eyes in the way only a dad could. "Take good care of my girl. She's my treasure."

"I promise you that, sir."

"Her heart belongs to you, but it belongs to God most of all."

"So does mine."

"If it didn't, I'd never be able to let her go. God bless you, Chase."

"He has, sir. More than I could ever hope for."

Tyler shook Chase's hand and surrendered himself as well, stepping back, but never away, joining Amy in the pew. With Pyper and Chase now facing forward, Ken Lucerne began the marriage service with the shadow of a large, brass cross covering them like a loving benediction.

"God designed this day before any one of us drew a breath. God chose this couple before they laid eyes on one another. God's power built a family into loving beauty from a field of ashes. God rescued sinners and gave them life anew. What greater way to celebrate a day of love than by saying, 'Amen,' and reflecting on His power with an opening prayer for the ordaining and sanctification of this marriage."

When time came for the vows, Pyper wanted to get the words out. They filled her chest, pushed and lifted, but as always, emotions and love got the better of her. She started—stopped—aching to share her deepest heart with the man of her tomorrows.

Naturally, Chase understood right away. He moved in slightly, visibly ignoring their surroundings, the church, the flowers, the stained glass. He wrapped his arms around her waist and whispered. "Look at me, Pyp. Just look at me."

When she did, the rest of the world melted away. Tears poured, but the words, her love, sprang free into a beautiful rainbow—a rainbow vibrant enough to compete with the patterns of sunlight bursting through the multi-colored glass of the windows all around them.

"A long time ago, when we first started dating, you posed a question. You wondered where God was taking me. Where He'd lead me—my dad, my mom, Mark. You. Us. Without your heart, without its beauty, its scars, its healing, I never would have found my way to the biggest blessing I've ever been given...and have ever received. Forgiveness. You forgave me for being shortsighted, bitter, and mean about my past. You allowed me to shatter and rebuild as a Christian, a daughter, a woman. I could have never, ever done that without you and all that you are, Chase. He led me to you...and I'm so grateful."

He swallowed hard, but kept focused on her eyes, nodding. Their pre-rehearsed vows had flown to the winds of spontaneity, erased by the power of their hearts joining together as God intended.

"Pyper, you've given me the gift of hope. You've believed in me enough to make me believe in myself again. You see the good parts, and you see and accept the bad parts. You see me the way God sees me, and you love me. That's something I promise to never take for granted. You're in my soul—and my heart."

From there, as family candles were lit, and a unity candle was born from its fire, a sequence from the song "Broken Road" filled the church along with a subtle breeze slipping in through half-opened stained glass windows. Pyper absorbed the brush of air, knowing for sure it was nothing less than a kiss from God, gifted from heaven, to her and her husband—His silken touch moving straight through their hearts and binding them together forevermore.

My dear reader friends ~

First of all, I want to thank you for sharing in the journey of Forgiveness.

When I first 'met' Pyper Brock, she was a downtrodden five-year-old, battling trust issues and the scars of emotional and physical abuse brought about by her father's addiction to alcohol. In the pages of my book Hearts Key we see her mother fall in love with a wonderful man named Tyler Brock. As a family unit they bring their own lives forward to a place of joy and grace and give Pyper a renewed foundation of loving trust, and faith.

In creating Hearts Key, then Forgiveness, I've learned the circumstances surrounding alcohol addiction are complex. Recovery can happen – just look at Chase Bradington's battle, and the way he won and maintained a victory over addiction. He does so hand-in-hand with God, and relies on his savior completely. Also, look what Mark Samuels created anew with his life once he faced God, warts and all, and was given the mercy of forgiveness and a calling to rebuild his shattered past by confronting his daughter and working tirelessly as a rehabilitation counselor. I loved showing the way authentic reform can be so transformative and hopeful—brimming with joy.

But as the story shows, the process is far from easy. The process begins with first steps—sometimes faltering, sometimes met with heavy resistance, doubt and intense pain. But the payoff of recovery is huge.

If alcoholism and its aftermath have touched your life, if you know of a person needing help with the issue of recovery, please pass along the following website, the National Council on Alcoholism and Drug Dependence. The site is full of resources:

https://www.ncadd.org/

In researching Forgiveness, I also gained a great deal of insight on faith-based recovery by visiting Faith Home, Inc.:

http://www.faithhomegwd.net/

Regardless of how a pathway to recovery begins, no matter how twisty and frightening the road may seem, my prayer is that people who are touched by this disease and come upon the pages of my story might feel compelled to make that first step, to move forward in hope and faith.

Christ will lead the way when He is invited, and welcomed. Trust that truth. Cling to it relentlessly. Recovery can happen. Recovery can work. Recovery can be won.

Blessings to you always, with Christ's love ~
Marianne

Thank you...

for purchasing this Harbourlight title. For other
inspirational stories, please visit our on-line bookstore
at www.pelicanbookgroup.com.

For questions or more information, contact us at
customer@pelicanbookgroup.com.

Harbourlight Books
The Beacon in Christian Fiction™
an imprint of Pelican Book Group
www.pelicanbookgroup.com

Connect with Us
www.facebook.com/Pelicanbookgroup
www.twitter.com/pelicanbookgrp

To receive news and specials, subscribe to our bulletin
http://pelink.us/bulletin

May God's glory shine through
this inspirational work of fiction.

AMDG

You Can Help!

At Pelican Book Group it is our mission to entertain readers with fiction that uplifts the Gospel. It is our privilege to spend time with you awhile as you read our stories.

We believe you can help us to bring Christ into the lives of people across the globe. And you don't have to open your wallet or even leave your house!

Here are 3 simple things you can do to help us bring illuminating fiction™ to people everywhere.

1) If you enjoyed this book, write a positive review. Post it at online retailers and websites where readers gather. And share your review with us at reviews@pelicanbookgroup.com (this does give us permission to reprint your review in whole or in part.)

2) If you enjoyed this book, recommend it to a friend in person, at a book club or on social media.

3) If you have suggestions on how we can improve or expand our selection, let us know. We value your opinion. Use the contact form on our web site or e-mail us at customer@pelicanbookgroup.com

God Can Help!

Are you in need? The Almighty can do great things for you. Holy is His Name! He has mercy in every generation. He can lift up the lowly and accomplish all things. Reach out today.

Do not fear: I am with you; do not be anxious: I am your God. I will strengthen you, I will help you, I will uphold you with my victorious right hand.
~Isaiah 41:10 (NAB)

We pray daily, and we especially pray for everyone connected to Pelican Book Group—that includes you! If you have a specific need, we welcome the opportunity to pray for you. Share your needs or praise reports at http://pelink.us/pray4us

Free Book Offer

We're looking for booklovers like you to partner with us! Join our team of influencers today and receive at least one free eBook per month. Maybe more!

For more information
Visit http://pelicanbookgroup.com/booklovers